A BLOW IN TIME!

JOHN R. CARDEN

Paperback: 978-1-965632-45-1
eBook: 978-1-965632-46-8
Library of Congress Control Number: 2024921640

Ordering Information:

Prime Seven Media
518 Landmann St.
Tomah City, WI 54660

Printed in the United States of America

A sweeping story spanning centuries of
Epic Courage, Bravery, and Valor
In the ICOPE Universe!

Translated and Authored
By John R. Carden
A citizen of the planet Earth

Parts of this Imperial historical document were translated from the written "Standard Galactic" language, the official language of the Interstellar Condominium of Planets and Empires; (ICOPE); and when Reptiloids are talking or telepathically communicating, they are translated from the standard Reptiloid oral, and telepathic languages into the reader's native language. The memoirs of many Imperial Magi were also used by special permission of the Caretaker of the Eternal Archives of the Imperial Seers; which are buried at a secret location 200 Imperial miles deep under the surface of Empire Prime, the Capital Planet of the ICOPE! The archives are accessible only by direct Mindar Teleportation by Imperial Seers with the correct training. (Again, as per Empire notation, telepathic conversation is indicated by italics and also written in the reader's native language.)

This novel is dedicated to the memory of Dr. Royal Raymond Rife and Dr. Otto Heinrich Warburg; gifted physicians who each dedicated their lives to finding a cure for cancer.

Did they each find a different cure for cancer THAT WORKS?!?

Research their names and their accomplishments for a few minutes on the internet and you will be able to answer that VERY IMPORTANT QUESTION; (WITH VERY USEFUL INFORMATION); that you can use yourself!

Famous Quotes from Empire Documents:

"In war; most of the time; bad odds will not make an air or ground combat mission a defeat; because good soldiers and good sailors and good flyers CAN SUCCESSFULLY DEFY THE ODDS SO THAT ANY MISSION CAN BE A SUCCESS!!"- Anonymous Imperial Military officer

= = = = = = =

"The Fates of the Time Stream will decide, Ran-Kee!"

= = = = = = =

"Who *or* **what** *is a 'Tanya' and* **what** *is a 'Rube'?"*

= = = = = = =

"Hang the danger; full speed ahead; no matter what happens; until Defeat; until Death; OR UNTIL VICTORY!" - The motto of a famous Imperial Admiral (IT WORKED MANY TIMES FOR HIM DURING HIS NAVAL CAREER!!)

= = = = = = =

"By the Eternal Flames of the Cosmic All, I hope we will meet again, Radak, AKA Thud!! I am not through with you yet!"

= = = = = = =

Simply put; any event in accepted 'History' can suddenly vanish as if it had never existed; because if one small event on one point on the Time Stream is somehow changed; it can affect and modify or totally delete or radically change any important Anchor Event Time Point or any other Time Point in the entire Universe!!- Imperial Seer Kantorie Smi-Th-Jo-Nes

= = = = = = =

"That will have to be closely studied; before it can be explained; Mumford!!"

= = = = = = =

Read the manual and find out, JB!

HISTORICAL NOTE

On a Day of Destiny, many eons ago; in the Imperial Seers Headquarters which was at that time; and still is today; situated two hundred miles under the surface of Empire Prime; a group of Magi were using their powerful mental powers to visualize ancient parts of the Main Galactic Time Line. As they visualized historical happenings that had occurred long ago, on Empire Prime and the ultra-important, but very small planet called "Earth"; several of them envisioned several facts about a Major Player in the present-day Imperial society; whose lineage long ago originated on Earth! They learned about the source of the Family Name known as "Blow"; which at that time was the name of a very famous Imperial admiral who was originally born on the minor planet Earth.

The facts concerning the origination of that name are very, very, intriguing! Long, long ago before civilizations had calmed down enough beings so that they could peacefully coexist with each other; groups of sentient beings had to regularly go to war with other nearby belligerent groups in order to protect their local families from harm. Each group or tribe elected a "war leader" or "chief"; usually the tallest and strongest warrior; which when necessary; would lead their group of warriors into battle! But another equally necessary position in a particular group of warriors going into battle was the fiery red-haired soldier who blew the ram's horn to give out the commands that were given by the war leader or chief. There were intricate signals to be blown to command the group to attack; retreat; circle around; and dozens of other commands for the warriors to immediately obey and carry out! The war leader gave the command to the soldier blowing the horn by telling him to "Blow. . . "; along with another phrase to specify the command for the "blower" to produce. As the years went by; because of faithful, meritorious service; the gallant and brave warrior in the tribe that used his lungs to produce the required very loud signals with the ram's horn before, during, and at the end of each battle; was honored for his faithful service to his clan and formally given the family name of "Blow"; with every member of his family also being given the same last name! And so it was that the family name of "Blow" continued to be used for hundreds of years by each of the horn blower's descendants; up to the present day and also far into the Future!!

TABLE OF CONTENTS

IMPERIAL PUBLISHER'S NOTE

This document in this important volume is covered under the Imperial Information laws passed by the Imperial Legislature in the year 452,176 A.F.E., (After the Founding of the Empire), concerning any stored or transmitted telepathic or oral, photographic, and written data that: 1.) could be insulting to any member of the Royal Line and/or that 2.) Contains sensitive information that could be dangerous to the Main Trunk of the Imperial Time Stream or any Auxiliary Time Line of the Empire if it is used to change any event in the "Past" in order to change the "Future"!

To quote an official expert on proper document procedure, Seer Ronka Wad-Dee, appointed Galactic Time Stream Watcher for Empire Prime, 563 Imperial years ago by the Emperor of a Million-Million Worlds, and at the present time, the ultimate source in this matter: **"Failure to follow the accepted legal protocol concerning publishing material detrimental to any members of**

Royalty or material dangerous to the Main Galactic Time Line will result in immediate and severe prosecution to the fullest extent under such Imperial laws!"

As always, as ordained in Imperial Law passed by the Royal Parliament, and also by the Decree of the Emperor and the Mental Laws of the Royal Seers; in any Certified Imperial or private Document or any mental projection that is allowed to be publicly published, republished by permission of the author or the publishing company, quoted, and/or publicly transmitted by the Imperial Ministry of Information: **Any mention of the controversial mythical "Winds of Destiny" in any non-fiction or fiction manuscript, any mental book, or any media public broadcast; does not mean official acceptance of their possible existence by Imperial authorities and/or Imperial scientists; it is merely indicates the author's own uniformed opinion about a famous age-old legend or is simply a technique to hold the reader's or listener's attention!**

INTRODUCTION

W hat is "Time"? To use an analogy to attempt to describe "Time"; does it exist as a "cloud" of "happenings" or as a "stream" of "events"? As "Time" passes and each sentient being in the Cosmic All "ages" and grows "older" as their bodies or energy clouds deteriorate or vanish; would it be possible for any Humanoid, Snakoid, Insectoid, Reptiloid; or even a "Colloid Cloud" energy being; to be able to "travel back" to a time in the "Past" or "travel forward" in Time to a particular position on the "Time Cloud" or "Time Stream" in the "Future"; in order to change their "Past Destiny" or "Future Karma"?!?

Back in the "Past"; at one Anchor Moment on the Time Line; because of meritorious service to his clan; a powerful warrior with fiery red hair; who was permanently assigned to blow a ram horn to signal the warriors in his clan or tribe to start a battle with the enemy; after a hard-fought victory; had been rewarded with a new Name of Honor by his chief! This caused all of the warrior's descendants in the "Future" to have the family name of "Blow"; which was to be spoken after their given; individual name was stated!!

If one could travel back and forth along the "Main Galactic Time Line"; suddenly living in a "Past position" or a "Future position" from where you first started and deliberately changing "Anchor Events" at either "Time Frame" while being in the other Time Position; what would be the consequences, both "Good" and "Bad"; of being able to do this heretofore impossible feat? Before such impossible time jumps are even attempted for the safety of the Universe; the important question has to be answered; just in case the time jumps are successful; just what would be the consequences of this heretofore impossible act being accomplished? As a result; could the "Future" somehow be slightly changed or even totally destroyed by a so-called "Time Traveler" from the "Future" changing happenings in the "Past" to instantly influence the "Future"; in order to change certain events that had originally already happened in the "Future"?!? But such impossible time acts are strictly against every Imperial Time Law of the Interstellar Condominium of Planets and Empires; because theoretically, doing such an impossible act would totally disrupt the Main Galactic Time Line!! Conversely; if such an event in the "Past" was changed; what would be the effect of such a "Time Voyager" changing events in the "Future"; then traveling back to the "Past" again? Wouldn't each of these "Time Voyagers" going back and forth in "Time" violate the "Conservation of Mass and Energy Theorem of Physics"; which states that: "In each galaxy; the sum of all matter and energy levels always remains the same at all points on the 'Main Galactic Time Line' for that particular galaxy"?

In other words; when a hypothetical "Time Voyager"; using an electronic device; or extremely rare mental powers; travels back and forth on the Main Galactic Time Line or any of its branches; when they emerge and stop moving on the Line; that point immediately has more mass and energy than the other points; breaking the Conservation of Mass and Energy Theorem; which states that "all points on the Universal Time Line must always have exactly the same amount of energy and matter as they do on any other Time Point"! So just what would happen if somehow the energy and mass at one point were out of balance and contained less or more matter and energy?!? Could any dangerous happening be averted if somehow an equal amount of matter and/or energy from the point the hypothetical "Time Traveler" reaches; could be exchanged with the point from which the "Time Traveler" came from; thus keeping the energy and mass of the two positions on the Main Galactic Time Line exactly the same? Would this make the shifting on the Time Line benign and harmless? None of the Imperial Magi or any other "Time Seer" in any other empire can answer that question; since SUPOSEDLY such an incredible event has never happened in the history of the Cosmic All!!

To find out the answers to these perplexing questions, read the following Imperial document which explores the adventures of such a hypothetical "Time Traveler"; then carefully ponder your own answers to the previously stated perplexing questions about the terrible dangers of "Time Travel" back and forth on the "Main Galactic Time Line"! For more information any Imperial Citizen may use the FTL communication facilities at their local Imperial library to research this intriguing subject! Then if you desire; you may then use the absolutely free FTL communication facilities at your local Imperial Library to contact an Imperial Seer on Empire Prime, the Capital Planet of ICOPE; in order to discuss your ponderings and/or discoveries about the effects of "Time Travel" on both the "Past" and the "Future"! The Imperial Magi on all points on the Main Galactic Time Line eagerly await input on this perplexing question; even if you are living in the "Past" or in the distant "Future"! (If in the "Future"; where the Imperial laws for time travel are always in effect; i.e.; do not relate events that have already happened on your Time Line; simply give your thoughts on the perplexing subject!)

PROLOGUE — WHERE DID IT COME FROM?

The vast Cosmic All can be a very dangerous place for any sentient being; be it a Reptiloid, a Snakoid, an Insectoid, a Humanoid, or even the supposedly extremely rare and very strange Colloid Cloud species; the intellect of each of whom is described as being made up of what looks like hundreds of floating "specks of energy"! On the myriad of planets; planetoids; and asteroids where sentient beings can live, there are a literally a million-million ways for an unarmed; unarmored; and defenseless being to lose its Eternal Soul, Id, or Cloud Consciousness; and immediately transverse and/or transposed to the next level of Cosmic Existence!

But somehow, a few select beings are seemingly more protected from such a fate than others; possibly by their position in the Time Stream, their strong will, their resourceful minds, or by their Karma, or "Ultimate Fate"; which seems to be "set in stone" on the "Time Steam" or, if you prefer; in the Time Cloud"! Such "protection" sometimes cannot be outwardly observed with visible sensors or even inwardly with the several thousand known "extra" senses of the mentally gifted species of the Universe in Totality!

Therefore; be it known for the Eternal Record; the following document is/will be; recorded in the Headquarters of the Imperial Seers; which is; and will be; buried at a secret location that exists 200 Imperial miles under the surface of Empire Prime, the Capital Planet of ICOPE! The particulars of this extremely important **ANCHOR EVENT**[18] are/will be; forever documented on imperishable opaque "Eternal Parchment" for the advancement and the education of the intellects of the Neophyte, Experienced, and retired Imperial Mages; as well as any Empire Citizen! Hence; a very unique "protected" intelligent being will be documented in the pages that follow!

It is recorded on the Eternal Pages of the Royal Seers: **"At a particular instant in the Time Stream of the Universe an extremely mysterious small interstellar craft, (which, as far as all Imperial Magi sources can visualize, had apparently been constructed using ultra-advanced unknown alien technology sometime at an indefinite and unknown place in the far future or distant past of the "Time Instant" in which it was presently residing); left an insignificant planet; called "Earth" by its inhabitants; and hurled outward at the fastest speed ever recorded in this Universe; to an unknown destination in order to perform an unknown extremely important and very dangerous mission! At the present position on the Main Galactic Time Line; just exactly where the unknown pilot or pilots traveled to; or** the actions the pilot/pilots accomplished when he/she/they emerged; apparently had no apparent lasting effect on the Main Galactic Time Line after it settled down!!! Added to this amazing fact is the fact that just what was/will be; accomplished by the pilot(s) and/or passengers of this unknown craft cannot be ascertained; either now or in the 'Future' because of unknown factors that somehow; at the present position on the Main Galactic Time Line; impossibly prevent any Seer from using their mental talents to visualize any facet of what this craft and its unknown pilot or pilots did on its unknown; but had to be; an absolutely incredible and utterly impossible mission--AN IMPOSSIBLE MISSION THAT; WHEN IT WAS OVER; APPEARED TO BE SUCCESSFUL--against all the odds; a victory against overwhelming enemy forces and superior enemy firepower; ranking with the odds of a snowball surviving in a blast furnace!! Such a phenomena of the Main Galactic Time Line somehow being kept from being viewed by any of the extremely powerful Imperial Seers has never before been observed and historically recorded in the Annals of the Imperial Seers at any time during the long five hundred thousand year history by any of the Imperial Seers! But there are obscure legends that such a phenomenon existed in the first few years after one of the first Emperors of the ICOPE established the Imperial Seers! But then over the centuries, rumors of such incredible happenings gradually faded out and were no longer spread around!

The information about the planet "Earth" quoted in this paragraph is from the visual and/or mental "List of Alien Planets" by the Royal Cartographers, A.F.E. 456,234; (After Founding of the Empire). The Royal Universe Mapmakers obtained the name of the planet from the "proxies"; or citizens of the Empire who were; and still are; covertly sent to live on the backward alien planet to observe and regularly report conditions back to Imperial Intelligence Headquarters. Such spies had been assigned to live on the small alien orb for many centuries to watch out for dangerous happenings and send back regular reports to Empire Prime; especially reporting on the level of military technology being attained by the alien Humanoids on the planet. Such "Intel" helped to protect the ICOPE from "unexpected happenings" which could suddenly appear unexpectedly beyond the Imperial Sphere of Influence. The Empire wanted information about happenings such as revolutions and wars between planetary civilizations having FTL warships, and unexpected scientific discoveries allowing planet-bound dictatorships to suddenly export their tyranny to other star systems. The system was designed to gather valuable intelligence about possible trouble on fringe planets so as to allow the Imperial forces to stop 'trouble' before it started and to help reinforce the Empire-wide peace which the ICOPE had strived for since its inception. Two Imperial Navy captains; Bordoe Gallant and John Cody; were also used to investigate events beyond the Empire's Sphere of Influence to also stop all sources of trouble before they could cause trouble for the ICOPE.

One Intel report which was constructed from many sources after an extremely important "Anchor Event" had occurred that suddenly caused the "Life Path" of one insignificant sentient Humanoid being to be violently altered; apparently caused by the unknown actions of the person or persons in the mysterious advanced craft; stated:

"The ultra-advanced unknown and unidentified craft; which apparently launched from the surface of the planet "Earth"; was initially documented by unnamed reliable sources to be on an important diplomatic mission to a faraway galaxy to attempt to get a hostage released from galactic terrorists on the extremely dangerous Thunder Worlds! There was only one problem and/or issue with the presence of such a sophisticated craft on such a technically backward small planet! The difficulty with this report was the fact that the technology of the planet had not yet produced even a prototype FTL craft capable of traveling even a few light years; or even barely above the speed of light; much less one that could travel between multiple galaxies at incredible speed! The small planet's best space fighter aircraft could literally patrol no more than a few million miles away from its sun; without having to refuel! Furthermore, it has been ascertained that the mystery ship's documented speed, range, protective electronic devices and armor, and maneuvering capabilities; were also beyond what the skilled Imperial naval architects of the Empire of Empires or any other ship designer in the Cosmic All could construct in their own most advanced courier ships, at that present time; or even 100 Imperial years in the future! The present Space-Time Propulsion Theories that are used to create the fastest ship possible cannot be used and/or modified and/or extended to produce faster speeds; since every facet of the equation has been totally exploited! Because of this fact; new physics propulsion theories; using different aspects and principals of the energy spectrum; acting on presently unknown properties of the space-time continuum; to produce faster movement on the Main Galactic Time Line; must be formulated in order to produce much faster propulsion systems as exhibited by the unknown craft!"

But where did this unknown impossibly advanced ship come from, and where could it possibly have originated from; if no known planet or civilization in this Frame of Existence could produce such a super craft with the impossible capabilities that it exhibited?!? Did it somehow come from some unknown advanced civilization in the Past? Did it somehow come from the Future? Was it from another dimension? Surely not in the Present; because such a craft simply could not exist in the present time according to all known military sources! Again, such fantastic performance will not even exist in the foreseeable far future; so how can it exist in the Present Time!

Never-the-less, to cover all possible sources of the ultra-advanced ship, the following questions have to be asked: Did the amazing ship somehow come across the planet's Auxiliary Time Line from the unrecorded ancient history of Earth; such as the now destroyed mystical kingdoms of Atlantis, Lemur, mythical Mu; or the advanced civilization that supposedly flourished on the continent of Antarctica on Earth before the planet's so-called "Ice Age" covered it up with three miles of ice at its south pole of rotation? Was it somehow from the far, far future where perhaps they have discovered how to "time travel" and use their advanced science to construct craft that can travel at the fantastic speeds exhibited by the unknown craft? Could it even be that it could be from another unknown dimension; which research by Imperial scientists seems to indicate may possibly exist? Even then, as now; with all their visionary powers, **THE IMPERIAL SEERS DID NOT KNOW; OR COULD NOT FIND OUT AT THAT TIME; AND DO NOT HAVE ANY MORE INFORMATION ABOUT THE EERIE SHIP EVEN TODAY AT THIS MUCH LATER "TIME POSITION" ON THE MAIN GALACTIC TIME LINE! THE REASON FOR THE LACK OF INFORMATION DESPITE CONTINUING MENTAL RESEARCH ABOUT THE INCIDENT ON THE MAIN GALACTIC TIME LINE IS THAT SUCH INQUIRIES BY IMPERIAL MAGI WERE, AND ARE; MYSTERIOUSLY STYMIED BY SOME**

UNKNOWN AGENT OR PHENOMENON!! FOR LITERALLY THE FIRST TIME IN THE FIVE HUNDRED THOUSAND YEAR-HISTORY OF THE IMPERIAL SEERS THEIR STRONG MENTAL POWERS WERE BLOCKED BY SOME UNKNOWN FACTOR!! FOR SOME REASON THE VISIONS OF ANY MAGI OF ANY MENTAL CAPACITY THAT COULD BE VISUALIZED ABOUT THE WHOLE FANTASTIC EPISODE BEFORE, DURING, AND AFTER; THE USE OF THE SHIP WERE EXTREMELY FAINT; TOTALLY BLACK; OR THEY COULD NOT BE VIEWED; i.e.; NOTHING APPEARED WHEN THE MAGI CONCENTRATED THAT COULD BE USED TO FATHOM AN ANSWER TO THIS PREPLEXING RIDDLE!! This was extremely unusual because since the actions of the unknown ship had already happened; hence on the Main Galactic Time Line they should have been extremely bright to any top-level Seer, but again; IMPOSSIBILY; AGAIN WE STATE THAT FOR SOME UNFATHOMABLE REASON; AT THIS POSITION ON THE TIME LINE; ANY VISIONS OF THE IMPOSSIBLE EVENT ARE EXTREMELY FAINT OR TOTALLY BLANK OR BLACK! I.E.; WHEN THE MOST POWERFUL MAGI ATTEMPT TO VISUALIZE THE TIME LINE OF THE MYSTERY SHIP; THE TIME LINES THEY CAN VISUALIZE ARE EITHER NONEXISTENT OR SO FAINT AS TO BE LITTLE OR NO USE! ONCE AGAIN; IT MUST BE STATED AGAIN THAT SUCH A PHENOMENON IS UNIQUE IN IMPERIAL MAGI HISTORY!!"

Perhaps the document to follow will ultimately enlighten the reader's path sufficiently to help the Royal Mages find the Ultimate Answer to this so-called "enigma wrapped in a puzzle surrounded by a paradox that is spinning forever on a Mobius Strip!" It is known at the present "Time" position on the Time Stream/Time Cloud that for many millennia into the far distant Future on Empire Prime, the Imperial Seers will ponder and futilely research just how this enigma of a ship came to be; just what the sentient being(s) and/or the AI[13] controlling the mystery ship did while in this "Time Frame"; where it eventually landed after it mysteriously disappeared; and the unknown skilled pilot who piloted the craft during its amazing and extremely dangerous trek through the hazards of descending to the surface of the capital planet of the Thunder Worlds! To sum up the situation. All the pertinent information about this amazing craft; its pilot or pilots; and just what was accomplished; is somehow hidden from the mental powers of the Imperial Magi and the science of the Interstellar Condominium of Planets and Empires!!

Let it be known to all researchers that there was, and still is; literally no sentient race of scientific beings in the Cosmic All with the ultra-ultra-ultra-advanced technology necessary to construct such a craft; whose capabilities seemed as advanced over the Empire's fastest courier ships as they were over the first Earthian rocket ships! So the answer to the "Impossible Question" of who built the eerie craft seems to be an enigma wrapped up in a shield of impenetrable corundum; that is destined to be unfathomable until the end of Eternity and beyond!!

WHO or WHAT could possibly build such an impossible craft? What scientific principles somehow unknown to Imperial Naval Architects, who always use the most advanced naval technology taken from all the planets in Empire's Sphere of Influence; allowed the unidentified ship to be so much faster than any known ship in the Physical Universe? After much research; the Imperial Time Seers pondered several Time Postulates that fathomed the possibility that the Impossible Ship could have possibly suddenly existed in this "Time Frame"; or could have somehow been "transposed" to this position on the Time Stream/Time Cloud because its Karma was needed to save the life of a sentient being that was important to the planet's Time Stream! When anyone tries to unravel the answer to this mystery; (which seems to be similar in structure to a Kor-Kian "Unknowable and Impossible Puzzle"); the so-called "facts", when taken together or taken separately; concerning the literally unattainable physical capabilities of the unidentified ship; seem to be like a jumble of senseless prose; wrapped inside a Thunder World's unworkable and impossible puzzle; and covered by a conundrum!

But, actually; to **veteran Imperial Navy Historians**; the answer to the seemingly endless puzzle; which seems to wrap in on itself and be literally impossible to fathom; is actually not difficult to figure out!! **To them; the answer to the baffling conundrum actually can be quite simple**; if one has followed the seemingly impossible-but-true exploits of the previously mentioned **Imperial Navy Captains, Gallant and Cody** through the Official Naval Logs of the Empire; and knows about the tried and true centuries-old **"Gallant Luck"** and the illustrious so-called **"Cody Coincidences"** of a similar age! If a scholar questing for the Truth; be it Reptiloid, Insectoid, Snakoid, Humanoid, or even an extremely rare "Colloid Cloud" being; is familiar with the two very famous advanced Humanoid beings who gradually acquired their legendary "Gallant Luck" and the famous "Cody Code" over several hundred Imperial years of very dangerous service to the Empire called the Interstellar Condominium of Planets and Empires; or ICOPE; **then the answer should be; and is; very; very plain!** When it is revealed that historical records show that **these two supposedly ordinary Humanoid beings were somehow involved in the unworkable puzzle about the mystery ship;** and there is no definite solution to the conundrum; then; to veteran observers; **THE ANSWER BECOMES QUITE SIMPLE!** Over the centuries, these two loyal Servants of the Empire have been known to pull off literally impossible feats of daring and courage; including having ships that seem to be slightly faster than the swiftest Empire Courier Class ships; (but not half as fast as the Mystery Ship)! So, since these two Imperial Spies are involved in the mystery, need we say more? **Somehow; some way; one or both of these two supposedly ordinary Humanoid beings have to be involved with the impossible and unknown Mystery Ship!** Because just like the unknown ship; these two Imperial spies have secretly and "off the record" exhibited impossible feats of strength, teleportation, and daring; for literally centuries as they served the Empire of Empires and their Emperor!! So when asked to do so "off the record"; Imperial Probability scientists have calculated that the probability that Captains Cody and/or Gallant know anything and/or were actively involved with the so-called "Mystery Ship" is approximately 98.99%!

BUT THERE IS A "CATCH"; i.e.; A VERY TOUGH "NUT TO CRACK" IN ORDER TO SOLVE THIS TRANS-GALACTIC MYSTERY!! The very large problem there is in asking either of the two Imperial spies about the subject of the unknown ship is the fact that both of them are covered by the Imperial Espionage Act of 150,277 AFE[29]; which makes it illegal for any Empire government official; interplanetary or interstellar news reporter; or any other person with an interest in publishing information; **to ask any Registered Imperial Agent anything about their past or present or possible future covert activities which now protect/will protect; the ICOPE from harm!** So this act effectively covers the two Captains from having to testify about the eerie subject of the impossible ship! Information that could be quoted from their now-sealed memoirs must wait until 1000 years after their deaths; (which because of the "Interferon 777" given to loyal Empire agents; won't be for possibly another 1500 or so years; (give or take a few centuries)!! So to find the Truth about the many astounding events that transpired during "The Impossible Happening", other unique and unexpected avenues of information must be explored!

The uncomplicated, actual, **TRUTH**, i.e., about the source of the Mystery Ship's impossible capabilities; impossibly and improbably lies in the planet Earth's far distant past; in the orb's present position in "time"; and incredibly; also far; far in the planet's distant future on the Main Galactic Time Line! So what is so simple about something existing simultaneously in three different places at once on the Time Stream-Time Cloud? How can this be?!?

Would that not violate the 'Conservation of Energy/Matter Time Rule' which states that at every instant in "Time"; all positions on the Main Galactic Time Line must contain exactly the same amounts of matter and energy? Yes? No? Sometimes? Maybe? A physically impossibility? Is this very perplexing question simply a riddle with either no answer; only one answer, or many answers? So just what would happen if any sentient being suddenly existed simultaneously; (and impossibly); at two, three, or more positions on the Main Galactic Time Line; "at the same Time"!?!? (In other words; a "Paradox Cycle".) In addition to this problem with this scientific hypothesis; to state one more time; wouldn't this also violate the "Conservation of Mass and Energy" Corollary" of the Sir Edmund Greco's "Main Thesis of Time"; which states that "all positions on any branch or section of the Main Galactic Time Line MUST contain the same quantity of regular matter; Dark Matter; and/or energy"?

BUT WHO CAN KNOW FOR CERTAIN; AND HOW CAN SUCH AN UNFATHOMABLE AND IMPOSSIBLE EVENT HAPPEN-- MATTER TRANSPORTED OVER THE MAIN GALACTIC TIME LINE AND LEFT IN ANOTHER SPOT IN TIME WITHOUT TERRIBLE CONSEQUENCES; SUCH AS AN EXPLOSION OR THE ENTIRE TIME LINE RUPTURING AND/OR IMPLODING?!? WELL . . . . perhaps the following document will help explain the Paradox Cycle which the previous description relates; of something or someone existing in several places at once on any portion of the Time Line! Again, after reading and pondering this document; if any reader has any revelations or questions about the whole subject of "Time Travel"; please openly or secretly; (whichever you prefer); using the **FTL** com system of your local Imperial library; contact the Seers on the Capital Planet Empire Prime as soon as possible! Under Imperial laws, the name, clan name, home planet; and all pertinent information about any Imperial Officer being recorded; and/or published; and/or broadcast by any mental or physical means is totally forbidden by a strict Imperial Edict by the Emperor many centuries before!

If necessary; any sentient being providing such important information about so-called "Time Travel" will be totally protected from mental and physical harm after any important data is officially accepted from any authorized Imperial Officer!

Now; remembering all the information you have been given in the previous pages; carefully read the following Imperial document and carefully ponder the possible effects on your future Life Path! Also; after you read this document and have pertinent information about any of the cataclysmic events that are documented; Imperial Magi would greatly appreciate contacting them to further illuminate the events so portrayed in the document you have read and pondered!!

CHAPTER 1

nd so; it came to pass on one ultra-important position of the Main Galactic Time Line; in the Cloud of Infinite Time Points, (or on the Main Galactic Time Line[31]); of the Universe; at the Earthian Aerospace Force Veteran's Hospital; an Anchor Event[18] was about to occur! The hospital was devoted to healing Imperial military veterans who had been severely injured or those former warriors of extreme age who have no family and have become extremely weak physically and/or disabled; and cannot take care of themselves. Two burly orderlies were conversing in very low tones near the side of an extremely old white-haired man who was eating a bowl of soup by himself in the cafeteria. The man had to eat very slowly because he had a very worn cyborg right arm which had a very weak internal motor that continually vibrated every time he used the metal arm to raise the spoon or his drinking cup to his lips; hence he had to be very; very careful not to spill something every time he raised anything to his lips. The motor was so old that the military supply store was no longer able to replace it and it would cost too much to replace his entire arm.

"Yea, that's him, Hank! I recognize him from my old navy days! How could I; (or any other veteran who served under him); forget a commanding officer who literally saved their lives and all the lives of the soldiers in the Imperial Navy forces under his command many times in battle with his daring maneuvers and forays to defeat the enemies who were determined to destroy our outnumbered forces and move on to invade Empire Prime? He was absolutely the best top brass that I was lucky enough to ever serve under; and now tragically; after all the centuries of distinguished Imperial Navy service; he is now reduced to eating thin soup alone in a civilian retirement center!! For some reason Admiral Blow never has any visitors or family to visit him at this location where he lives! What a tragedy in the life of such a compassionate and caring man!! The admiral always took care of all of the men and women and Reptiloids and Snakoids and Insectoids under his command; before he took care of himself; and all of us were extremely loyal to him because of it! So, unfortunately; the rumor going around the place about the famous Admiral Blow being secretly admitted here is true! I can hardly believe it, but he's the grizzled old man slowly eating soup alone at that corner table! Looking at him, you wouldn't believe that harmless-looking; shriveled; elderly gentleman with a dilapidated cyborg right arm; is actually the former Admiral Jonathan Baines "Hurricane" Blow; the famous and gifted military leader that once had the reputation to be able to make the Mountains of Orion on the Thunder Worlds shake with his anger and rage when he was in charge of the Combined Terran and Imperial Fleets; and any bureaucrat or official on Empire Prime crossed him! But even so; with such a reputation for being hard, he never could get over the botched raid to rescue his patrolman from the Thunder Worlds, losing his right arm in that conflict, and also the tragic death of his beloved wi. . ."

But suddenly, as the two medical personnel talked, there occurred a unique and **LITERALLY IMPOSSIBLE** event that had **NEVER BEFORE HAPPENED** in the Entire History of the Cosmic All; either in any previous Creation; (before the so-called "Big Bang"); or in this present age after a very evident "Intelligent Design" of the Cosmic All!! In the atoms of every sentient being in the entire Universe for an Eternal Moment there seemed to vibrate an enormous sound like the Heart Strings of the Universe were plucked, and every iota of the "Main Galactic Time Line"; (or if you prefer, all of the "infinite time points existing in the Cosmic All's Time Cloud"); was forever altered; with every being in the Veteran's Hospital or in the entire Cosmic All totally unaware of the change!! The next quadrillionth of a second, because of one of three other different "related events" on three other widely separated points on the Eternal Time Line; the old man quietly eating soup in the cafeteria literally faded out of existence and out of the memories of anyone who had even known him, as if he had never existed; because he had not ever been born; (**WHICH WAS NOW TRUE!!**) Every past accomplishment of the old man when he was in the Terran and Imperial militaries for literally centuries; the record of his birth; all his school records; all his medical and governmental military records; his very tragic short marriage due to his wife having cancer and dying suddenly; and all of the effects of his existence had all suddenly ceased to exist! At the exact 6instance of the disappearance of the Humanoid known as "Jonathan Baines Blow"; **EVERY PHYSICAL TRACE AND EVERY MENTAL TRACE AND MEMORY THAT HAD BEEN RECORDED IN THE MINDS AND HEARTS OF LITERALLY MILLIONS AND BILLIONS OF HIS ACQUAINTANCES, MILITARY ASSOCIATES, FRIENDS, FAMILY, LOVED ONES,** and Reptiloids, Snakoids, Insectoids, Colloid Cloud, and/or Humanoid sentient beings who had ever read or heard anything about the man; **SUDDENLY CEASED TO EXIST! ALL PARTS OF HIS PAST AND FUTURE BLOODLINES IMMEDIATELY VANISHED; ALONG WITH ALL OF THEIR DESCENDENTS, ADINFINITUM; THEY ALL INCREDIBLY AND IMPOSSIBLY; CEASED TO EXIST-ANYWHERE IN THE ENTIRE CREATION!!** Thus it came to pass that instantly; in and along that particular sub Time Line; (or Floating Point in the Time Cloud); the formerly-famous naval veteran and devoted husband; had never been born; with all the resulting cataclysmic effects!

But the next quadrillionth-of-a-quadrillionth-of-a-second at another extremely close point on the Time Line-Time Cloud; because of another "drop-in event" caused by deliberate actions on another position on the Time Line; **ANOTHER LITERALLY IMPOSSIBLE UNIQUE EVENT** happened; which incredibly reversed **MOST; (BUT NOT ALL); OF THE EFFECTS** of the previous ultra-important Time Line Happening! The new event impossibly recreated all of the infinite data, bloodlines, memories in the minds of sentient Reptiloids, Snakoids, Insectoids, Colloid Cloud, and Humanoids; as well as all the material objects, and/or intricate happenings that had been virtually erased from all across the Cosmic All; WITHOUT ANY SENTIENT BEING IN THE ENTIRE COSMIC AWARE THAT THE UNIQUE EVENT HAD EVER OCCURRED; AND WITHOUT CAUSING ANY HARM TO ANY PORTION OF THE ETERNAL TRANS-GALACTIC TIME LINES!!

(But now as ordinary mortal beings; we must continue to travel along the present Time Stream/Time Cloud location at the regular speed of "Time" on our planet and in our home solar system! Some of us will reach the exact point of the "impossible event" happening much later in our future Life Line; if our lifespan is long enough and/or we are authorized to take the Empire's Humanoid age-extending wonder drug called "Interferon"; which; when properly taken; can literally bestow immortality!)

At the first instant in Time that the lonely old man had ceased to exist; the two orderlies who had been observing him in the cafeteria were suddenly working with other patients somewhere else in the hospital when their charge suddenly ceased to exist; with no memory of having known or ever assisted the Important Event Figure; and all hospital records documenting that the old man had ever been a resident of the hospital also instantly vanished; as if they had never existed!! But why did the important aerospace military veteran vanish from his position in the orderly Time Stream-Time Cloud as if he had never existed in the hospital; and the next quadrillionth of a second suddenly reappear at another different point on the small Time Stream-Time Cloud of the unimportant planet known to its relatively primitive inhabitants as "Earth"; without any sentient being aware of what just happened? The answer to this new literally hidden mystery; (which would be forever unknown to almost all of the quadrillions of beings in the entire Cosmic All); was/and is/ and will always be; like a mystery wrapped inside a maze; inside an impenetrable conundrum; residing in another dimension; i.e.; impenetrable; unknowable; and unfathomable to (almost) any sentient being in the entire Cosmic All; except perhaps; one or two specific Earthian Humanoid scientists who specialize in "Time Travel Equipment" and one "Citizen One"[11] being!!

Again it must be related that the paradoxical reason for that radical alteration of the Universe is because of three; (perhaps four or more literally "Impossible Events"; caused by the so-called "Watson Time Avalanche Effect"[17]); at widely spaced positions in the Time Continuum of the Cosmic All! It is known that material objects and sentient beings that are shifted on the Time Line can affect one or more other positions on the Time Line! Somehow, some way; using Time Principles unfathomable to all but the top echelon of the Imperial Time Mages and one ordinary Earthian Humanoid; the answer to that previously mentioned "Kor-Kian Puzzle" impossibly and improbably exists simultaneously in Earth's far distant past; in the suddenly "new" present position in "Time"; and also far; far in the "new" distant future "Time Track" that suddenly; and using what was previously thought to be a virtually impossible "transaction"; had replaced the old "Past" and "Future" Time Tracks permanently; and after an eerie intervention by a "Citizen One" being[11]; with absolutely no repercussions or damage; or any sentient being on the Main Galactic Time Line or any of its branches knowing that anything had changed!!!!!

But **WHY DID THIS UNIQUE EVENT OCCUR?!?!?**

Well, as the popular fictitious protagonist known as "Professor Crime"; the well-known "Crime Scientist"; i.e., "Crime Fighter"; frequently says to Mumford Mullens, his so-called "sidekick" on the episodes which are shown weekly on "The Stranger Still Zone" that can be observed on the famous Martian Sci-Fi Channel; **"That will have to be closely studied; before it can be explained; Mumford!!"**

So Imperial Citizen, read the following Imperial Document and be prepared to be amazed at what it verifies--incredible events that will happen/are happening/have happened; in our section of the Cosmic All; and our section of the Main Galactic Time Line; that have never occurred before!! Historically; they have never been reported before; and probably never will happen again in our dimension and all across our entire Cosmic All! But did these incredible impossible incidents that are about to be revealed; actually happen in the "real world" to ordinary sentient beings as visualized by the Imperial Magi; or are they just fantastic constructions of an author's imagination?!?!?

Well. . . . . there is a saying that is very appropriate in this unique situation! To quote a saying that is often stated by Earth Aerospace Force Master-Sergeant Sammy Parks; a minor protagonist that is seen very regularly on an eerie science fiction program "The Star Marines!" to his "sidekick" comrade Johnny Baxter Storm-Cloud; and all the men under his command!

"Read the manual and find out, JB!"

In other words, read the following Imperial document; then ponder the situation and contact the nearest Imperial Seer if you have any questions or you want to provide any additional information!!

CHAPTER 2

And so it came to pass that on a particular point on the Main Galactic Time Line an infinitely important "Anchor Event"[18] was approaching fruition that would affect literally every living being in the entire Cosmos!! Thus, at a very important position on the Main Galactic Time Line; the stars shown in all their eternal glory as the almost completely automatic long-range EAF patrol ship "Sam Houston" solely manned by veteran Patrolman Johnny Trevor, approached its maximum search range a little beyond the orbit of the so-called "dwarf-planet" Pluto and its large moon Charon; and prepared to gradually turn 90° to continue its patrolling of the unmarked frontier span of the small solar system. As the young aerospace pilot started programming his course computer to change his trajectory the instant he reached "Point Beta", he looked down on the picture of his fiancée, Susan Wagstaff; which he had taped to the side of his forward instrument panel. But even as Johnny looked up to continue his chosen trajectory; because the young Earthian did not possess the mental powers of an Imperial Magi, he could not feel the Winds of Destiny start to swirl around his craft; indicating that something very; very important was about to happen--either something very, very good; or something very, **very BAD!!** (The final description of the forthcoming "Galactic Anchor" Event would depend upon certain important events that had happened/were happening/would happen on the Main Galactic Time Line in the Past/Present/and/or Future; with the verb tense to use depending upon the reader's position on the Main Galactic Time Line!)

Just before that moment for altering its path arrived, the ship's primitive, but powerful "sadar"[1] sensor picked up an enormous contact at long range! An instant later the contact became a tremendous mile-long alien craft; with dozens of what appeared to be weapons pods and platforms attached to all of its sides; that was floating less than a few thousand feet from the "Houston's" prow! Instantly, following standard protocol, Patrolman Trevor fired off a white flare, on a trajectory away from the unknown alien craft; indicating peaceful intentions! He then started transmitting peace signals on all known frequencies to let the unknown beings on the huge warship ship know that he meant no harm! Then he powered up all his defensive screens and offensive weapons; (although against such an apparently large and powerful ship, he knew they would be as useless against the unknown vessel as using a thimble to bail out the ocean)! Next he programmed the AI navigator to start an evasive pattern of travel; then coolly sent an emergency message to Earth; along with automatic second-by-second reproductions of every one of its internal and external sensors! (Lastly he tried to send a short personal message, but its signal was cut short by powerful jamming fields projected from the enormous alien craft.)

On Earth, at the headquarters for the Aerospace Defense force at the famous "Chuck Yeager Air Force Base"; as the emergency signal and the "Houston's" sensor data started coming in and was immediately noted by trained observers; back in faraway space; several important events in and around the "Sam Houston" happened very quickly! First, the ship's automatic internal sensors reported that the pilot had mysteriously vanished; then it recorded and transmitted the sadar tracings to headquarters as the unknown invader moved away from the ship! After this, the alien ship then apparently accelerated to a large percentage of the speed of light to exit the solar system; heading in the direction of the Milky Way! For only a few seconds the sadar tracked the raider as it covered almost a million miles away from the sun; long enough for the military computers on Earth to compute where the enormous ship was headed. As the invading ship disappeared from the transmitted sensor readings, it appeared on the automatic long range sensors on the dwarf-planet Pluto and then on the ship's sensor recordings that were being received. The next instant the sensors reported that apparently the "Houston" was suddenly entirely vaporized by what looked like a pale red beam of light coming from beyond the range of the scope; just as Patrolman Trevor had just started an apparently personal message; "Tell Susan that I lo. . . .". One moment the sensors reported that the patrol ship was a solid object; the next nanosecond the readouts indicated only a large cloud of rapidly expanding gas!!

For a split-second the color video and audio sensors on the doomed ship showed that a powerful ray of enormous energy briefly touched its hull; and apparently the entire ship's Tytano steel hull instantly ceased to exist; incredibly, all the plastic; metal; and paper substances in its hull all evaporated to nothingness by the extremely powerful energy beam!! Immediately the ship's automatic beacon signal that had been sending a continuous position indicator to its base; and all other data transmission ceased! On the ship's military base; the termination of the signal caused Trevor's commanding officer to try to contact his young pilot; with no luck! The pilot's personal communicator frequency was dead and even the rugged emergency transponder hidden in the ship's life boat was not functioning!

Following standard emergency protocol, using all the visual and audio data that the Aerospace Defense Headquarters had received from the doomed ship's communications suite and the sensors on the dwarf-planet Pluto; AI tactics computers working in tandem with Humanoid experts came to several conclusions. First, it appeared that the patrol ship "Sam Houston" had been completely destroyed and literally vaporized by an extremely powerful energy beam of unknown design and projected by unknown forces from far outside the solar system of Earth! Secondly, the ship's audio and visual transmissions seemed to indicate that immediately before the ship had been totally destroyed by energy weapons employed by unknown forces, Patrolman Trevor had somehow been removed, or "transposed" from his ship; apparently just like in all the popular science fiction movies on the Sci-Fi channel! As the impossible facts about the disappearance of the young patrolman were inserted into the official record by the computer-aided conference of Humanoid military experts and the AIs used by the Aerospace Defense forces to increase their efficiency; against all odds; similar ironic thoughts almost simultaneously popped up into the minds of the seven Humanoid members of the conference! After hearing and seeing all the data about what happened to Patrolman Trevor, they all remembered that an amazingly similar fictitious event had happened only a few weeks before on an episode of the tremendously popular high-definition television sci-fi program, "The Stranger Zone"! It that episode of fantasy, space aliens from the planet "Blockon" had kidnapped a crippled Earthian baseball player; making it look like his automobile had been totally destroyed; and after taking him in time stasis to their planet; healed him with their superior medical technology so that he could perform an important job for them on "Kildorf"; an enemy planet! The space aliens could not safely descend to the surface of "Kildorf" because of extremely advanced enemy electronic and biological counter-measures that would quickly crumble their space suits; then degenerate and destroy particular enzymes that existed in their cell structures; causing instant death! Hence; they physically could not safely go without their bodies being literally dissolved and totally destroyed! **But each of the Humanoid military experts who remembered this story line immediately realized that the incident that had just happened was not a fiction story projected for the enjoyment of television viewers; it was actual events happening to sentient beings![21]**

With no hard evidence as to what force destroyed the "Houston" and where the unknown enemy force would strike next, the defense conference had some hard choices to make! The defense forces of Earth did not possess enough ships, sensors, and equipment to guard the whole frontier out beyond the orbit of dwarf-planet Pluto; therefore Supreme Fleet Admiral Blow and the top officers of the Earth Aerospace Force would have to pick their patrol and sensor search areas very carefully and hope for the best! As the defensive preparations went forward, none of Earth's primitive inhabitants could feel the fabled Winds of Destiny surge at record levels around every square inch of the tiny, but somehow important planet! But, since the planet did not, at the moment; contain any "home-grown" Humanoids with "Telepathic Quotients" high enough to be trained as Imperial Seers; who without any training could have intuitively "sensed" the wisps of energy surging around them; that important fact was missed by the billions of beings that populated the small planet! But there were some beings on the tiny orb who were painfully aware of the sudden surge of the sub-atomic energy beings known by the Imperial Seers as the "Winds of Destiny"! Several of the "proxies"; or Citizens of the Empire that had been sent to the Earth in order to allow the Empire to keep track of its scientific accomplishments; were instantly aware of the energy gale and had to instinctively raise their mental shields in order to protect their upper "brainar" facilities from being totally destroyed! The Magi proxies then immediately transmitted an emergency message about the tremendous surge of the Winds of Destiny to Empire Prime using their covert FTL com units; and waited for instructions from their superiors! But neither the clandestine Imperial spies; nor their military and civilian contacts on the Capital Planet so far across the Universe; could figure out just what was happening or what had happened to cause the Winds of Destiny to rise to gale force! The Imperial Magi could only keep their protective shields up and wait for the Winds of Destiny to ebb so that they could visualize the Time Line to determine what had just happened!! Alas! All the sentient beings that were being affected by the surge of subatomic energy could do was **WAIT!!** And all one Admiral Jonathan Baines Blow could do was **ALSO IMPATIENTLY WAIT;** as the powerful Winds of Destiny surged up from their subatomic homes; sped out into interplanetary and interstellar space at thousands of times the speed of light; and on past Empire Prime in just a few minutes!!

CHAPTER 3

The previous events in space that were documented in the previous sections of this Imperial document created a dilemma for Earth's top Space Force Admiral!! Because for one of the extremely rare times in his long life of military service; Supreme Fleet Admiral Jonathan Baines Blow was stumped by something that had happened to personnel under his command and he literally did not know what to do! Communications had just arrived that indicated that for the first time in many years; he had lost a ship under his command to what the official report said was "unknown enemy action"! The reported combat action was reported to be at the extreme range of his unit's assigned theatre of operations; out past the far reaches of the solar system; beyond the orbit path of the dwarf planet known as "Pluto-Charon". The Admiral's problem was that he had no evidence or idea just who or what destroyed his craft; other than ultra-long range enhanced telescopic pictures; and thus he was helpless to retaliate against the unknown hostile force that had destroyed his patrol craft without warning! The craft could have been destroyed by an equipment failure; but that hypothesis was immediately discounted! Upon receiving the report of the possible attack; Earthian forces immediately scrambled every ship that could raise gravity and the area where the patrol craft was apparently destroyed was thoroughly investigated with every sensor and technique known to Earthian science! But the only clue that the Earthians had about the invader was a transmitted recording of several seconds of the "Houston's" sadar which could be used to predict a trajectory for the unknown ship's destination.

Day after day; and a large percentage of each night; the very stubborn Admiral Blow used all the official resources at his command, and a few of the "unofficial ones"; trying to put all the tantalizing pieces of evidence together to figure out just what happened far out in space resulting in the loss of one of Earth's finest patrol craft, but more importantly; the tragic loss of one of its finest young men! Johnny Trevor was an extremely talented officer that to all of his commanding officers seemed bound for greatness! The young navy man had an almost genius IQ; he got along with everyone; and he had used "old-fashioned" common sense in everything that he did! Because of all these qualities; he was being primed by the cooperating Admirals and the Generals who commanded the Earthian Aerospace Forces for quick promotion to join them on the upper levels of command because Earth needed his mental and physical capabilities!

Because of the destruction of the patrol craft by unknown forces; the high command; following the laws set forth in the Earthian constitution of 2215; declared martial law; organized all planetary citizens to defend the planet in case of attack; and prepared the planet's defenses in case of another sneak attack!

Under emergency protocols, every military and scientific ship that had the capability and that could be spared journeyed to the orbit of Pluto to search for Intel--any sign of the destroyed Earthian patrol ship or the unknown invader. An organized search using a host of civilian and military ships scoured the area where the "Houston" disappeared for many days with every sensor that they possessed set on emergency overload! The net result was that they found nothing pertaining to the case! The searchers did find a few burned out obsolete rocket cases; several primitive scientific satellites dating back to the dawn of the Space Age which had been sent out to explore the outer planets; a few unidentifiable metal items; and other archaic military items; all dating back to the "Cold War" which had ended several centuries before. No trace of the missing ship; either liquid, solid, or plasma residue; was ever found! It was as if every atom of the ship had been destroyed and turned into energy; or maybe the ship had been captured by the huge ship! But the indication of a large explosion on all the visual sensor data seemed to make it appear that the "Sam Houston"; (named for the Texas hero at the historic Battle of San Jacinto); had been totally destroyed; the first ship under Admiral Blow's command that had been lost in many years; and he took the loss very, very hard!

As such, exactly like he had since the first day he had gained command of the fleet and immediately considered it **HIS** fleet manned by **HIS** personnel; the Admiral took it very; **very personal** that someone or something had killed one of his men without warning and with no chance to for the man in his command to defend himself! And deep, deep down in his Id; his Soul; or the Gestalt that made up one Jonathan Baines "Hurricane" Blow; a terrible resolve began forming: **WHOEVER OR WHATEVER DID THIS DESPICABLE ACT OF INVADING THE SOLAR SYSTEM AND DESTROYING HIS SHIP AND KILLING HIS PATROLMAN WOULD SOMEHOW; SOMEWAY; SOMEDAY; REGRET THE ACTIONS!! JOHNNY TREVOR WOULD BE AVENGED; EVEN IF IT TOOK ALL OF ETERNITY TO PAY THE UNKNOWN ENEMY BACK!** And as any former associate or naval person who had ever been under his command could attest; when Admiral Blow purposed in his Heart to do "take care" of something very important like the terrible act that had just occurred; **HE WOULD EITHER ACCOMPLISH IT PERSONALLY** or sometime in the future, one of the persons under his command would carry out the highly-rated assignment! In the unlikely event that the "job" could not be done or if the "responsibility" could not be completed at that point in time; the Admiral would wait for a more opportune time to get the job done! When the perpetrators of the unprovoked attack were identified; at the earliest possible time; the Admiral would use every resource that he had to strike back in order to repay such a terrible deed!

Throughout his long military service as a top commander, the veteran Imperial Navy man had a very plain "modus operandi"! Ever since the "Skee-Kan-Toe" raids beginning around 2063 Anno Domini, Earth time, (465,934 A.F.E., Empire Time); when he had first covertly met Captains Gallant and Cody from the gigantic Interstellar Condominium of Planets and Empires, and had secretly given them help; Admiral Blow's official military protocol to be followed for all foreseeable and unforeseeable situations was "set in stone"! After his relatively small navy, with the help of the two captains; had defeated the raider's fleet after years of conflict; every one of his subordinate staff knew what he would do under all military campaign circumstances! If it looked like that revenge on the Earth's unknown enemies that destroyed the patrol ship could not be accomplished in 10 years, or 50 years, or 100 years, or 200 years, or even 1000 years; the Admiral would "make a permanent note"; and for the rest of his life he would look to somehow find a favorable opportunity to personally attempt to accomplish it, or let one of the skilled soldiers or sailors under his command volunteer to do the job if such an opportunity presented itself! When a "note" was unpaid for several years; Admiral Blow made plans to have the note "refinanced" by someone else. i.e.; if his span of Earthian Navy service was too short to "pay the debt"; i.e., he retired or died; then the "note" would be automatically given to his successor to pay off and exact revenge!

But finally; after many long hours sifting the evidence with his military advisors and his scientific experts to guide them, the Supreme Commander of Earth Forces had to come to the final conclusion that barring an extremely unlikely catastrophic equipment failure: A). The patrol ship "Sam Houston" had been either captured or totally destroyed by an unknown force and B). There was nothing that could be done to either find the missing man or retaliate against the unknown forces which had invaded the solar system! Earth forces were helpless! They did not have the technology to either identify the assailant, or have the means to travel the long light year distances in order to seek out its home planet; which lay far out in the galaxy; far beyond the range of Earth's short range space vehicles!

But following the personal modus operandi that he had used all his life, one Jonathan Baines "Hurricane" Blow stubbornly refused to face the hard facts and quit searching for answers that were not there! All his life he had always believed that when stumped by a problem, if he researched and dug, ultimately; he would find the answer to any problem, if he kept on "plugging"; kept on trying; and **did not quit!** Obstinately, he kept on trying to find an answer to the riddle of the terrible loss; which from the first report of the attack; he had "taken very personal"; i.e.; **EXTREMELY "PERSONAL"!** Night after weary night, after attending to his normal command duties; he stayed in his office and tried to gleam additional facts from the sparse data that was available; comprised mainly of several seconds of sadar images, and pages and pages of extremely dry scientific computer reports which always indicated that the researchers had found nothing. He tried enhancing the available images with computer programs; but that only blurred the images even more than the original pictures, making them even more useless to obtain pictorial data about the deadly unprovoked attack on his patrolman. He researched all the logs of all the other patrol craft on duty at the same time as the doomed ship and again found nothing that could be used. He checked all the radar and sadar video tapes of every military installation in the solar system for the period of a week before the incident; and a week after; looking for any possible unreported contact before and after the deadly attack. The Admiral found nothing to help his quest! As he stubbornly, (and seemingly senselessly); refused to quit; unknown to his ordinary Humanoid senses, the Winds of Destiny gradually rose in intensity around him; indicating something of Galactic Importance was happening or about to happen!! But never-the-less; with absolutely nothing to indicate who or what had destroyed his ship; the seemingly useless one-man research effort continued unabated!

Day after day; night after night, seven days a week, after finishing his regular command duties; the famous Admiral with fiery red hair named Blow ate; slept; and worked in his office instead of taking off to relax for a short time at his home with his beloved wife; Mary Pearl Blow; who was undergoing very painful chemo and radiation treatments to attempt to cure numerous cancer tumors in her body that had metastasized from a large tumor that had been removed several years ago! Some nights she would bring a meal up to his office and they would have a quiet evening together; just enjoying each other's company. When she got drowsy, Mary Pearl would sleep the entire night on a cot in the office so she could be close to the man she loved; while her husband continued to work in order to solve his Very Important Problem; with no letup! As he had the entire time of his military career; when faced with a problem, the admiral absolutely refused to quit and accept defeat; he kept on striving to find the information that he needed in order to "balance the books" against the unknown forces that had invaded the solar system and kidnapped and murdered his pilot **FOR ABSOLUTELY NO REASON!!!**

Having been very happily married to her husband since he was a first year military college student and during the very difficult period that he was a cadet pilot; his beloved wife Mary Pearl understood and tried to keep the home fires burning for the Admiral; even when her chemo treatments for stage four cancer made her extremely ill and unable to eat; and made every strand of her long blond hair fall out; causing her to wear a long blond wig until end of the chemo treatments and hopefully her hair started growing again. (The couple was not able to have children because in the early days of their marriage in order to save her life; after extensive surgery for cancer; she had to have chemotherapy almost continuously up to; and beyond; the present time to keep the cancer that the surgery could not get from spreading.)

Time after time, over and over; using his trained photographic memory; the Admiral reviewed each small bit of pertinent data scanning thousands of individual ship's combat reports, seeking to find something that he had missed the dozens of times he had reviewed the data before. Then late one Tuesday night, he almost, **HE ALMOST**, accepted defeat! (The "key word" is **ALMOST!!**) Sitting at his desk the man known as Admiral Johnathan "Hurricane" Blow; (because of his tremendous, but controllable temper which he always put to good use to focus his entire being on solving a problem); put his head in his hands; looked up toward Heaven, and started silently crying and praying! *Why? Why did this terrible thing happen? Why can't I find out whom or what did this terrible deed! HELP ME!* He asked and prayed over and over again as the days went by! Then; one fateful night, he became silent in his mind and finally accepted final and total defeat! For one of the few times in his personal and military lives, **HE HAD BEEN DEFEATED, BUT STILL HE WOULD NOT GIVE UP;** as he forcefully vowed in his mind!!!!

Then finally, the Admiral screamed to the walls; since he knew that he would not disturb anyone because his beloved Mary Pearl was at home and there was no one left on duty in the large building; with all the doors locked and the electronic security system on to prevent any intruders; either by smashing in a door or by transposing directly into the building! Then he came to a fateful decision and vowed: *#BY THE ETERNAL COSMIC ALL, IF I SOMEHOW LIVE TO BE ONE THOUSAND YEARS OLD WITH THE HELP OF EMPIRE ADVANCED MEDICAL TECHNOLOGY; I WILL NEVER STOP TRYING TO FIND OUT WHO DID THIS SENSELESS ACT AND I WILL RETALIATE WITH THE PROPER FORCES AGAINST THE PERPETRATOR! IF I CAN NOT FIND OUT WHO DID THIS NEFARIOUS DEED DURING MY LIFETIME, I WILL LET MY SUCCESSORS ALL CONTINUE THE CRUSADE UNTIL ETERNITY IS REACHED AND THE UNKNOWN PERPETRATOR IS FINALLY BROUGHT TO JUSTICE BY THE SUPREME BEING!!#*

As the Admiral's vow was completed; the EAF building was very silent; as if the vow would do nothing to solve his problem! But the old Anglo-Saxon proverb that **"The darkest part of the night means dawn is about to break!"** was; and is; **STILL VERY TRUE--BUT ALSO, THIS HISTORIC WISE SAYING IS <u>TRUE</u> <u>"IN MORE WAYS THAN ONE"</u>!!!** As his eyes blurred with the tears of his frustration, a strange; very small pinpoint of light suddenly appeared on the top of his desk amid his papers and his communication equipment! It quickly expanded; and then just as quickly the brilliance faded to nothingness! But as the light faded; then disappeared; a medium-sized envelope suddenly appeared just in front of his quivering hands! Wiping the hot tears of frustration from his eyes so that he could see, the **MAN** known by the service persons under his command as the one and only Admiral "Hurricane" Blow; grabbed and opened the ordinary-looking envelope with hands that no longer quivered! For some strange reason, the instant he touched the envelope; after weeks of inner turmoil; he was suddenly at peace in his Soul; because somehow he felt that his hard work; his pleas; and his fervent prayers had somehow been miraculously answered! (It had to be "miraculous" because envelopes just do not appear out of thin air above ones desk; except during episodes on fictitious satellite television shows such as "The Stranger Still Zone"!) Carefully tearing open the envelope's flap and pulling out the contents, he found that it only contained one page of very precise; very small; closely-spaced hand-written words; the writing of which was very familiar and red letters and numbers on the page looked like he had somehow written it! All of the closely spaced words on the sheet looked exactly like they had been constructed with the same unique writing techniques that he always used! Quickly scanning the strangely familiar page; the Fleet Admiral's brain soaked up the detailed information on the sheet like a sponge; as he read the most important message in the entire history of the Earth and its relatively-new Space Fleet!

His photographic memory was important because the split-second his eyes scanned the last letter of the last word in the message, the page and the envelope vanished; to be replaced with a small amount of very hot material; which dropped through his hands and then proceeded to burn a small hole through the desk and drop on the floor to slightly mar its surface!! But the Admiral did not give the extensive damage to his expensive desk and slight damage to the floor a trillionth of a second's notice as he had quickly read and understood the data written on the page using a strangely familiar printing script, (**WHICH HE KNEW INSTANTLY, WHEN HE SCANNED THE FIRST LETTER OF THE FIRST WORD, HAD INCREDIBLY BEEN WRITTEN IN RED "BLINK-O" BALLPOINT PEN INK BY HIS OWN HANDS; USING HIS FAVORITE WRITING SCRIPT; SPACING; AND SLIGHTLY DIFFERENT TECHNIQUE IN SHAPING CERTAIN LETTERS!) ALL OF WHICH MEANT THAT HE HAD SOMEHOW IMPOSSIBILY SENT THE MESSAGE TO HIMSELF FROM SOMETIME IN THE FUTURE WHEN CERTAIN IMPORTANT EVENTS INVOLVING HIM HAD TRANSPIRED!! (FROM THE TONE OF THE INSTRUCTIONS, THE FUTURE EVENTS HAD NOT TURNED OUT SO WELL FOR EARTHIAN FORCES!!)** So through an apparent miracle; which he did not at the moment understand; he immediately had all the vital information about what his forces could do and must do to protect Earth from attack and attempt to rescue his missing pilot on the Thunder Worlds; because of the exact instructions on the sheet; which seemed to imply that Earthian forces had been "whupped" by the Thunder World forces!!

The strange note also advised him to stop his wife's initial radiation and chemo treatments and take her to another cancer doctor that employed the techniques of Dr. Regal Strife that used microwaves tuned to kill the cancer cells and leave ordinary cells unharmed; instead of the customary combination of extremely destructive surgery, radiation, and chemotherapy!! The note said that the customary daily and weekly chemotherapy and radiation treatments used to eradicate the cancer would eventually kill his wife; but several Strife microwave treatments would cure her cancer with absolutely no side effects; including not losing her beautiful blond hair!!

He believed what the page said because, again; impossible as it seemed to be; HE RECOGNIZED HIS OWN UNIQUE CHOICE OF WORDS; SHAPING OF CERTAIN LETTERS; (LIKE PUTTING AN ARROW AT THE TOP OF EACH J; AND OBSERVING HIS OWN UNIQUE WRITING STYLE); ALL OF WHICH MADE HIM TRUST THE INFORMATION EVEN THOUGH IT SEEMED TO BE AN IMPOSSIBLE TIME PARADOX TO BELIEVE THAT SOMEHOW; SOMEWAY; SOMETIME IN THE FUTURE HE SOMEHOW HAD THE MEANS TO SENT THE NOTE BACK IN TIME TO WARN HIMSELF AND GIVE DETAILED INSTRUCTIONS ON HOW TO RESCUE HIS PATROLMAN AND PAY BACK THE INVADERS WHO HAD DONE THE TERRIBLE DEED! ERGO, IF HE COULD NOT TRUST HIMSELF; WHO COULD HE TRUST? THEREFORE; JUST LIKE EARTHIAN HISTORY RECORDED THAT THE FAMOUS MARSHAL SAMSON BLAIR[12] HAD ALWAYS DONE BACK IN THE OLD WEST WHEN HE PLAYED THE EARTHIAN CARD GAME OF "POKER"

WITH HIS FRIENDS! ERGO; TO SAVE HIS PATROLMAN; HE WOULD FIGURATIVELY SHOVE ALL HIS "POKER CHIPS" INTO THE CENTER OF THE TABLE BY PUTTING LITERALLY EVERY SHIP EARTH HAD INTO SERVICE; AND WOULD LITERALLY BET HIS LIFE AND THE LIFE OF PLANET EARTH THAT THE INFORMATION ON THE EERIE DISAPPEARING NOTE WAS 100% TRUE!! (WHICH IT WAS!!!!!) He would bet his life because the note said to just send in one small ship, instead of every warship that Earth could muster; hence he would be the one to put his life on the line in order to save his patrolman; and not all the personnel in the Earthian fleet; which had apparently caused the loss of many ships and personnel!!

If the Admiral had thought about the strange event more; he would have remembered and recognized a plot line from an episode from one of his favorite shows called "The Stranger Zone"; (the predecessor of "The Stranger Still Zone"); which had aired a few years ago! The name of the author of the eerie episode was listed on the show's credits which appeared on the rolling credits after the episode was over as "Norman Chance"; which was actually a "pen name". The writer's real name was John Chance Watson; AKA[16] **THE** Doctor Chance Watson; who many years ago; had a real life experience on the subject of "Time Travel"[2]!

What happened next did nothing to tarnish the rock-hard reputation of one Fleet Admiral "JB" Blow! The present ranking Flag Officer of Earth's space fleet, from his earliest days in the military of what had been the North American Federation; was never one to hesitate when it came to doing the tough jobs that were necessary! So a split second after the last letter of the note faded from sight; Blow opened a small round recessed cap that was on the top of his desk, which exposed an oddly shaped key hole. Reaching into one of his front pockets, he extracted a large ring of keys and inserted an oddly shaped key on his large keychain. He then pushed and turned the plastic key at the same time in a certain manner to accomplish his purpose. (The key being partially made of plastic instead of metal kept an electronic circuit from being activated which would have detonated a large explosive charge!) An instant after the combination key was finished turning and was taken out, there was a small click, and a small panel slid back from the unadorned left side of his command desk; revealing what looked like a keypad of different colored round and square buttons of various sizes. Without hesitation Blow pressed a small recessed insignificant green button that was inside a circle of larger red buttons. The immediate result of pressing the unimportant-looking button was turning on every emergency claxon horn within every Earth military installation to sound in a certain pattern! That particular patterned signal put each military base on its absolute top alert status and required all personnel to immediately go to their Emergency Post to await further orders!! Immediately as every emergency signal each base and installation possessed was turned on; every one of their exterior lights came to full power! In the minutes that followed, the Admiral then used his laptop computer to construct and automatically send detailed orders for every living military officer and enlisted person on the affected bases and installations! The orders sent the entire Earth defensive and offensive forces to execute "Emergency Plan Beta"; which was one of several emergency plans that he could have ordered by pressing different buttons under the concealed cover! In his heart, he had no qualms about trusting the strange message which was somehow; SOME WAY; IMPOSSIBLY SENT THROUGH TIME; SENT INCREDIBLY BY HIMSELF IN THE FUTURE TO HIMSELF IN THE PAST; SO THAT HE WOULD BE SUCCESSFUL IN THE RESCUE OF HIS PATROLMAN AND THE HEALING OF HIS WIFE'S CANCER!! THE NEVER-GIVE- UP; NEVER-QUIT ADMIRAL "HURRICANE" BLOW HAD SOMEHOW; SOMEWAY; IMPOSSIBLY COME THROUGH AGAIN "IN THE CLUTCH"[23]; ACCOMPLISHING THE IMPOSSIBLE FEAT OF SENDING HIMSELF A MESSAGE FROM THE FUTURE WHICH TOLD HIM WHAT TO DO; INSTEAD OF GOING AHEAD AND DOING AN ALL-OUT ATTACK ON THE THUNDER WORLDS WITH THE ENTIRE EARTH FLEET THAT APPARENTLY HAD NOT WORKED; AND BEGINNING MEDICAL TREATMENTS FOR CANCER ON HIS BELOVED WIFE THAT APPARENTLY HAD NOT WORKED!! THIS CAUSED ALL THE EVENTS OF HIS FUTURE LIFE PATH; THAT HAD BEEN VISIBLE TO IMPERIAL SEERS ON EMPIRE PRIME; TO SUDDENLLY BECOME BLANK!! THEY NO LONGER SHOWED ADMIRAL BLOW FRUITLESSLY TAKING HIS BELOVED WIFE TO A LOCAL HOSPITAL FOR USELESS CANCER TREATMENTS THAT EVENTUALLY CAUSED

HER DEATH! THE TIME LINE ALSO DID NOT SHOW THE ADMIRAL TRYING TO RESCUE HIS PATROLMAN AND EITHER BEING KILLED WHEN THE REPTILOIDS DESTROYED EARTH; OR BEING CAPTURED BY THE THUNDER WORLDS FORCES AND IMPRISONED FOR THE REST OF HIS LIFE WITH HIS RIGHT ARM MISSING!! AT THAT INSTANT; EVERY POSSIBLE FUTURE LIFE PATH OF ADMIRAL JONATHAN BAINES BLOW WAS EITHER BLANK OR TOTALLY BLACK; WHICH INDICATED THAT THE REST OF HIS LIFE PATH DEPENDED UPON HIS ACTIONS AFFECTING EVENTS THAT WOULD HAPPEN IN THE NEXT FEW MINUTES OR HOURS OR DAYS OR YEARS!! In the future; when they tried; the experienced mental powers of the most powerful Imperial Magi could not fathom the time interval in which they would take place!!

Ultimately; when the "Time Scenes" on the Main Galactic Time Line slowly returned; they would show a change in the Admiral's Future Life Path from probable Death or Imprisonment to a possible Life Path of joy and pleasure! It would also cause the Orbit Paths of every galaxy; the Future Destiny Paths of every empire and planet; and the Life Path of every sentient being in the whole of Creation to suddenly be somehow altered! Because of his altered Life Path; every Galactic Time Line and Sentient Being Life Path in the Cosmic All suddenly became dark or vacant; causing the Imperial Magi to issue an Empire-wide alert and the Imperial Naval Headquarters on Empire Prime to put every Imperial planet and Naval Ship on

Emergency Patrol duty with every sensor on emergency power until it could be ascertained exactly what was causing such a ruckus on every Life Path and Destiny Path that existed in the Whole of Creation! But how long would this dangerous time of uncertainty last?!?!? The Imperial Magi did not know and at the moment; since the Main Galactic Time Line was blank; they could not use their legendary mental powers to find out!!! All every Imperial Seer and Citizen could do was. . . . WAIT; TO ULTIMATELY VISUALIZE THE MOST IMPORTANT "ANCHOR EVENT" IN THE HISTORY OF THE WHOLE CREATION! AN EVENT THAT ALL OF THE ENTIRE FUTURE MAIN GALACTIC TIME LINES WOULD LITERALLY "SWING AROUND"! IT WOULD BE AN EVENT THAT WOULD EITHER TOTALLY DESTROY EARTH AND ALL TRACES OF THE PLANET ON THE MAIN GALACTIC TIME LINE OR THE UNIQUE EVENT WOULD GREATLY STRENGTHEN ITS PLANETARY OFFENSIVE AND DEFENSIVE FORCES! BUT WHICH ONE?!?!?

No sentient being knew; or could fathom just what was going to happen; where it was going to happen; or whose life path it was going to alter/and/or influence in some unknown manner!!

CHAPTER 4

The Admiral trusted the message because he knew that somehow, some way, at some unknown time in the future; when he had found out just **WHO** or **WHAT** had attacked his patrol craft; then at that time in the future he had somehow; some way, managed to find a way to send back a message to himself in the Past so that he could "even the score" with Thud and also save the life of his beloved wife Mary Pearl! That had been the modus operandi of Admiral "Hurricane" Blow since the earliest days of his career in the Earthian space force! When faced with a problem or superior enemy forces or an impossible problem; **SOMEHOW; SOMEWAY; HE WOULD SOLVE THE PROBLEM; DEFEAT THE ENEMY FORCES WITH THE RESOURCES THAT HE HAD; AND SOLVE THE "IMPOSSIBLE" PROBLEMS FACING HIM WITH THE FORCES THAT HE HAD!**

So now with what he knew in his Heart was the correct "Intel", the Admiral's highly-trained military brain fit all the pieces together and started reworking his future personal and military plans!! First he called and cancelled his wife's first appointment for conventional cancer treatments at the local base hospital. Then he looked up Dr. Regal Strife's office address and phone number; and made an initial doctor's appointment for his wife immediately after his next important mission that he was about to set in motion! Then he called Mary Pearl and explained to her just what was going on and simply telling her that her regular cancer treatment had been canceled and a new treatment would be tried after his next mission. Mary Pearl was pleasantly surprised at news, but she had not been looking forward to withstanding all the side effects of the standard cancer treatment; nausea, swelling of limbs, losing her beautiful long blond hair, as well as several other unpleasant side effects!

With his much-loved wife's treatment schedule taken care of; the Admiral started moving his military forces around like chess pieces on a chess board; the only difference being the "pieces" involved were not on a two-dimensional board of a few square feet, they were on a three-dimensional span of outer space possibly several light years across; and the "pieces" were the personnel and the equipment of the EAF; which were being moved to defend planet Earth from the unknown enemy forces that had destroyed the "Sam Houston" and killed Patrolman Johnny Trevor!

Next, using the information which he had quickly read and memorized on the vanished sheet, the MAN sent an emergency request to the Egyptian government to be allowed to excavate a certain remote section of the Nile River to obtain certain Aerospace Force property which had been deposited at that location during a secret mission! Because Admiral Blow was on very good terms with the Egyptian Navy, and Army; his request was quickly granted and the necessary legal papers were immediately faxed to him.

His good friend, General Mohammed Shrini Vassan; faxed that he would meet his friend's force on the spot, as soon as he could; in order to help them all he could!

The Admiral also sent detailed orders to certain local platoon leaders and the commander of the military engineer group on the base. They were ordered to meet him ASAP on the base's flight line, the attack platoon—armed and fully combat ready; and the military engineer group bringing all their equipment to the flight line!

At the instant that the "Plan Beta" alarm sounded, the Earthian Defense Level at every base and aboard every ship was automatically raised from green to red! All military leaves were canceled and every person on leave was instantly contacted on their personal coms, home vids, satellite phones, or cell phones and told to report immediately back to duty **AS SOON AS POSSIBLE!** Every trans-Pluto fighter and long range patrol and sensor space craft on the ground at every base was fueled; armed; then launched and ordered to stay aloft on patrol until further notice! Tankers and ground-based fuel stations would keep them on station 24/7 until further notice! The Supreme Joint Chiefs of Staff immediately met and formulated offensive and defensive plans based on the new information presented by the Supreme Admiral of the Fleet!

But strangely the most important military mission being started to defend the planet also involved a very large hypersonic VTOL transport craft of a very advanced design which had been operational for only a few months. The craft had inertial dampeners; (compliments of reverse-engineering the Roswell artifacts); which substantially lowered g-forces when the plane took off and landed; when it accelerated to Mach 5 and decelerated to land; and when it had to maneuver at hypersonic speeds! The craft also had antigravity systems which substantially lowered the mass of the large plane; allowing it to transport very heavy cargo; and its main ramjets to propel the craft with greater efficiency. It had the capacity to carry the very important heavy cargo that the Admiral would first obtain on the African continent; then transport to a certain point on the North American continent. His complex actions had to be completed in order to allow his new; very complex overall plan to rescue his kidnapped patrolman a very slim chance to work! And at this point on the Main Galactic Time Line; even the Winds of Destiny had never before seen scattered events on the Main Galactic Time Line somehow interacting with each other to produce unknown effects on Future and/or Past events concurrently! Never in the history of the Cosmic All had the Winds of Destiny witnessed three or four unrelated Anchor Happenings on the Main Galactic Time Line somehow ''mesh'' and interact together simultaneously to produce unknown effects on one or more other Anchor Event Happenings!

But what effect would this have on literally all the Time Paths of every event and Life Path of every sentient being in the Universe; all of which were now still either blank or totally dark on the Main Galactic Time Line in every galaxy and all its branches?!?!?! Even the Imperial Magi could not fathom the answer to this important question; and they could not figure out what was causing the UNPRECEDENTED

TOTAL BLACKOUT of the Main Galactic Time Line!!! In the entire five hundred thousand year history of the Mental Magi, such a fantastic phenomenon had never before occurred; hence, because what would ultimately happen was impossible to predict since so many, many things could happen; virtually all Life Paths on the Main Galactic Time Line and all its smaller branches were blank or darkened; hence the Imperial Magi were literally powerless to visualize just what was going on!

CHAPTER 5

After confidently issuing all the necessary orders, the Admiral walked down to the nearby flight line and met the group of combat-ready soldiers and the military engineers; complete with all the heavy equipment which he had ordered that they bring. On the line, he commandeered the very large hypersonic transport to send the armed combat force; along with the military engineers; to a certain point on the Nile River in the African continent. As the troops and the engineers were climbing on the transport and the engineers were loading their gear, Blow made sure the combat force was well armed and the engineers loaded heavy-duty mining equipment, which was capable of quickly digging a wide, stable tunnel; while at the same time, being able to send all the excavated dirt efficiently back to the surface. It had to be "heavy-duty" because his information said that the goal of their excavation was several hundred feet down under a very dense and very hard layer of native rock and weighed several tons! While the engineers were digging in the dangerous region, the armed troops would be around to make sure they were not disturbed while doing their assigned job.

At the area where they would bore down; internationally famous Archeologists Doctor David McBroom, (a very good name for an archeologist!), and Doctor Chesley Blacklock; had used small whisk brooms to patiently and carefully work that same riverbank on the Nile River for thirty years; searching for important Egyptian relics and fossils. When the two men originally had decided to become partners and had selected an archeological site, they had determined that they would continue to dig at that site until they found something important, or they both died; with the other partner continuing to dig on the same spot until he died; all for the advancement of science and Egyptian archaeological knowledge!

McBroom and Blacklock paid the local help they hired very good to cart away and help them examine and sift everything that was brushed from their carefully marked off spots. Over the long years they had made it down approximately thirty feet using Whisk brooms to brush away the hard baked clay; with literally every speck of dirt examined. For three long decades they had worked a schedule almost 12 months a year and 6 days a week through the region's dry, hot seasons, and its hot rainy season; tirelessly searching for important historical discoveries and ancient Egyptian artifacts. The two competent scientists did their work the "old-fashioned way"; slowly and tediously mapping everything they found; using electronic instruments to examine each microscopic speck that they found, examining microscopic pollen and fossils; and hoping to someday discover something important historically; and faithfully recording literally mountains of absolutely useless data in their laptop computers and emailing thousands upon thousands of reams of absolutely worthless information to their college's mainframe data banks back in Virginia! Up until the exact moment that the Anchor Event started, after many years of dedicated; back-breaking; and dull archaeological work; the two archeologists had found absolutely nothing of historical or monetary value! But was that about to change?!?

But that Fateful Day, McBroom and Blacklock were totally unprepared when; without warning or any radio messages from Egyptian authorities; a very large VTOL transport plane with unfamiliar "Earth Aerospace Force" markings on its tail assembly approached their position at high speed; abruptly stopped in midair high over their archeological site; then vertically landed on a wide rocky ledge near their excavation site on the Nile River! At the same time, Egyptian Army jeeps commanded by the famous General Mohammed Shrini Vassan quickly arrived at the archeological dig location and ordered heavily armed combat teams to secure the area! Exiting very quickly from the unknown and unexpected transport plane; a large Egyptian government-authorized Aerospace Excavation Team, also heavily armed; with all of the necessary written authorization documents from the Egyptian Antiquity Minister to help them; descended on the precious archeological site of McBroom and Blacklock and; with very little notice; told them and their excavation team in no uncertain terms to quickly grab all their tools and equipment and get back out of harm's way! As soon as the archeologists and their diggers scrambled out of their excavation diggings with their whisk brooms and all their equipment; the unknown force unloaded enormous digging equipment from their plane. Then the operator turned on the powerful machine and its powerful headlights to illuminate the area of the river bank where the tunnel would be constructed; and proceeded to start digging precisely on their precious archeological site where Blacklock and McBroom had uselessly toiled for over thirty years without finding anything of historical or monetary value! Up until that instant all they had ever found was worthless desert sand, sedimentary rocks, and silt! But now; someone was going to quickly start at the spot where they had toiled for three decades and find something valuable that they would have eventually found using their patient archaeological techniques!! IT WAS NOT FAIR! MCBROOM AND BLACKLOCK'S RESEARCH TEAM WERE THERE FIRST!!! THEIR TOILING OVER 30 YEARS EXACTLY IN THE SPOT NOW BEING EXAMINED BY THE HUGE DIGGING MACHINE SHOULD BE WORTH SOMETHING! IF AND WHEN THE UNKNOWN INVADING FORCE FOUND SOMETHING BY USING THEIR ROPED OFF SEARCH AREA TO BORE INTO THE DEPTHS OF THE EARTH FOR SOMETHING THAT HAD TO BE VERY; VERY IMPORTANT; THEY SHOULD SOMEHOW BE REWARDED!

The foreign engineers used totally unfamiliar digging equipment to quickly construct a large steel-reinforced "concrete lattice" tunnel down from their cherished digging spot to far below the bedrock of the desert! A few hours later several hundred feet down, the advanced rotor digging machine; which used ground-penetrating radar to navigate and control its effective large rotating drill bits; its spinning suction rotors to gather up and swiftly expel dirt; heavy-duty steel lifting forks; and a heavy-duty conveyor belt to efficiently bring the dirt to the surface; came upon a very strange black structure beneath the ground! The operator of the digger very carefully dug around the immense object to completely uncover it. Then he used the machine's lifting forks to place the unknown object on the conveyor; and safely send it undamaged to the surface! To the watching archeologists; who had carefully dug at that spot for decades; it was as if the digging team impossibly already knew what was down there and had somehow made sure that their equipment that they brought along could safely dig around the unknown object without damaging it; and then carefully pick up the extremely heavy unknown object that had apparently been buried for many millennia; and safely transport it to the surface!! But how did the foreign digging team know that the object was down there?!?! No document about Egyptian artifacts ever published even hinted about such a large black object somehow being buried at this location; so how did the EAF engineers know about it?!? HOW COULD THEY POSSIBLY KNOW ABOUT IT?!?! IT WAS IMPOSSIBLE! IT WAS EERIE! SOME OF THE EGYPTIAN HELP CONFERED AND DECIDED THAT IT WAS JUST LIKE THE EERIE TELEVISION PROGRAMS "THE STRANGER ZONE" AND "THE STRANGER STILL ZONE" SCIENCE FICTION PROGRAMS THAT WERE TRANSLATED FROM THE ENGLISH LANGUAGE AND BROADCAST ON EGYPTIAN TELEVISION NETWORKS EVERY MONDAY AND FRIDAY NIGHTS!

McBroom and Blacklock watched from a distance with binoculars as the digger machine was used to carefully dig around the important archeological find; while carefully using quick-drying lattice cement mesh to swiftly construct walls to prevent the soft clay from caving in! After many intricate maneuvers the skilled operator of the machinery soon completely uncovered what appeared in the machine's powerful headlights to be a strange heavy cylindrical black container with a flat bottom. The unknown object was carefully lifted using the machine's steel forks; placed on the conveyor belt; and sent slowly traveling to the surface on the conveyor belt. When the work detail had the peculiar object safely deposited on the surface; following written orders which somehow incredibly accurately described what they would find; and where they would find it; all of the intricate machinery was quickly stowed on the large VTOL transport aerospace plane and all the personnel and all the heavy digging equipment were quickly removed from the excavation site! The advanced transport had the lifting power to move; and the room to house; all of the troops and equipment that it originally brought in; along with the capability to retrieve the mysterious object that was somehow impossibly found several hundred feet under hard Egyptian clay! The huge machine dug from exactly the same spot that McBroom and Blacklock had worked on for over thirty years; and extracted the large black object from a depth that the two archeologists would have reached in about thirty more years digging very slowly with their small whisk brooms; if they had not died of old age or mutated Nile Fever!!

When the entire crowd of foreign and Egyptian military personnel had left the digging site almost as quickly as they had arrived; standing by the gaping hole exactly where they had been working for decades; for the first time in many a year; McBroom and Blacklock had literally nothing to do! Digging at the spot where the two archeologists had been slowly and carefully digging all their archeological lives, in only a relatively few minutes, the invading engineers had literally completed their lifetime job for them; and had found nothing on the way down to the very eerie large black object! As the strange excavation team was leaving; they had politely asked McBroom and Blacklock if they wanted them to leave the tunnel or fill it in. After conferring briefly to answer the question, the two archeologists started wondering if they should switch sites or start again using their small brooms a few hundred feet down in the wide tunnel that had been provided! After carefully inspecting the tunnel walls beyond the bedrock and finding nothing of interest, they wisely decided to check with the Egyptian Archeological Commission and pick out another more promising site in which to dig for literally the rest of their lives! So they politely told the unknown force that had quickly built the tunnel that since it appeared to have no useful artifacts evident, they wanted it filled in for safety. When everyone was safely clear, a few ounces of C-14 explosives did the job; and after checking that the tunnel was safely filled in; the strange foreign excavation team was quickly on its way in the huge VTOL jet plane!

Back on the river bank; standing around what had been their working area with the large filled in hole in the center; the two archeologists were perplexed and confused about the very eerie events of the past few hours! Their life's work had literally been taken from them! Dr. Blacklock voiced what they both were thinking, "David, I don't know how that Aerospace Force military group got permission from the Egyptian Antiquities Government Agency to disturb our site, and how they knew that something was down there; but I think they actually just saved us at least thirty more years of fruitless digging until we gave up, retired; or both of us died of old age or some mutated Nile or Asian Fever! I am very thankful that they came to our digging site because they sure did us a favor! As they were digging using that conveyor belt to take out the dirt, we both observed that there was nothing except ordinary clay and sand on the belt; no pottery shards; no fossils; no rotten wood; no nothing; other than plain old sand, silt, and clay! We would have slowly gone down to where that strange black container rested without finding anything and wasting our lives for nothing! **But something tells me that after decades had passed and we got to where the container was at this particular instant in Time; it would not have been there!** This whole incident sounds like something that would happen on an episode on the eerie new 'Stranger Still Zone' that is broadcast on the Egyptian Sci-Fi channel every Saturday night; with the actors speaking Egyptian Arabic! Since this spot has been shown to contain nothing of value; we can now try digging at that site on the Nile where that Swami mystic told us to dig after we used some of our quinine to cure his son of malaria; or we can opt for that other promising site we almost picked thirty years ago before we started digging; instead of picking this one because you said that 'Salina', the name of the area printed on our map; sounded like your mother's middle name!"

"Yea, Chess, I agree that we need to choose another site! Let's drink some water and cool off in Cairo for a few days and think about what we should do now!" McBroom was heard to say as they left the area with their faithful, and well paid native guides and diggers to pick another site at which to dig; with the permission of the Egyptian government.

The two famous archeologists wisely chose another site; instead of spending any more time on the site which they could see contained nothing of archeological significance. They chose another promising site which local legends seemed to indicate that a prehistoric civilization once existed in the area. But hard luck continued to be all the luck that they ever had during their very long and unprofitable archeological careers! After digging for another fifteen years without finding anything; Dr. McBroom peacefully died in an Egyptian hospital with his faithful wife; Dr. Blacklock; and all their crew around him.

Then, going by his previous oral agreement with his dead colleague; Dr. Blacklock continued his quest for another fifteen years; without finding anything; except a small triangular medallion; made of what laser spectra analysis indicated was an unknown alloy of aluminum; and having unknown writing on its side. Despite being examined and its strange markings analyzed using every archeological data base in the world, the writing was never deciphered and can be still found in the London Historical Museum in London, England; planet Earth. In a few thousand years, when archeologists search under the extremely thick eternal ice covering Antarctica with laser excavators; they will find similar markings on artifacts which will document the former presence of an advanced civilization which existed long before the last Ice Age; which was literally covered up by three miles of ice when the last Ice Age started and almost the entire Earth was covered by ice! At the end of that enormous Ice Age, most of the ice melted except for clumps on the North and South poles and the permafrost in the northern and southern latitudes near the North and South Poles.

But such is the life's work of dedicated archeologists seeking to advance archeological knowledge about mankind's past! Sometimes they are lucky and discover important artifacts; and sometimes they "strike out" and find literally nothing; which makes the Life Paths of archeologists very; very interesting! If you don't think so, ask retired archaeologist Dr. Chesley Edmund Blacklock; who now lives in New York City in an exclusive retirement home for retired archaeologists! He can fill you in on some very interesting information that is not in any official history book; such as information about what really happened at the Roswell crash site; and tell you all the details about the ultra-secret "Aztec UFO" which was found hidden in a cave in the far reaches of the Grand Canyon, Arizona; in the early 1900's; then somehow information about its discovery and its exact location were lost to history!! Other retired archeologists at the retirement home had shared with Dr. Blacklock about the secret archeological finds they discovered and all the eerie events that had occurred during their exciting careers that had been kept secret by government bureaucrats and military brass! Dr. Blacklock also shared with his friends at the retirement center all the amazing facts about what had happened to him on the banks of the Nile River! With all the formerly secret information being exchanged openly between the members of the retirement center; the banter between all the retired persons was never dull!!

CHAPTER 6

The transport plane flew nonstop back to Yeager Aerospace Base and deposited its strange cargo at the extreme edge of the air base; behind a heavily-guarded compound. The Admiral thanked the combat troops and the engineers for their excellent work and told them that he would put a "Highest Commendation Award" letter in each of their files! For their gallant effort that day the Admiral told them that they each would be permanently promoted one grade level; effective the next day! He also told them that the entire mission they had just finished would be officially labeled "Ultra-Top Secret", because it involved the safety of the entire planet; and any information about it could not be discussed among themselves or with anyone else for the rest of their lives! If it were ever found out by military intelligence that anyone had 'spilled the beans', **IMMEDIATELY** 24/7/365.25; the military MPs would come looking for them for "swift and fatal" prosecution! With Admiral Blow's tough reputation; every soldier and every engineer believed him about the MPs coming to get them if; and when; they blabbed anything about the ultra-secret mission that had just been completed!! Because of the Admiral's reputation and their firm loyalty, any information about the mission was never leaked by any of the men that were involved in the undertaking! Decades later; when several men involved in the mission started having their memoirs published; nothing was ever said about the strange military mission to Egypt; or the eerie events immediately after the plane landed back at their base; peculiar happenings seemed to come out of a "Stranger Still Zone" script!

With his people taken care of, and rewarded for their excellence in carrying out the strange mission, covertly, skillfully, and without asking questions; the Admiral took the next step of his over-all fantastic plan! With several high-ranking base officers behind him, Blow approached the black container as if he impossibly knew what it was; and exactly what it contained! Slowly walking around the muddy black object; seemingly just a black oil or gasoline tank with a flat bottom for stability; the veteran military man kept closely examining the side of the artifact as if he were looking for something specific. Using his right hand to wipe away the heavily-caked dirt on one particular section, he finally found what he was seeking; a rectangular section of very shiny metal.

Then he slowly turned around, looked each of them in the eye, and spoke the words that his loyal troops would remember until the day each of them died: **"Men, this is so important that I must state that until the day you die, you are sworn to absolute secrecy about the things you will see in the next few minutes! You may never understand exactly what has previously happened; what is happening at this time; what will happen in the future because of our actions; and how this concerns you! But know this! This** mission concerns the safety and well-being of our planet, and as such, it is classified Ultra-Top-Secret!! Is that understood?" Blow loudly commanded while continuing to glance around to look each man straight in the eyes.

In response to his order, as he looked each officer directly in the eyes, each man looked at him back without flinching; saluted him; and said, **"YES SIR!"** very convincingly with their whole Heart!

After the last man gave his oath of secrecy, Blow put his hand on the strange shiny metal face plate that he had uncovered; just like the written instructions that he had apparently sent to himself instructed him to do!! Immediately, at his touch, the large black rectangular container completely disappeared from off the face of the Earth; exposing an incredible sight! All of the officers present were combat pilots and they had seen unusual airplanes at Edwards Air Force Base; in Area 51; and in the new secret testing zone in the interior of Alaska called "Area 102"; but they had never seen such a craft as what was suddenly sitting on the ground before them! The aerial combat veterans were literally awestruck and speechless by the object's sleek lines and majestic beauty! The young officers were witnesses to the fact that the ship that sat before them had just emerged from a seemingly solid metal container that had somehow mysteriously silently disappeared without leaving any trace or residue! They were also witnesses to the incredible fact that the eerie black container itself in the last few hours had just been excavated in Egypt under several hundred feet of sand and clay; and as such; it had to be at least thousands; perhaps hundreds of thousands of years old! Yet the artifact before their eyes appeared to be the most advanced air or space vehicle that they had ever seen! It was colored the blackest black and because it was apparently a streamlined "lifting body" and did not have wings; it looked like it was flying hypersonic while just lying on the ground! The aircraft was so black that was hard to see because it seemed to absorb all light around its shape! Amazingly; its exterior was vacant of any clear canopy around the cockpit! Its entire fuselage was seamless and lacked any projecting sensor arrays or openings! Each of the veteran young pilots observing the craft wondered how the pilot of such a craft could navigate without the pilot being able to look out a clear surface or have television or any type of vision screens with which to steer! The technology to allow such a craft to be successfully navigated without the pilot being able to observe his or her surroundings was a total mystery! Its exterior had no inscriptions or military markings, except for a small inscription partially covered by mud; under the left, front side of the fuselage which incredibly was written in very familiar script! It simply said "*Tanya*" in flowing English cursive writing script!! So how could they read what should be Egyptian calligraphy thousands of years old? Virtually all of the writing systems used at that time did not exist when and where this amazing craft apparently came from--several thousand years in the Past and before that particular script was ever created! The technology required to construct this amazing aircraft did not exist at the time of the Egyptian Pharaohs; which is where this craft apparently originated! They wondered if the craft came from Mu; or from mythical Atlantis?!? Was the source of the ultra-advanced craft the extremely ancient civilization discovered under the three miles of ice on Antarctica?!? Was it some other unknown advanced civilization that perished under the deep waters of some Earthian ocean or sea that had flourished in prehistoric times and then vanished under the fiery lava flow of a super volcano; the towering wave of a tsunami; or a super earthquake sending the entire civilization to the bottom of one of Earth's seas or oceans; covered with a thick blanket of lava and mud?!? The young soldiers and airmen could not fathom any answer to that conundrum; as well as wondering if the writing really a woman's name or did the flowing script mean something else? This question and dozens of others flowed through the minds of the young men as they patiently awaited orders from the Admiral as to what they should do next!

Blow broke the spell by saying, "Colonel Ballesteros, please come with me! Colonels Cody Smith; Bill Baxter; and Donell Carr, Jr.; please guard the perimeter around the ship!"

As he started walking up to the small ship, a hatchway suddenly opened before him, exposing a very bright interior. Colonel Ballesteros, the son of the retired aerospace veteran Marty Ballesteros, Senior; loyally followed his commanding officer through the cramped opening and into the command center of a ship that he had never dreamed of; except while reading science fiction novels; or watching an exciting serial episode of "Captain Space" featured on "The Stranger Still Zone" Sci-Fi series on the Science Fiction High-Def Channel!

"Here, Marty, you are my witness! Like I said outside the ship, everything you have seen and will see here will have to be kept secret indefinitely, for the safety of the entire planet Earth! Because this matter involves the safety of the entire planet, this order supersedes and countermands any order that anyone will ever give you; (including me if I am under duress or I am controlled by drugs); and bounds you to secrecy; even if you are court-martialed and pressure is brought on you to make a statement about the matter; or face a court-ordered life-time sentence of incarceration on the moon; with no chance of parole!" Blow stated as he picked up an intricately printed piece of paper; read it for a few moments, and handed it to the young man. Amazingly and impossibly; on the first line the paper stated in readable words that it was an official "Imperial document"!! It was written in formal writing script; using the same style that "Tanya" on the side of the craft was printed; in what appeared to be the same legal document written in several different languages! It was formally signed by what the one script that Marty could read; called the "present Emperor Jones XIII; of the Interstellar Condominium of Planets and Empires"; and it gave legal ownership of the AI-controlled ship named "Tanya" to one "Admiral Jonathan Baines Blow" for one extended combat mission until he returned it back to his home planet Earth; either in pristine condition, slightly damaged, heavily damaged; or totally wrecked! If the ship were totally wrecked and lost during the combat mission; there would be no penalty! Coming back in any of these conditions the ship could be legally transferred back to the previously mentioned "ICOPE", for a total refund of the original purchase price!"

The young Colonel was dumbfounded! "But....sir! How did you know about this ship, Sir; which apparently has been buried under the Egyptian soil for at least thousands of years?!?!? Who was, or is; or will be; 'Tanya'? How can we read that paper containing what should be Egyptian script thousands upon thousands of years old? Again, how could you know beforehand the exact location that it was buried; apparently for thousands of years? Because of its location so far beneath the surface of the river bank, this ship has got to have been buried for hundreds of thousands of years, buried with mud from the Nile River; yet when you somehow took it out of the container; it looked new! It is physically and impossible 'time wise' that it could contain a so-called legal paper, signed by some 'Emperor Jones XIII'; apparently thousands of years ago; giving you ownership of this advanced ship! How did such an unknown alien ruler; probably hundreds of thousands of light years away; and thousands of years ago; possibly know you would be at this obscure position in an unknown desert on a planet virtually unheard of beyond its orbit? Who could have possibly known all the factors that would allow them to produce such a paper; and making statements that were impossibly true? How could you do it? How could anyone do it? What I have witnessed here is literally impossible! It would even be almost impossible to believe even if it were seen on an eerie episode of the science fiction show on the new literally far-out 'Stranger Still Zone' called 'Far Space!'! Any writer of that great Sci-Fi show who produced such drivel would be immediately fired by Mel Blankenship, the show's great producer; for producing such an unbelievable show!!" Colonel Ballesteros sputtered; not believing that such an impossible event could possibly happen!

"Stop spouting and repeating yourself, Son! **Relax**!! I know you don't understand exactly what is happening! Please listen to me; and calm down!! **You don't have to understand what is going on for this very important ultra-secret mission to be a success!!!** But all you have to realize is the fact that; **for you and everyone else in our group;** for you; **whatever happens on this mission is totally CONDITION GREEN; NO SWEAT AND NO PROBLEM; NOW AND UNTIL THE DAY YOU DIE!** For you, everything about this military exercise is **OK** because as your commanding officer, this mission is totally my responsibility; **NOT YOURS!** You have been; and at the present time; are acting completely under my orders and under my command! You don't have to worry about anything about this ultra-secret operation; which you know nothing about because it's totally my baby and my responsibility! **Since you are following the legal orders of your superior officer, you can never; ever be prosecuted for anything that you do on this trip; since everything that you have done or will do is legal and harmless!** Again, I will tell you that you and your fellow officers are simply following legal orders given by a superior officer; **ME**! For emphasis, again; **I'm telling you that everything is in the green and everything for you is LEGAL, so please relax; stop worrying; and SMILE!** You and your friends are not doing anything that you can be prosecuted for; so calm yourself down and hang loose! I hope that someday I will be able to tell you the whole story about what we have just accomplished! If and when I do; you will be the first one that I will tell and I guarantee that you will be proud! Until then; you have to act like a clam about what you have seen and heard that is Ultra-Top-Secret!"

Blow stopped talking a moment in order to look around; then he continued, "You have known me, and I have known you literally from the first second of your life; your parents asked me to witness your birth; and I hope that when this mission is over, you and your daddy will be able to serve under me until the day you both retire!! He knows, and you know; that I am an officer of integrity; I have never, and will never do anything illegal; and **I literally always take care of the people under my command; before I take care of my own needs!!** So for this one very important time in which you cannot know just what is going on; for now you have to trust me; with no other support for following my orders, other than what you know about me! Again, I solemnly pledge to you that this secret operation is about protecting the Earth and it is not something illegal! Again, I hope that someday I can tell you just what was, what is; and what will soon go on far beyond your sight and senses in order to save our planet! Until that future time when I can release you from your oath of secrecy, you are under strict orders not to tell anyone what you have seen, or discuss it with anyone else on this mission! As a career military officer, if this is the only secret thing that you will have to carry to your grave; **you will be extremely lucky!** As you get more seniority, you will start carrying many such heavy 'baggage' concerning military secrets that must be kept quiet until the day you die!!!" Blow cautioned his young officer.

The very logical explanation of the Admiral finally penetrated the thought processes of the young Marty; and finally he stood back and said, **"YES, SIR! Thank you, SIR!! I understand, SIR! Please excuse me for running off at the mouth!"** Colonel Ballesteros stated as he stood at attention and executed a snappy salute.

The Admiral returned the salute; then said, "No problem, son!! Dismissed! As you exit, tell the other officers to stand clear! This baby has a slight blow-back when it goes FTL in a planetary atmosphere that will knock you down if you are too close to the FTL propulsion field!"

As the Admiral entered the ship, the Winds of Destiny rose to gale force; indicating that what was about to happen was very; very important!

"Let's go, Tanya! Let's get this show on the road; so we don't get the road on the show!![27] **To quote Captain Tim Time on his show 'Time Trooper'; 'Time is a-wasting!!'"** All the young officers near the ship heard the Admiral say just as the ship's door closed. Marty also seemed to hear a woman's voice saying, **"Yes, Si. . . . "**! Then the door closed, and he could near nothing else!! Hearing the Admiral apparently speak to someone in the ship; not knowing about the ultra-secret Imperial Navy Time Stasis fields; each of the young officers wondered how anyone could possibly exist in that ship that apparently been buried under the Egyptian soil for an extremely long time! To their knowledge, the Earthian Aerospace Force did not possess what apparently was a very advanced FTL craft; so how could the veteran military Earth man know how to fly the unknown craft when he had never seen it before!?!?!? Ergo; how could Admiral Blow know that the ship had "a slight blow-back when it goes faster than light in a planet's atmosphere"? But why would he lift the advanced craft and go FTL from the surface of the planet; since doing so was apparently an extremely dangerous maneuver that Earthian science said would destroy the ship and/or the whole planet? The Admiral should know better than to perform such a dangerous maneuver!! But perhaps the Admiral did know that his ship would harmlessly lift off from the surface of the planet and not pulverize the immediate area or literally the whole planet!!

Kurt "KC" Casey, the so-called "Science Geek" on "The Stranger Still Zone"; who gave out science facts every week at the end of each eerie episode, once stated; after a show featured a space ship that supposedly could travel faster than light; that scientifically it would be impossible for such a craft to start going faster than light while on the surface of a planet or near the planet in its "gravity well"! The reaction and "push" of the ship's FTL drive against the planet's mass would either cause a reaction strong enough to blow up the ship; or the electronic thrust and reaction of the FTL drive impulses against the planet's gravity would cause "gravity waves" that would crumple the planet's crust under the ship down to its liquid core causing widespread volcanic eruptions; or both of these projections would happen and destroy both the ship and the planet! So if this was an established scientific fact; how could the Admiral do it without causing his death or widespread destruction on Earth? Against all the odds; deep down in his Heart, the young Marty trusted his Godfather and believed that somehow; some way; nothing would happen!

It was all very strange; but as Colonel Ballesteros quickly again reviewed everything unusual that had happened recently in and around the commanding officer that he had literally known since his birth; young Marty was content because he believed the Admiral, and deep down he knew that ''everything was in the green'' and that he would totally trust the Admiral with his life; and the life of his home planet Earth!!! He knew that the Admiral would not start up and fly the amazing black aircraft from its present location if that would endanger either the ship or his men standing nearby or the entire planet!!

As he watched the ship about ready to take off, young Marty again pondered the incredible situation! With such disjointed strange events, it seemed impossible that the Admiral could know just what was going on; but all the personal information that Blow had said was true; the young officer had known the veteran navy man literally from the first second of his life! His parents told him that the **MAN** now about to leave in that eerie craft had actually been at his birth and also at his christening; and was his legal Godfather; i.e.; if anything had happened to both his mom and his dad before he came of age, the Admiral would have become his legal guardian! As it was; Admiral Blow had managed to be at most of his graduation ceremonies, along with his beautiful wife, Mary Pearl! (He had heard she was destined to start the usual cancer treatments for very advanced level four cancer and because the disease was so advanced, the treatments could slow down but not cure the tumors and she would probably die of cancer several years in the future). His dad had served under

Admiral when he was only a captain and now he was still serving under the navy man; at the moment serving covertly elsewhere. His dad, Marty Ballesteros, Senior; had told him that he liked serving under Admiral Blow because the **MAN** always somehow knew exactly what was going on around him and also at every level of his command! He also always seemed to know what was about to happen next; in ordinary day-to-day matters or in deadly combat; as if he could somehow visualize the future; and he always used this information to protect the men under his command; not for personal glory; and not to protect himself until all the persons under his command were safe! To the Admiral, his men always came first! He would never leave any of his men behind during any operation; everyone on any mission went out together and every person came back together! This idea that the Admiral could see the future was almost too far-out for young Marty to believe! But since his earliest memories he and his dad had worked with, played with, eaten meals with; and had completely trusted the **MAN** known as Jonathan Baines Blow! Since the day young Marty was born and as he was growing up; the Admiral had always seemed like one of his uncles; not his Godfather or his dad's military superior!! Young Marty had completely trusted his dad and since babyhood he had always trusted his Godfather; so because of his upbringing and his long association with his present commanding officer; the young man had faith in his commanding officer and his friend; and believed that the veteran navy man somehow; someway; impossibly had a complete knowledge and a complete command of the eerie events that had just happened; were taking place now; and would probably happen in the future!!! He also believed the naval veteran when the Admiral stated that the information would be used to protect Earth, and not for personal gain! He did know that Admiral Blow was a man of integrity; therefore; he would obey orders with no questions asked and he was prepared to carry the events of this day to his grave; even if tortured or court-martialed to get him to reveal what happened during this incredible mission; which like Admiral Blow said; was ultra-top-secret information; especially since it involved such a top-secret; highly-advanced; apparently prehistoric; aerospace plane from who knows where!

After giving his officers time to get clear, Blow strapped himself in and started the short automatic procedure to command the AI to raise ship; which had been briefly described on the paper that mysteriously appeared in his office; apparently being sent by himself from the "future" to himself in the "past" so that he could attempt to literally salvage his sorrowful empty Life Path and allow him to save his wife from cancer by choosing the right medical treatment to completely remove her cancer tumor with absolutely no side effects!!

A few minutes later, to the small group of men on the ground, the small ship; instead of taking off like a plane or a rocket ship; seemed to simply vanish from the surface of the planet; with a loud noise as the atmosphere imploded into the area where the ship had been only a millisecond before; and temporarily leaving the Winds of Destiny behind! Incredibly the loud "pop" was the only effect of the eerie ship's departure! Contrary to what was supposed to happen; the ultra-advanced FTL[22] drive of Captain Gallant's ship;

that he had given the Admiral to use on this important mission; did not create a dangerous reaction with the Earth as it vanished into space!! A few minutes later, moving faster than any other natural or being-made object in the history of the tiny solar system; (including those of the ancient country of Mu hundreds of thousands of years ago at the Earth's south pole before the Ice Age; and those produced by mythical Atlantis before volcanic eruptions totally destroyed its advanced civilization); the ship crossed the orbital path of the so-called "dwarf planet" Pluto! It was extremely fast, even for an AI-controlled Imperial courier ship! In fact, it was faster than any AI ship or even the two ships of Captains Gallant and Cody had ever traveled before! Decade after decade; then century after century; as their ships gradually improved in speed because of alien technology gradually being added to the FTL drive components; the two Captains did not have the time; and also had no reason; to see how fast their ships could travel! But on this mission, things were different! The ship the Admiral was using was straining to reach its incredible top speed for a very good reason! It had to be fast, for the sleek vessel had an extremely long way to go in order to attempt its assigned rescue mission! It would need literally all its unrivaled speed to get to the Thunder Worlds in time for Admiral Blow to attempt to save Patrolman Trevor! But would the Admiral's complex plan work; and would it be in time?

As the Winds of Destiny caught up with and blew around the small ship, the eerie energy creatures knew that the rescue plan being attempted by the Humanoid known as Admiral Baines Blow would **probably** be "in time" for him to <u>attempt</u> to save the patrolman under his command; if he used "TIME" correctly at three different points on the Time Line/Time Cloud; which would alter the Main Galactic Time Line to completely change the Life Paths of Patrolman Trevor and Admiral Blow! But the Winds could visualize several "branches" of the Admiral's Karma; indicating what could happen if Blow's mission was a total failure; a partial failure; a partial success; or a complete success; (which was very, very unlikely)!!!

Among the strongest and most likely of their visualizations was the Life Path that showed the fact that if Blow did not "use TIME correctly"; the mission would be a failure and both the Admiral and the patrolman would be executed by the Thunder Worlds Reptiloids! The Admiral for having the audacity to invade their planet; and the patrolman for attempting to escape! All the other "branches" and manifestations and visions of the Main Galactic Time Line caused by unprecedented manipulation of the Time Line were extremely dim; indicating that the odds were stacked against the Admiral's chances for even a partially successful mission or a completely successful "time operation"! But even if the Admiral had known this information; he would have continued the mission anyway; because of his motto that skilled pilots and soldiers can overcome bad odds and obtain victory with just their daring and their skill!

So with the Main Galactic Time Line and all its branches in flux because of the major changes going on in the Life Path of one Jonathan Baines Blow; all the Winds of Destiny; the Admiral's men; and the Admiral could do was . . . . . **WAIT--WAIT** to see what would happen to Admiral Blow who was piloting the mysterious black ship! But also wait to see just what the Admiral could do to save his patrolman from the Thunder World Reptiloids and safely make it back! Would **The Man** who always seemed to know exactly what was going on around him and what was about to happen; totally succeed in his quest; or totally **fail?**

Also, how would his actions affect the Main Galactic Time Line in their galaxy and all the other galaxies; by either helping each and every sentient being in the Cosmic All; or by hindering each one because of the several disruptions of the Time Continuum caused by the Admiral's never-before-used "Time Manipulations" over several positions on the Time Line at the "same time"; sent from points in the Future to several points in the Past; which should disrupt the future events? Not even the Winds of Destiny knew exactly what was going to happen when Admiral Blows "time shenanigans" literally kicked in!!!! Such unique manipulations of the Main Galactic Time Line could; and PROBABLY WOULD; produce violent quaking of the Line THAT WOULD TOTALLY DESTROY EVERYTHING!!!

But since the time manipulations had already been done; nothing could be done to stop the cavalcade of Anchor Moments that were about to happen--Anchor Moments that would forever change every sentient being; every planet; every solar system; and every galaxy that existed in the entire Cosmic All--forever!! But would "good" or "bad"?!? Would they be constructive or destructive to the Life Path of one Admiral Jonathan Baines Blow?!?

No sentient being or even the Winds of Destiny knew; or at that pivotal moment on the Main Galactic Time Line; COULD KNOW!! At that instant in the history of the entire Cosmic All, to any being with the "Magi Gift" of being able to visualize portions of the Main Galactic Time Line; in order to obtain vital information about Future Happenings; the Life Path of the Admiral was as blank as a newly manufactured chalk board; which meant his Future Life Path would be influenced by his actions in the next few minutes; hours; days; or some unknown time interval!! All every one of the sentient beings able to visualize the Future could do was . . . . . . WAIT! Wait for a "Doomsday"; imprisonment on the Thunder Worlds; escape with terrible injuries, (like losing an arm); or the unlikeliest--a happy "Break-Out Day" for one very important sentient being by the name of Admiral Jonathan Baines Blow!! But which Fate would it be?!? Not even the Winds of Destiny could fathom what was going to happen; as the small Ship of Destiny sped closer and closer to the impenetrable Thunder Worlds to attempt to pull off an impossible rescue!!!

CHAPTER 7

When the ship was well beyond Alpha Centauri, Blow was given a complete tour of the totally automated ship; guided by a solid hologram figure of a beautiful young woman produced by the ultra-advanced controlling computer AI who Captain Gallant had named 'Tanya' when several centuries before he had given the personable computer the necessary electrical circuits to be able to totally control his ship, 28/8^{25}!! The life-like holographic image of the very attractive Humanoid woman graciously allowed him to temporarily rename her 'Mary Pearl' for luck; then she familiarized him with all its unique features and all the equipment that Cap had left for his use. The ship had ultra-advanced curved holographic viewing screens molded in the shape of the front, sides, and top and bottom of the cockpit which gave the pilot a 360° view on all sides and up and down for unprecedented visibility, without a transparent canopy to the outside; or any instruments penetrating the ship's surface anywhere! The screens could smoothly move around the ship's front and side surfaces so that the pilot could observe any direction when in flight. Somehow the sensors that observed just what was going on outside the ship in all directions could somehow look through the solid walls as if they were made of glass and provide a 360° vision for the pilot!! Blow was amazed about this fact and hoped he could remember to ask the AI how this was accomplished when the mission was over and things settled down! (Magi note: He never did--YET!)

First; Tanya, the beautiful solid holographic young woman, checked him out in the cockpit, showing him what each lever; button, and holographic indicators controlled, which he instantly filed in his photographic memory! Her hands seemed warm as she touched and guided his hands in the intricate maneuvers needed to guide the ship. She gave him a complete checkout of the secret alien devices that made Captain Gallant's ship "special". As previously recorded in other documents, the Key-Coo-Kan Reptiloid species on one of the Thunder Worlds gave him the device that increased the efficiency of his ship's warping field by 5% after he saved the life of their Ruler Elect on a hunting expedition. The Captain still bore the scars of that encounter with a "Thunder Tiger"; never having taken the time to have the scars removed by a doctor's medicine cabinet while on Empire Prime! Several decades before; the Banko species of Insectoids living on the strange "Belt Planets" near the "Great Dark"; gave him the circuits that increased the output of his neo-electric generators by 6% when he exposed a traitor in their Planetary Cabinet. Another Snakoid planetary government near the northern edge of the Great Dark gave him electronics that improved the shape of the warping field by a staggering 4% after he gave them warning of an impending Hunan attack that literally saved their planet from total destruction!! Several other extraordinary devices had been added through the centuries that each time supposedly would improve his ship's speed only a few percentage points. But over the decades as many grateful species covertly rewarded the two Imperial Captains for their service; each incremental improvement of only a few percentage points had the effect of geometrically expanded the capacities of the other parts of the propulsion system; which vastly increased the speed of the ships of the two captains until they were literally faster than the other standard ships in their ship class as other standard ships in the class were over the other primitive Terran ships!! The devices were all deliberately designed by the alien races to be able to be quickly detached and safely locked in the ship's kitchen cargo hold when the Captain's ship was about to be periodically inspected and refurbished by Imperial shipyards, so as to keep the secret devices, **SECRET!**

Secondly; the newly renamed AI gave him a quick "hypnotic" course which allowed him to instantly be familiar with exactly what maneuvers the ship could do, and the ones that the ship could not safely do without causing damage and destruction.

Third; it also briefed him about the advanced Imperial defense belt that he would wear; along with all the details of the coming dangerous mission.

Lastly; it gave him a complete history lesson about the traditions, laws, and the titanic Reptiloid beings that inhabited the Thunder Worlds. It also made him proficient in speaking "Thunderese" the major dialect of the Reptiloid race from the Thunder Worlds; which controlled a large volume of space north of the twentieth parallel of the northern Galactic Axis; which happened to be next to the Empire's Sphere of Influence. Such important information would come in very handy very soon when he would have to parley with the Reptiloid ruler and his warriors for the life of his patrolman!

While waiting for the ship to reach its destination, Blow used the time well; practicing on ship control equipment that used virtual reality and mental projection technology to become very, very experienced in piloting the advanced craft and proficient using every capability, original and alien; that had been designed into the beautiful interstellar cruiser! For the coming mission he realized that he would need to use the full capability of every facet of the ship's operation in order to succeed; so he trained as hard as he could on the real-life training equipment!

Tanya also trained him to use the Imperial defense belt; which gave him amazing mental and physical powers that he would need on this mission! But as advanced as he knew the ship was, he again realized that he would need virtually every feature of the ship and every piloting skill that he possessed to come out of this mission alive and with the captured patrolman! But even with such a technically advanced ship that used neo-electricity that could not be detected by ordinary electrical sensors; made with a science hundreds of thousands of years beyond that possible on Earth; he realized deep down in his soul that the combat odds were against him and that he probably would not make it off the legendary Thunder Worlds alive! **But knowing this fact, he searched the depths of his Id to figure out why he voluntarily choose to go** anyway, even if he realized that he probably would not come away alive from the Thunder Worlds of the Reptiloids! Why did he risk his life, after calling in "debts" that other men owed him and was now about to travel alone hundreds of thousands of light years; simply to try to personally rescue one of his men; instead of allowing younger; more capable men to try the literal suicide mission? **WHY DID HE DO THIS?!?** He was getting too old to act like one of the super-duper heroes that were regularly featured in science-fiction shows on "The Stranger Still Zone"; and Captain Rex Reed's "Thunder Mountain"! Over and over he pondered to answer the question as to why did he do this? Why did he act like the actors on that show when he knew that what was broadcast on satellite television was only a fiction story and this was reality? Why had he not asked Captain Gallant or Captain Cody; or even one of his skillful men to attempt this deadly mission? He knew that anyone of the faithful men under his command, or either of the two Captains from ICOPE would gladly accept the foolhardy mission that he was attempting if he had asked them! They were used to succeeding in accomplishing extremely dangerous missions; he was not!

HE DID NOT KNOW WHY HE INSISTED ON ATTEMPTING THIS MISSION; EVEN THOUGH HE WAS FOLLOWING THE STANDARD PROCEDURE THAT HE HAD USED ALL OF HIS LIFE IN UPPER MILITARY COMMAND! He always took things too personal; wanting to solve problems and do things by himself, instead of waiting and using the sometimes superior talents of his men to solve problems and do the necessary work!

He would have to take an extremely long time in deep meditation to carefully examine his Soul to fathom the answer to that perplexing question, but he realized that at the present location in the Time Stream he simply did not have enough "Time" to fathom the strange events that were happening around him, and the unknown forces that were driving his actions! Was it simply because he realized or believed that since the captured pilot was under his command; this made it his "Duty" to attempt a rescue? Why? What was the driving force that made him pilot an impossible ship past the Great Dark and many light years beyond; to try to rescue a young man that was under his command that he hardly knew? Why was he doing this? **HE HONESTLY DID NOT KNOW!** With the rescue mission in progress, he did not have enough time before his ship reached the Thunder Worlds in order to spend enough time to successfully fathom the answer to that riddle; even as the Winds of Destiny paced his ship; amazingly moving at many times the speed of light!

But as the ship traveled through the Cosmic All; literally moving faster than any other manned ship in both unrecorded history; (i.e., Atlantis; Mu, the nation that once existed under Antarctica's three mile layer of ice; and several others originally on islands or sunken islands across the vast Pacific Ocean; whose names have not been discovered); and recorded history; the Admiral did not know that he was not alone as he tried to complete his rescue mission! Because he did not have the mental powers of an Imperial Seer; he could not feel the fabled Winds of Destiny; as they surged all around him; moving as fast and faster than his present record speed; indicating that somehow; for some reason, the rescue mission that he was attempting was of galaxy importance; and might possibly affect the Life Path of each and every being in the entire Universe! Was this the reason he was somehow literally driven to save the captured pilot? Only the fabled Winds of Destiny knew; as the sleek dark ship traveled at record speed so that one Admiral Jonathan Baines Blow could complete his rendezvous with Destiny and completely change his Life Path literally 180°; from one of pain and sorrow; and his beloved wife dying of cancer; to a bright path of gladness, joy, and health for his many future children; his wife; and himself; not to mention dozens and hundreds of personnel who had served around him and loved to hang out at his large estate! But it all depended upon how he completed his coming impossible mission! The odds were totally stacked against the Admiral; with all of his possible Life Paths either dark; very dim; or nonexistent; (which meant that the rescue mission would probably be unsuccessful!) But one thing the Admiral had done all his life--he did not believe that such odds were final--he believed that the person attempting any dangerous mission himself or herself; MADE THE ODDS THAT WOULD MAKE THEIR MISSION A SUCCESS--THE IMPOSSIBLE ODDS DID NOT MAKE THE PERSON ATTEMPTING A SUPPOSEDLY UNACHIEVABLE MISSION SUCCEED OR FAIL; ONLY THEIR SKILL OR LACK THEREOF; WOULD CAUSE THE MISSION TO FAIL!!

So as the Admiral and the holographic young woman sped through space; moving faster than any object in recorded and unrecorded history; other important events were amazingly happening at the same time in other parts of the Cosmic All's Main Time Line--events that could totally destroy; help; or hinder the Admiral's goal of completely changing his Life Path from sorrow to joy; or from sorrow to OBLIVION AND DEATH! PLUS events were simultaneously happening which could totally destroy all extensions of the Main Galactic Time Line; WHICH WOULD TOTALLY DESTROY AND PULVERIZE THE ENTIRE UNIVERSE AND LITERALLY EVERY THING IN IT!

But which event(s) would affect the Main Galactic Time Line and which would be harmless?!?!?

LITERALLY -- "TIME WOULD TELL" WHICH SCENARIO WOULD OCCUR AND WHICH SITUATIONS WOULD NOT!!!

CHAPTER 8

As the small ship entered a very large solar system and approached its goal, the large dark target planet appeared to be covered with dense clouds moving at extreme speed in jet streams all over the globe, from one end to the other. It also seemed like hundreds of lightning bolts were continuously ablaze all over each continent from one pole to the other; which was why it was one of the fearsome "Thunder Worlds"; controlled by large reptile-like creatures; who could withstand its treacherous natural conditions which would immediately kill any unprotected creature known to ICOPE science! The bolts would instantly execute every creature known to Empire scientists; except those fearsome Reptiloid beings that were native to the Thunder Worlds! These powerful sentient beings had very electrical-resistant nervous systems and could withstand a direct hit by any of the bolts with absolutely no damage to their nervous systems; their four eyes on thick stems; or their physical scaled bodies!

As it entered orbit high above the Capital Thunder World, Tanya the controlling AI of the small Earth ship somehow verbally transmitted the correct procedure on the correct command frequency to ask for permission to land! Amazingly, the Artificial Intelligence controlling the ship somehow also knew how to communicate in flawless "Thunderese"; the main language of the planet's Reptiloid race! The failure to correctly use the correct code grouping to identify the ship and correctly pronounce the complex "Thunderese" intonations would have immediately caused the planet's powerful AI-controlled defenses to immediately vaporize the interloper! But somehow Tanya used the correct protocol; permission was immediately granted; and the tiny vessel's Humanoid commander; instead of the holographic young woman; started trying to flawlessly pilot the ship down into the treacherous atmosphere of the planet toward what was apparently the only space docking facility on the planet. Failure to be absolutely perfect in its trajectory through the safe channels would cause immediate destruction in the ultra-dangerous lightning-filled environment below the vacuum of space! Any deviation from the "safe channels" of the planet's atmosphere would immediately cause the small ship to exceed its design parameters and cause it to instantly crumple and descend at supersonic speed to ultimately crash on the rocky surface of the capital planet of the Thunder Worlds!!

At the upper part of the planet's atmosphere; ascending jet streams of hot air and moving over 300 miles per hour were followed by pockets of swiftly-descending rivers of frozen gas; followed by swiftly ascending rivers of super-heated gas going in the opposite direction! This combination of up and down hot and cold jet streams was happening simultaneously all over the planet! The effect of this swift exchange of extreme heat and extreme cold balanced out the temperatures on the surface of the planet; between the ultra-cold Polar Regions and the ultra-hot belt of territory around the equator of the planet. The skillful pilot of the ship had the extremely difficult task of the guiding the craft's movement through the aerial barrier of swiftly moving extremely hot and cold gasses and safely reaching a docking pad somewhere below.

At the same time the ship was piercing the planet's protective atmosphere; at the bottom of the dense layer of storms and lightning surrounding the dark planet; in a very large armored palace, Ran-Kee, an underling of Thud; the Supreme Ruler of the Thunder Worlds; was telepathically speaking to his Most Exalted Ruler in subservient tones. *#My Liege! Amazingly the interloper appears not to have any advanced systems with which to guide its descent through the atmosphere or its landing! To our long-range sensors, it seems not to possess any land sonar, radar or sadar; and it does not emit any microwave, infrared, or Z-band energy that indicates that it has any offensive or defensive sensors to help its navigation! The ship seems to be absolutely devoid of any systems except primitive electrical circuits to control its ordinary landing rockets; and yet our sensors indicate that the single creature that is piloting the craft is apparently doing so without any artificial electronic aids to guide him through the treacherous wind currents of our planet! Yet; apparently without any external or internal aid; the small ship is coming down straighter and steadier than your battle cruiser with our latest equipment and controlled by the most experienced pilot in the fleet; who knows the exact positions of all the hot and cold jet streams! What manner of* *creature is on that ship that it has the necessary powerful mental capabilities and unknown senses to pilot such an obsolete ship without any sensors; without any automatic directional controls; and without any vectoring help from our planet?!?! The being has to somehow sense the surrounding conditions in all directions from its ship and instantly make course corrections; being absolutely correct every time or the ship would have been lost the first second it reached our planet's usual atmospheric maelstrom!#* Ran-Kee, Radak's aide telepathically asked and stated to his Ultimate Ruler.

#The Fates of the Time Stream will decide the ultimate fate of that ship, Ran-Kee! If the unknown being makes it to the planet surface; he is still in danger!! Then we will wait and see if the being's senses can guide him safely through the lightning fence; past our planet's dangerous native creatures; and through the maze surrounding the palace; without falling into the many holographic traps awaiting him! If he is successful in making it to the planet surface; surround that advanced ship and confiscate it! We might find out a few military secrets of the alien's race; in addition to how he pilots so well through the dangerous vortexes of our planet's atmosphere! If he is unsuccessful in his descent; our present problem will be solved! Ergo; the scheduled execution of the captured Earthian spy will proceed on schedule! Afterwards my pets outside the walls will have an exotic meal; with at least two courses, instead of one!# the very deep mental voice of the Reptiloid ruler answered the underling.

Almost in record time; aided by control systems and sensors powered by a recent Imperial scientific breakthrough known as "neo-electricity"[26]; (sadio impulses of which the sensors of the

Reptiloids could not detect); the small ship successfully pierced the treacherous atmosphere of the Thunder World, as if the lone pilot had been there before; and successfully landed next to a very large structure which stretched far into the distance. Trusting his "battle sense" the pilot of the small ship cruised along the outside of the alien building until something prompted him to land his small craft next to what appeared to be a small hill next to the structure.

After the small Humanoid exited the craft; he mentally signaled the holographic AI being still on the ship, *#Good-bye for now, 'Mary Pearl'! Thanks for letting me call you that on this trip while I was inside! If I don't make it back; which I probably won't; leave this barren world; give my regards to **THE MAN** and thank him for loaning you to me to try this foolhardy rescue; and tell my beloved Mary Pearl that I loved her to the end! If I somehow impossibly survive; we will meet again; soon I hope; at one of the Emperor's galas when you accompany 'The Man' as a beautiful Humanoid woman dressed in a sparkling Royal Gown! If and when we both make it; I claim the first dance with you after you dance with the Captain!! But to get back to being serious; I will electronically call you at this very spot; when I successfully make it back after rescuing the young man who was under my command when he was kidnapped! If I am unsuccessful, after a certain length of time, the time controls in your ship will bring you back to the present and you can immediately forget me and return to Captain Gallant!#*

*#Wilco, Admiral! **GOOD LUCK AND GOOD HUNTING!**# Tanya the AI controlling the ship mentally told him. #I hope you make it back so I can dance with you at the next Emperor's Ball! I'll leave*

dancing with the Captain and claim the first dance with you; with the permission of your beautiful wife!!#

After that telepathic message; the Admiral touched a spot on his defense belt; and with absolutely no sound or visible light; the small black ship appeared to totally dissolve into primeval subatomic dust that was soon scattered across the entire planet by the ultra-fast wind belts! Such a senseless act apparently left the Admiral without any way to escape the planet! But in all past operations; Admiral Blow always had a backup plan; **BUT DID HE HAVE ONE THIS TIME?** (Seemingly his ship had been totally destroyed; blowing away in the wind; and at that instant; there were no other Imperial or Earthian ships within several thousand light years! How could he escape even if his rescue mission was successful? Perhaps only the Winds of Destiny knew at that particular instant!)

As the gleaming dust apparently vanished forever into the wind; taking with it supposedly his only way off the planet; Blow looked around to observe two things. In the side of the large black structure there suddenly appeared to be an open door; as if he were invited to enter. Secondly; he observed what appeared to be Patrolman Trevor's patrol ship covered with a tied down ECM tarp that had prevented his sensors from detecting it; pushed into the hard ground what he estimated to be 20 or 30 yards away from the door; as if the ship had crash-landed on the eerie planet! Knowing the techniques of the Thunder World Reptiloids; they had probably just pushed the primitive ship out of their battleship; not caring about the primitive ship since it did not have any technology that the reptiles did not already have!

#Well, I'll be jiggered! Those aliens snookered us! They did not destroy our ship; they apparently projected solid holographic scenes of our ship exploding in order to convince us that the ship was destroyed in order to apparently try to obtain valuable information on the ship's electronic systems about our relatively primitive defenses, without our knowing they had the Intel!# Blow surmised to himself. *#Then they just dumped it out close to one of the entrances to Thud's palace!#*

Putting all thoughts aside, Blow turned on his Imperial defense belt; powered directly by Zero Point Energy; with an atomic battery backup in case the Reptiloids had a protecting energy field blocking Zero Point Energy from being used as a power source. Then he turned it up to full power and walked toward the inviting door and moved closer and closer to his Ultimate Destiny; even as the Winds of Destiny invisibly surged at record levels around him!

At the same time; unseen and undetectable around the surface, the Winds of Destiny again rose to record heights around the Thunder Worlds; who at that time only had a handful of mental adepts who could sense their presence because of political beliefs in the past history of their empire that most of the time telepaths and anyone who exhibited any mental ability were traitors! So the few beings on the Thunder Worlds who had the extremely rare mental powers that could sense that something important was happening raised their mental shields; **KEPT THEIR VERY LARGE REPTILOID JAWS SHUT**, and did not say anything; since Radak supposedly did not like Reptiloids having the mental powers like the Imperial Magi!

Moving many times faster than light, The Winds surged around all the Thunder Worlds; then blew past distant Empire Prime; equally mystifying the Imperial Magi; who also had to raise their mental shields to prevent extensive mind damage!!

Every mental adept being able to sense the surge of the Winds had the same thought: *#Just what was happening somewhere in the Universe that would make the Winds blow so hard at near record levels?#* In past history, such an outpouring of the Winds had been caused by a barbarian invasion of Empire Prime; a supernova about to occur near one of the Pleasure Planets; and one such indication of an Anchor Event that was still a mystery! But in this particular happening; only the passage of regular "Time" would unveil and reveal the cause of this surge of the eerie Winds of Destiny--an Anchor Event in progress that had totally blanked the Main Galactic Time Line to the mental powers of the Imperial Magi and an Anchor Event that would radically change the course of the Main Galactic Time Line until Eternity started and all radioactive materials in the entire Cosmic All had transmuted to lead!!

CHAPTER 9

The door in the side of the large structure opened to a lightless corridor whose end could not be fathomed, as the dark shaft in front of the Humanoid seemed to travel to infinity! Microscopic video sensors hidden all along the corridor watched as the small being that left the ship started walking along the steel hallway without the assistance of a portable light, as if it could see in the dark; which it could with infrared sensors. The alien Humanoid being quickly transversed the maze of tunnels between it and its ultimate goal as if he could sense the quickest way through the dark corridors around it for many feet in all directions; (which the Admiral could using the sensor features of the suit)! Finally the unidentified being was faced with a very large metal door. After a moment's hesitation, the Humanoid known by his comrades; and the men and women who served under him many light years away; as "Blow"; concentrated a moment and then swung his right fist at the seemingly impregnable door with what Earthian "sports writers" had described during the last century in what was called "newspapers"; as a **"Sunday Punch"!!** The instant the Humanoid's fist struck the door the blow produced an extremely loud "THUNK!"; and then suddenly there was an immense hole in the Tytano Steel surface as the door was forced inward like it was made of Earthian balsa wood that was struck by a pile driver; to the utter astonishment of the Reptiloids watching him on monitors inside the throne room and the other reptile beings observing the Anchor Event from in the building's control room!!

#The Tytano battle-door was locked, and a 100-ton Hunan Ultimate Battle Tank could not have forced it open like that small Humanoid incredibly just did! How could the puny alien being open it with just its bare hands?!? With his small Humanoid physical power he should not have been able to dent the door; much less destroy it and force it inwards so that he could enter! Our sensitive close-range sensors still have detected no electrical impulses or destruction beams coming from the unfamiliar belt on his waist! Amazingly our detection devices cannot penetrate a micron into its depths! Somehow the unknown being produced enough physical power or maybe even telekinetic power to do the job; or what appears to be an ordinary Humanoid is an unknown type of being from a high gravity planet and possesses super-Humanoid strength; which he just exhibited!# Telepathic voices forcefully asked and stated in the Throne Room of the Ruler of the Thunder Worlds which was beyond the ruined armored steel door that was over two Imperial feet thick!

As the Reptiloid telepathic and electronic voices continued to babble in the throne room; Blow started down a very large dark hallway; walking very fast since he could see in the inky blackness of the building's passageways using passive and undetectable Imperial neo-electricity sensor technology! Confidently walking in total darkness using the defense belt's advanced infrared, sonar, and microwave devices; the Earthman slowly penetrated an immense labyrinth of tunnels which lay outside the palace of "Thud", the Thunder Worlds Ruler. The Admiral quickly spanned the confusing maze of darkened passageways in record time; without any help from the Reptiloids who were waiting for him inside the throne room on the other side of the confusing spiral of tunnels.

Finally reaching his ultimate goal; while in total darkness Blow stopped before a very large ornate door; which opened wide as he approached; (probably to prevent its destruction)! A very large and brightly lit room lay beyond the entrance; which he knew was Radak's throne room! Blow deliberately walked into what he knew was a trap to attempt to save his man; **even though he knew that he probably would not leave the enemy's stronghold alive!** There were too many of the huge Reptiloids to defend against; even with Captain Gallant's powerful suit he could not defend all directions at the same time!! He accepted that fact when he appointed himself for the rescue mission that he probably would not leave the Thunder World alive. But even if he did not survive; Blow wanted to make sure that he was able to fight well enough so that the totality of the Thunder Worlds would traditionally sing their War Songs about his exploits against their huge Reptiloid warriors for a hundred thousand years! Glancing around the literally alien scene in front of him; and quickly memorizing the location of every Reptiloid warrior; the veteran military man quickly sized up the situation! There were two parallel lines of Reptiloids leading across the very large throne room to where he needed to go! Then just before the Reptiloids probably would attack him; Blow said a short prayer; then he mentally went over the tactics he planned to use. The Admiral vowed to follow his own personal "War Rules" concerning being heavily outnumbered before a conflict! Ergo; when he was attacked and the conflict broke out, the Lone Earthian would use all the weapons in his suit; he would physically fight the huge Reptiloids as best he could; and afterwards he would **"LET THE CHIPS AND THE REPTILOID BONES AND SCALES FALL WHERE THEY WOULD; UNTIL TOTAL VICTORY OR DEATH WHEN HIS OWN HUMANOID BONES FELL TO THE FLOOR"**!!! He continued to act unafraid and started walking confidently between the two rows of Reptiloids; across the very large ornately decorated room in order to reach his goal that he could see far across the large room; a very large Reptiloid seated on an ornate throne at the end of the long lines of reptiles. Blow kept on toward his goal even though he was traveling between two lines of armored beings of the Reptiloid species that looked like very tall and heavily scaled Earthly alligators having slightly shorter mouths and "snouts"; which he knew would instantly try to stop him if he ever turned around to try to escape! After several hundred yards of walking between the deadly Reptiloid warriors; he stopped in front of his final objective; an extremely large Reptiloid being clad in a very ornate military uniform with what looked like several dozen military metals pinned to the front of the livery. The fearsome being was seated on a very intricately carved throne; with end of each of the two lines of heavily armed warriors ending at each side of the front of the ruling area!

At such a perilous time in his life; a phrase suddenly sprang into Blow's mind: ". . . **yea though I walk through the Valley of the Shadow of Death, I will fear no evil!!!. . ."** If there was to be a battle; his chances for escaping alive with his man were very; very slim! Ergo, he would have to either talk his way out of this jam; and if that did not work; Blow again vowed that **he would fight so that the war songs and war chants of these Reptiloids would declare his bravery and fighting skill against the Reptiloid warriors for at least the next hundred thousand years!!** All these thoughts about the situation took only an instant; then Blow had to return his attention to what the Thunder World Reptiloid warriors were doing around him!

When the Reptiloid on the throne; and all of his warriors that were lined up around the room ignored him and nothing immediately happened; Blow took the time to look around and observe what would probably be his Death-Scene; and again brought up the fact in his Heart and Soul that if all these Reptiloids came at him at the same time; there was no way he could defend himself from all of them at the same time or escape; even with Cap's defense belt! But through the years as a raw recruit; an officer commanding a small number of troops; and finally as an Admiral with men and women under his command; he had always chosen to always tell the truth; take care of his personnel; and always do his **DUTY**, no matter what the outcome! So to the watching Reptiloids; outwardly the Humanoid soldier appeared to be very cool and confident as he calmly looked around the Ultimate Room of the Reptiloid Emperor of the planet; finally resting his gaze on the nightmare creature seated before him on the very ornate throne.

Inwardly, it was another story! The veteran military man felt cold and clammy in the pit of his stomach, and had a strong sense of foreboding; all of which could mean that something important was about to happen; maybe good or maybe bad! But like all good soldiers and airmen from time immemorial,; he would let this inner feeling of fear actually improve his performance by causing the release of adrenalin into his bloodstream; if and when physical or mental combat presented itself!

From intelligence reports Blow knew that the Reptiloid ruler that he was observing was named Sar-Kon-See. . . Radak, The whole name of the Reptiloid Ruler was composed of several hundred names; comprising his Official Royal Lineage from the name of the first ruler of his plant at the dawn of his planet's history thru the present; although the present ruler sitting in front of him had been nicknamed "Thud" by Captain Gallant several hundred years before; because as he had dealings with the Reptiloid; he became convinced that the nickname was appropriate; and he did not like spouting dozens of Reptiloid names every time he formally addressed the reptile ruler!

The huge lizard-like being sitting on the throne before the much smaller Humanoid had been an avid hunter of dangerous game all his adult life of 600 or so years; but for only the second or third time in his existence; his battle instincts indicated certain things to him about the being before him!! Thud did not like the sudden feeling deep in his Id that he was being the **"HUNTED"**;

instead of the "**HUNTER**"! The feeling started as the small Humanoid first came into view; then it grew stronger as the puny Humanoid being came bravely closer to his throne; walking past hundreds of his warriors like he was walking alone through a forest! When he first looked into the weak; puny-looking eyes of the small; apparently unarmed Humanoid standing before him apparently unafraid among the hundreds of Reptiloid warriors; he immediately got the very uncomfortable feeling that he was the "pursued" instead of the "pursuer"! But that was ridiculous! The Reptiloid knew that he was the total and absolute Master of the Planet and the whole realm of the Thunder Worlds! There was no way the puny Humanoid could escape!! The weakest of his warriors surrounding the apparently unarmed; unarmored; and totally defenseless Humanoid could take the alien out in a millisecond; and yet. . . . . just how did that weak Humanoid smash that steel door in order to enter the building?!? He had the uncomfortable feeling that something... was. . . . not. . . . . quite. . . . . . right! SOMETHING WAS WRONG!! SOMETHING WAS VERY, VERY **VERY WRONG!** His veteran battle senses indicated that apparently the short being was not afraid; even a little bit! In his previous dealings with Humanoids over hundreds of years; Radak had become an expert in evaluating their "body language" and the chemistry of their sweat to evaluate their level of fear! But this being was very different from any he had ever met! This being literally exuded confidence and his body language amazingly exhibited a total lack of fear or uneasiness! There was a complete lack of "fear" pheromones emanating from the strange Humanoid's body; indicating that the puny being was somehow extremely confident of the outcome of what to him should have been a hopeless situation with so many Reptiloid warriors around him; waiting for the command to kill him with an avalanche of arrows and spears too numerous to defend against! Realizing this fact; the Reptiloid ruler searched his extensive memory of battle tactics trying to figure out why the weak puny being could possibly think that he would ever leave the room alive! Just who; or more importantly; **WHAT** was this being? Thud knew that Captain Gallant; Captain Cody; and the eerie being that only looked Humanoid; called "Ajax Chrome"[3]; using their ultra-advanced protective equipment; could look like any creature or any Humanoid they wished! Could this very confident Humanoid actually be one of those superior beings in disguise? No, he surmised; if it were one of those three powerful beings; they would have no reason to disguise themselves; they would have simply broken the door down and commanded him to release his prisoner; **OR ELSE!!** If this had happened they would have had the power to force him to do it; defeating all his warriors either one-at-a-time or all-at-once with their powerful mental thrusts and titanic overwhelming physical strength! Then the powerful warrior would have left with his former prisoner; and nothing his forces could do against the powerful being would have been able to harm him! Therefore; the being before him was not one of the literally untouchable invulnerable beings with unusual powers and ultra-advanced super weapons! But just what famous invincible warrior stood before him? Was this a new powerful Humanoid warrior standing before him trying to make a name for himself?!?!? He had no answer to that very dangerous question!! But probably the best question to ask was: **WHO OR PERHAPS; <u>WHAT</u> WAS HE?!?!?** Was he an unknown super-powered warrior from far across the Universe that was just trying to make a name for himself? Was he one of his political rivals; just another Reptiloid in disguise trying to unseat him from his throne? The powerful Reptiloid ruler of the Thunder Worlds could not answer that question—**YET**! But it was an extremely important question that needed to be answered--**VERY QUICKLY!!**

But at that moment all his underlings just outside the throne room were working furiously with every sensor and telepath available on the planet to answer that vital question! Since the eerie Humanoid arrived on the planet they had attempted to penetrate the unknown being's mind and that strange belt on his waist; but so far with no luck! His underlings were still trying to use every telepathic and sensor forces they possessed in order to find out anything that could defeat the strange Humanoid invader; but they also could not penetrate either his mind or what appeared to be an unpowered defense belt on his waist! But the dozens of sensors of the Reptiloid soldiers situated inside and around the outside of throne room still could not detect any electronic activity anywhere in or on the belt! They also could not detect any weapons on the alien's body! Without any information about how the alien was armed; Thud could not safely order his warriors to attack the eerie invader; because the invader would not come into this room without being heavily armed and prepared to fight to the death against his much bigger and stronger warriors!! If and when any of his underling scientists were able to contact him through his com-piece on his ear with the vital information that would allow him to correctly assess the situation; then he would act! Until then, he would wait; simply bide his time; and see what the interloper wanted.

As he pondered the situation; Radak; AKA Thud; again let his normally fearsome gaze roam aimlessly around his throne room; ultimately letting it rest on the small eyes of the apparently defenseless creature standing so confidently in front of him; acting like **HE**, and not the powerful armed Reptiloids around him, were in control of the situation!!

The very tall reptile seated on the throne was the strongest; most powerful Reptiloid being on his home world; hence by the Royal Law of the Thunder Worlds; he was THE Supreme Ruler! Only as long as he was the Strongest Reptiloid; able to defeat all physical challengers; would he be the Supreme Power and be instantly obeyed by any of his men! Accordingly; some fateful day in the future; when he stopped being the largest and strongest Reptiloid on his planet; by tradition; another stronger and more capable warrior who defeated him in the Royal Arena would take his place on the traditional Throne of His Fathers! This was how it should be; according to age-old Reptiloid tradition and law!! On the future day that he was defeated; the new ruler would add his name to the Official Royal Lineage and rule the Thunder Worlds with an iron hand until he too was eventually defeated! This was the way his Reptiloid people chose their fittest ruler; such was the Royal Tradition as it had been; and such as it would be until the last sun burned out in the Cosmic All and all radioactive material had turned to lead!

But at that instant; as he set on his ornate throne; at that Anchor Moment during his long reign; the Reptiloid had never before had such a deep-seated feeling of helplessness and physical inadequacy!! It had first started when the Humanoid first came into view and he first looked into the eerie gleaming bright orbs of a creature that he was probably about to attempt to kill in the next few minutes; with absolutely no mercy! And as the unknown creature stood before him; every time Thud glanced again into those two spooky Humanoid eyes with his four Reptiloid eyes; the feeling got worse!! But why should he not order his warriors to kill the unknown being because of his transgressions?!? The unknown sentient being was worthy of death because the interloper had literally invaded the Thunder Worlds by successfully navigating the extremely dangerous alternating jet streams of ultra-hot and ultra-cold air with no damage to his ship! Then he landed on this planet with no authorization; and knocked down the thick steel door guarding the labyrinth by hitting it with just one blow with one of his small Humanoid fists!! Then he somehow made it through the confusing maze of dark tunnels; and entered the throne room without authorization! Thus; following the ages-old traditions of the Thunder Worlds; the penalty for these illegal actions of entering the Royal Palace Grounds without permission was always **DEATH;** using one of several deliberately slow and very painful methods used by the Reptiloid warriors against their enemies!!

And now unfortunately; it was his duty to judge the unknown alien and give the proper orders to his warriors to ensure that Thunder Worlds Justice was carried out!! But at that instant; Thud absolutely did not know what to do!! He did not want to order his warriors to attack the warrior having unknown powers and possibly have them all killed or defeated!! This would not be good for his reputation as a warrior leader!! If that terrible event happened; his own people would rise up and demand that he abdicate the throne! So at that Anchor Moment in the Throne Room of the Thunder Worlds; as the invisible Winds of Destiny swirled around Thud; he did not know what to do or what to say to such an unknown warrior as was standing unafraid before him!!! **WHAT TO DO; WHAT TO DO; WHAT TO DO!! HE DID NOT KNOW!!**

Again, the thoughts passed through his three brains that since he did not know the powers and weapons that the warrior standing before him possessed; if he ordered his warriors to attack him; anything could happen! All his warriors could be defeated and if the unknown Humanoid did not kill him; his own people would tell him to resign his throne!! He casually glanced at the room and stopped when his eyes centered on the unknown warrior's eyes! Nothing in his experiences had ever affected him the way the eerie gaze of the Humanoid Earthling did; not even the luminous hypnotic gaze of the Ka-Kantor snake just before it bit him while he was hunting on Thunder Moon II several decades ago!

Then all of a sudden; unexpectedly; his problem was solved when the supposedly invulnerable Humanoid did something extraordinary! Using the hidden Imperial defense belt which heightened his mental powers, the Admiral penetrated the old-fashioned mechanical mind shield of Radak and delivered a telepathic message to the Reptiloid who was probably about to give orders to his guards to kill him! *#My family name is Blow! I am a military man from the planet Earth; seeking revenge and retribution for your recent craven and unwarranted offenses against my Home Planet and my forces! You apparently have one of my men; whose only offense was that he was captured by your forces while he was scouting for our fleet at the edge of our own solar system; several hundred thousand light years from here! He was only protecting his home planet and he did not attack you; you attacked him first! You were the invader; you were the aggressor; NOT HIM!! HE DID NOTHING TO WARRANT HIS ABDUCTION AND KIDNAPPING!! Your ship captured his craft with a tractor beam and brought him here; with no reason to abduct him or charge him with any crime! He did nothing to warrant execution; which you are apparently planning; by feeding him to your so-called pets! This will not happen!!!! I am here to take him back to his Home Planet!#* the Humanoid being somehow projected into the receptive centers of all the Reptiloids on the planet! But Radak still remained silent!!

The admiral continued telepathically communicating when there was no immediate reply. *#If you will release him into my custody; Earth will consider the case closed; especially if you will also release his patrol ship; which you apparently confiscated before you put it in a stasis field and created a dummy explosion so that we would think it had been destroyed! You attacked him even though he was transmitting peace signals on all known frequencies and languages,* *and he had fired a white projectile; which in our neck of the galaxy meant that he would not attack you and meant you no harm! If you do these things; no harm will come to your planet! If you will not agree to these terms; I cannot guarantee what will happen to you; your warriors; or to your planet!#*

Even the least of Radak's guards could withhold their laughter no longer; and the very large hall cascaded with both the very loud oral and the powerful telepathic versions of laughter that was peculiar to the Thunder Worlds; caused by the puny Humanoid's fantastic speech of worthless, unsupported, and senseless arguments!

#How can you make such an unsupported threat; Earthman! You are one puny Humanoid against hundreds of my warriors that are in this room and thousands also on call and available; if they are needed; in mere minutes!!# the deep telepathic voice of Radak projected on a short-range basis.

#It is not an empty threat; oh Radak; it is a promise, a real promise of real and terrible retaliation to you and your planet! Again I state that this man; acting under my authority to patrol the outer edges of our solar system; did nothing to warrant you taking him or his ship! He did nothing to rate being kidnapped by your raiding patrols in our quadrant next to our home planet; then thrown into your famous Prisons of Darkness like a common criminal; to be mercilessly tortured for no reason; and ultimately scheduled to be executed by your infamous hooded executioner; and then fed to your pets! YOU were the aggressor in our solar system;*

not he! YOU were the invader of our peaceful solar system; NOT MY MAN! YOU had no reason to capture MY soldier and illegally bring him to your home planet for execution and feed him to your pets; *WHEN HE DID NOTHING TO BE GIVEN SUCH A SENTENCE FOR SIMPLY DEFENDING HIS SOLAR SYSTEM WHICH YOU HAD JUST INVADED!!!#*

The very angry Earthman paused; then continued *#I am here because of one reason and one reason only! Our fleet has a general iron-clad rule when it comes to combat operations! In combat; for all our forces; after a mission; it is the DUTY of every person in every unit and ship assigned to that mission to make sure that everyone working that mission all come back together; or we all die together! Therefore; for this combat rescue mission; I choose to state unconditionally that with or without your permission; no matter what you or your forces attempt to do; I will either walk out of your dank and dark palace with this man who was acting under my orders to defend our planet when you kidnapped him; OR MY DEAD BODY WILL REMAIN HERE WITH THE BODY OF MY BRAVE PILOT AFTER MANY OF YOUR WARRIORS DIE; BEFORE THEIR WEAPONS SEND ME TO WHAT YOU CALL VALHALLA!#* the Admiral stated; then continued; *#After which; you and your planet will take the consequences which will then literally be out of my hands; since I will be dead and not commanding the forces which will immediately attack your home worlds because of your rash acts of piracy assault!!#*

Radak started to give an angry retort to the alien and order his soldiers to kill him; **but then a cold realization hit his consciousness!** How could the unknown alien speak and telepathically project the Reptiloid dialect spoken on this planet through his sturdy mind shield which had never before been breached by any mechanical probe or powerful telepathic being since he started using it several hundred years before? How did this being know his battle name? How did he know all this guarded information about his secret Thunder World Battle Procedures? Was the confident alien an extremely rare Humanoid telepath that could decode the brain patterns of a Reptiloid and "read" his thoughts; or did he use some other undetected device to accomplish that amazing feat? Did the small being only look Humanoid? Was he somehow a legendary "shape shifter"; or a Trecian Warlock; able to transform his body into any shape and size which had the physical or mental characteristics necessary to perform the task that he was assigned? The Supreme Ruler of the Thunder Worlds did not know and none of his advisors in constant mental and com contact with him told him that they knew either! At that instant Radak's "combat sense" kicked in and he started having a deep sense of foreboding that unless he did something to appease this unknown being; something **BAD** was about to happen--to him; his warriors; and all his empire's worlds!

To add another facet to the puzzle before him; still, amazingly; none of his Reptiloid telepaths could sense any of the alien's thoughts! Also; after trying for many minutes since the alien first appeared; none of the advanced sensors of the Reptiloids could detect any electronic signals or power systems anywhere on the alien's body; ergo; everything he did had to be using his own strength and mind power; without electronic help! Just how did he knock down that steel door?!?!?! Amazingly; the alien had broken down the invulnerable outer door to his palace maze; and could read his thoughts with just his innate abilities without any electronic devices! Also, just how did a primitive Humanoid from supposedly what was a pre-FTL culture know about the execution traditions regarding enemy spies of his Reptiloid race and know about the ferocious "pets" that he loved to have around the palace to keep the place clean of vermin? How did the eerie and confident alien know exactly what had happened before; during; and after the incident in which the Earthian Humanoid was captures? How could what looked like a primitive Humanoid living in a pre-FTL civilization; suddenly obtain an advanced interstellar cruiser; navigate hundreds of thousands of light years alone through uncharted space; and somehow make it safely through the deadly atmosphere of this planet without any electronic help to stand confidently before him and act as if the weak alien owned the universe! Something was terribly wrong! Something was not right! In addition to the sense of foreboding that was slowly increasing in the bottom of his 5th stomach; his keenly honed "battle sense" also told him that something dangerous was about to happen to him and/or his entire planet; **and he could not fathom exactly what it was!!**

So Radak; AKA Thud; started going over again the incredible chain of events that brought him and his warriors to this tense moment!! He again reasoned that there was no way a helpless;

weak being could impossibly make it through the Thunder Worlds defenses; break down a steel door with apparently no physical or electronic help; and although outnumbered thousands to one; fearlessly make such fantastic demands; apparently with absolutely no physical or mental indication of fear; without the help of something missing factor or force; or the small Humanoid was some other ultra-powerful being who was hiding his capabilities!!! **SO WHAT WAS THE VITAL FACTOR OR FACT THAT WAS MISSING?!? HOW COULD WHAT LOOKED LIKE A WEAK HUMANOID PERFORM SUCH IMPOSSIBLE FEATS OF STRENGTH AND MENTAL ACCOMPLISHMENTS?** The situation was completely insane! It was unreal!! It was literally impossible! It could not be happening; **YET SUCH A CAVALCADE OF UNLIKELY EVENTS WAS HAPPENING; RIGHT BEFORE EACH OF THEIR FOUR EYES!!** A combat veteran with several hundred years of battle experience; Radak sensed that some deadly invisible force or entity was present in his throne room, and he realized that he and his physically powerful guards were helpless to defend against it! Even as the Reptiloid nicknamed "Thud" wrestled with this mysterious being; even as the Winds of Destiny was at gale force around them; all his tactical advisors were still at work; feverishly using every one of the military tactics computers all across the Thunder Worlds to try to ascertain just what was happening; to no avail!!

In addition; he reasoned that there were too many impossible events that had recently happened that had enabled this; this frail being to suddenly come before him and voice threats that could not be backed up. . . .**OR COULD THEY?!?!?** Over and over he kept rolling the impossible facts through his mind to somehow make sense of the unsolvable riddle that was right before his four Reptiloid eyes! Coming down into the Capital Planet's atmosphere the alien somehow knew the correct planetary access codes and had verbally transmitted them in the very complex language of Thunderese to allow the planet's defenses to allow his ship to safely descend to the surface of the planet without being destroyed by the powerful automatic weapons all around the planet's surface! Again and again Radak pondered the incredible fact that in front of the recording vision screen apparently using only his own strength; the small being had impossibly ripped open his Tytano steel door to come inside; either with telekinesis or by some unknown and undetectable device hidden in his belt; which their powerful sensors could not penetrate!! Then the alien had then successfully transversed the dark maze around his palace in record time; somehow walking from the outside entrance; through the bewildering labyrinth; to the entrance outside his throne room by the shortest route possible!! Added to these impossible events; the Humanoid's brain was unreadable by any of his powerful Reptiloid telepaths who had been trying to penetrate the alien's mind since he approached the planet, with no success; even when the alien was not using an electronic mind shield! Since so many literally impossible things happened together, again he weighed all the facts and again and again came to the same deduction as his original conclusion: that the weak-appearing Humanoid **was not what he seemed!** He could not be a "primitive Humanoid"! He had to be something else to have an unreadable brain and know such hidden information about the Reptiloid! He had to be an ultra-advanced; physically and mentally powerful Humanoid being, or an alien being able to control its body to be able to look like a weak Humanoid! **HE COULD BE A SHAPESHIFTER[4] OR A POWERFUL WARLOCK[7] FROM THE TRECIAN WITCH PLANET[4] MARVANA!!** If the alien was so powerful that he could offer such threats alone, the Reptiloid ruler knew that he had to be extremely careful; since the eerie being had indirectly threatened his entire planet; which; with his unknown powerful weapons; he probably could quickly destroy!! In his cognitive areas of all three of his primary brains, the Reptiloid realized that he had to find out more information about the strange Humanoid before he could order the execution of the one already in custody and the one that stood fearlessly before him! The safety of his Empire was at stake and he had to find a way out of this maddening riddle which threatened to destroy the Thunder Worlds!!!

For some strange reason; Radak again fathomed that the ultimate safety of his Reptiloid People on all the Thunder Worlds was at stake! (Imperial Seer's note: **HE WAS RIGHT!**) For this ultimate reason, the reptile ruler knew that he must be extremely careful! The **Prime Anchor Event of the Millennia** for the Thunder Worlds continued to unfold as the Reptiloid pondered his reply and response to the challenge of the powerful being that apparently only looked like a puny, soft, and weak Humanoid! Unfelt by almost all of the beings in the palace, the Winds of Destiny again rose from strong to gale force around the entire planet and speeding on to Empire Prime at many times the speed of light; as the few Reptiloids who were mentally adept and could sense their presence still remained quiet; with their mental shields on maximum so that the tremendous surge of energy would not literally fry their brains!

After pondering the problem for many seconds, Radak came upon what he thought was a brilliant solution to his two problems! To his experienced military mind, it was the **ONLY SOLUTION** to the impossible situation, which seemed to offer no safe way out for either him; his warriors; or his planet! He signaled in the emergency battle sign language to Ran Kee and his guards so that the small Earthman could not know what he was going to do, although he could probably read his mind and know what was coming off! With combat hand and claw signals he signaled his guards: *#We are going to release the captured Earthman to this alien who calls himself Blow and then see if the two Humanoids can escape all the physical and electronic defenses of our planet; WITHOUT A SHIP!! They have no ship with which to use to escape and no physical way to escape our clutches! The dumb Earth person apparently destroyed his ship before he came into the maze so that we could not capture it while he was inside! Watching them fail will be a tremendous joke! When they ultimately fail; with the sheer numbers of our attacking warriors; we will ultimately overpower him and feed the two aliens to my pets!#*

The fate of the Thunder Worlds hung in the balance as the Radak began to implement his chosen logical plan of action! But in the lowest depths of his cognitive inner brain he wondered if even such a logical plan would it be enough to save his world from the threats of this mysterious and apparently extremely powerful Humanoid!! Unknown to his keen ordinary Reptiloid senses, at the moment; only the swirling Winds of Destiny knew the answer to his private question! (Because the Fate of Thud's Empire hung in the balance; since it is important enough, some of the most powerful Imperial Seers on Empire Prime should be able to visualize this Event at some instant in the near or distant Future as an extremely sharp or extremely faint vision and be able to chart the future effects of its nuances on the course of the Galactic Time Line/ Time Cloud!)

But for now; at this instant on the Main Galactic Time Line; the die was cast!! At this instant on the Main Galactic Time Line the "players acting out the Anchor Event" on the capital planet of the Thunder Worlds; both the single Humanoid and the hundreds of physically powerful Reptiloids around him; would have to play out their designated roles; with no help; or hindrance; any other force in the Cosmic All!!! There would be no help from the forces of the ICOPE fleet; Gallant and Cody the two prominent powerful Imperial spies somewhere in the cosmos; the Reptiloid fleet which was orbiting the planet and patrolling the solar system of the Thunder Worlds; the Imperial Seers on far away Empire Prime; or the Winds of Destiny swirling unseen around the "players"!

What it boiled down to was that the brave sentient being standing in the Reptiloid throne room that was involved in this important event would have to literally "go it alone"!! Ergo; to be able to escape with his severely injured patrolman, Admiral Blow would have to escape from and defeat the hordes of the Thunder Worlds solo; without any help from anyone! **But could he somehow do it?!? The Earthian was TOTALLY ALONE; WITH NO APPARENT MEANS OF ESCAPE!!!** Blow could not leave the planet because he had apparently destroyed his space ship right before he entered the maze!! Ergo, he was without any help; resources; or strength and power other than what he had on his person at that fateful instant on the Main Galactic Time Line?!? So just how could he escape?!?

Well. . . . . . . to quote an old Imperial Marine phrase: "Would that be a tough fight or would that be a tough fight---for the Reptiloids!?!?!" (YES; IT WOULD BE AS FUTURE HISTORY WOULD RECORD UNTIL THE LAST SUN IN THE COSMIC ALL BURNED OUT AND ALL RADIOACTIVE MATERIALS HAD TRANSMUTED TO LEAD!!!)

So now; the die was cast; and the two major players of this conflict were about to continue their battle of wits and brawn; amid the powerful gale of the Winds of Destiny swirling around all these 'players' of this deadly situation and surging on out past the Capital Planet so far away! It was a moment and a cavalcade of brave actions that would be talked about among the Reptiloids of the Thunder Worlds for millennia! Their bards and singers would also keep the Event of the Ages alive until Eternity began! But what would the Earthian side of the coming conflict say about the

Anchor Moment about to happen? Would Admiral Blow be able to escape the Reptiloids?!? Plus, would he be successful or fail in turning around his Life Path from sorrow to joy and saving the life of his wife?!?

So at this Anchor Moment on the Main Galactic Time Line; a Moment of Destiny that not even The Winds of Destiny knew what could; or would not; eventually happen to each of the combatants; Radak; aka Thud finally decided how to solve his problem and . . . . ACTED!

CHAPTER 10

#**B**ring the Humanoid prisoner into the throne room!# the tall Reptiloid Supreme Ruler commanded, both mentally and in sign language as the Winds of Destiny swirled around him.

At the imposing reptile's command, the very weak and severely injured EAF Patrolman Johnny Trevor was brought to the throne room; roughly carried like a ragdoll by another tall Reptiloid and literally dumped at Blow's feet!

"The prisoner is released to you; a Humanoid supposedly named Blow; or whoever or whatever you are! You may leave the planet; but first you have the problem of how to get you and your injured soldier out of the palace! Then, how do you propose to leave our planet without a ship; which you destroyed before you entered our maze?" Radak forcefully stated and asked.

In response, without saying or mentally projecting anything; the Earthman boldly picked up the wounded man who was still unconscious; as if he were a small stone; and rapidly walked out of the room between the two rows of warriors; unhindered by the hundreds of heavily-armed Reptilian guards around him! The tall warriors left Blow alone and did not attack him; since their Supreme Commander King Radak did not command them to attempt to stop him! **But why would the brave Reptiloid warriors do this?!? Just why did they not attack the escaping Humanoid?!?** What was the reason?!? The tall Reptiloid warriors did not move because during the time Blow spoke with Radak; after each of the guards in the room had looked into the literally blazing eyes of the Humanoid being; they did not want to get in the way of what apparently was a superior being having unknown powers; especially since they had not been ordered to do so by their king! Each of the reptile warriors had been trained from the time they hatched from an egg to follow King Radak's orders **EXACTLY**; doing nothing unless so ordered by their king or one of their superior officers! As the Admiral left with the patrolman, Radak ordered his guards in the nearby control room to send a small recon tank to follow Blow to allow him to watch the Earthian's movements from the throne room and send orders to his troops using the speaker and the small video screen on top of the tank!

In only a relatively few minutes they watched the alien again successfully make it through the totally dark corridors of the bewildering labyrinth with his burden; walking straight through the darkness without any hesitation as if he had somehow memorized the way through the confusing pattern of tunnels! Hidden sensors along the corridor, and the small unmanned armored scout tank following behind Blow; kept Radak continuously informed of the alien's progress; and behind the rolling camera on treads; a large force of guards also kept a safe distance behind the enigma of a supposedly powerful Humanoid who had been allowed to leave the throne room without Radak ordering them to stop him! Finally after successfully retracing his steps back through the dark maze, Admiral Blow exited through the ruined steel door; continued a little longer outside the building; then stopped and carefully deposited the severely wounded patrolman near the spot where he had apparently dissolved his ship to prevent its capture by the Reptiloids! In response; dozens of guards that had also come through the door stopped and formed an impenetrable circle around their quarry! The Reptiloid spy tank also stopped amid the guards and using its external audio speaker and its video outlet; Radak transmitted a message to the two aliens appearing on a screen in his throne room and the small screen on top of the tank.

The transmitted message was very loud and to the point! "You somehow made it back again through the labyrinth that is around my palace, but how will you get off the planet, Earthling? You are marooned and completely at our mercy, even if you do have permission to leave our planet with your pilot! The ultra-advanced ship that you came to our planet with is gone because YOU dissolved it so we could not force our way into the advanced ship to capture it and get valuable intelligence data! Now, what will you do? The weapon systems and the navigation power systems on your nearby obsolete ship have been dismantled by our intelligence forces; so you cannot use it to escape! Our planetary sensors indicate that there are no Imperial or Earthian ships within several thousand light years to help you and apparently you have no communications equipment with which to contact them! Even if you could contact another ship come rescue you, it could not get here in time to save you and it could not successfully make it through our mighty planetary defenses without being totally destroyed!" Radak sneered in Thunderese.

In answer to the question, in the relative calm just next to the ruined armored door, the Humanoid known as Blow opened the folds of his jump suit and pressed two buttons one side of his defense belt in a complicated pattern! Instantly, from all parts of the horizon, gleaming bits of matter somehow forced their way through the howling winds and appeared to coalesce a few feet from Johnny Trevor's boots back again into Captain Gallant's very small black ship; with "Tanya" printed on the left front side!! It was in exactly the same spot that it had occupied when it was seemingly reduced to dust! (Actually when Blow pressed the small button on his defense belt the first time before he went into the labyrinth; Captain Gallant's ship was sent exactly one second into the future through a time warp portal created by the defense belt! The optical illusion of the ship's entry down the Time Stream; (or if you prefer, Time Cloud); made the ship seem like it was turned to dust!) Quickly Blow again easily picked up his man as if he were a small sack of Earthly potatoes and started toward the ship's hatch.

As the Admiral walked along; using the defense belt; he telepathically sent a very important message to Radak and his hordes! For a thousand mile radius around the ship and up into space; Reptiloid telepaths; and even nontelepaths; winced as they picked up the powerful mental message directed to the Ruler of the Thunder Worlds by the unknown Earthian Humanoid warrior!

#By the Eternal Flame of the Cosmic All, I hope we will meet again, Radak; AKA Thud! I am not through with you yet! Sometime in the Future I will make you pay for what you have done!! I relish meeting you in battle to obtain revenge!! If it takes a year, a thousand years, or until Eternity starts; either I personally; or future descendants from my world; will somehow make you pay for your unwarranted and barbaric treatment of MY pilot; who did NOTHING to warrant such cruel and brutal treatment! He was in Earthian territory when he was viciously attacked without any cause by YOU the invader of his solar system!! You had no right to capture my patrolman; take him back to your Thunder Worlds; and have any reason to execute him for simply defending his home planet!! By the way; you can keep the patrol ship you captured; it is one of our very old models; so examining its primitive electronic systems will not help you! We on Earth no longer use such obsolete short-range FTL equipment! It does not contain our latest FTL propulsion system which can run continuously because of the shape of its advanced field core which reduces heat tremendously! We will be ready the next time if and when you invade our section of the galaxy! SO FOR YOUR OWN SAFETY AND THE SAFETY OF YOUR THUNDER WORLDS; STAY AWAY!

I WILL NOT BE SO KIND NEXT TIME IF YOU INVADE OUR SECTOR OF SPACE! IF THERE IS A NEXT TIME; I WILL NOT HOLD MY FORCES BACK UNTIL THEY HAVE TOTALLY DESTROYED YOUR FORCES; THEN WE WILL INVADE YOUR HOME WORLDS AND TOTALLY DEFEAT AND DESTROY ALL YOUR REPTILOTIC FORCES! When we spread the news about your defensive incompetence though the galaxy, it will more than pay us back for the cost of our outdated ship!# Blow telepathically drilled into Radak's Reptiloid brain as he assisted the injured soldier through the small entry hatch and immediately carefully placed him into a medical cabinet; where he was soon under anesthesia and his many wounds were attended to by the Imperial ship's very able AI "robot doctor".

But Thud was not finished dealing with Admiral Blow; as he shouted in Thunderese, **"Wait, alien, you can't leave this planet because YOU ARE TRAPPED!!!** All our impenetrable planetary defense energy screens are in place above you and **nothing in the universe can leave until they are dropped; which we will not do until you surrender!** Also, it is a well know scientific fact that a ship cannot go FTL in a planet's gravity well without its drive and/or the planet blowing up! If you try to go FTL; you will die when your ship's propulsion system blows up! If you don't use your FTL drive; you cannot rise fast enough from the surface of our planet to escape our automatic defenses which are now aimed at your ship and will blow you to atoms the instant you move! Admit defeat now and let us end this farce; foolish alien! Surrender immediately! Admit it! You are wasting your time trying to escape our planet! There is no way out through our powerful electronic screens because they are impenetrable; being designed to stop material objects and also protect the planet from energy weapons! Our military tactics computers have calculated that even an Imperial Tytano battle ball ramming them at over 1000 times the speed of light could not force its way through them without the ship being totally pulverized and destroyed; with no damage to our planet!! THE SCREENS ARE THAT STRONG AND FORMIDABLE BECAUSE OF THEIR VERY POWERFUL GROUND-BASED ZERO-POINT ENERGY SUPPLY! THERE IS NO WAY THAT YOUR TINY SHIP CAN PENETRATE THE POWERFUL DEFENSE SCREENS ABOVE OUR PLANET!!! Admit your defeat and immediately surrender! You are doomed no matter what you do! Surrender and I promise you and your pilot a quick and relatively painless death!" the Reptiloid sneered again over the ship's ground intercom.

"You are wrong, Reptiloid! WE ARE NOT TRAPPED AND WE ARE NOT DOOMED BECAUSE ESCAPING THIS PLANET IS NOT IMPOSSIBLE FOR TANYA, RUBE!" was the Admiral's quick thunderous reply which used an Earthian derogatory slang word and Tanya's name that the Reptiloid's computers could not translate! After the short retort; the hatch of the small ship quickly closed and a faint hum pervaded the area as Tanya quickly analyzed the planet's protective screen above them to find out if they could escape or if they would have to surrender to the Reptiloids! After a split-second analysis of the screens the AI told the Admiral that since the screens only gave "one-way" protection, they could escape; with only the planet's defensive screens totally destroyed by a tremendous counter-surge of power!

As the ship prepared to escape the Thunder Worlds; even though the young patrolman was in the medicine cabinet getting his many injuries attended to; the Admiral shouted, **"Hang on, Johnny! Tanya says she has just analyzed the screens above us and she can penetrate the energy shields protecting the planet because they are 'one-way'; and designed to only protect against objects coming in; not going out! If she can't; we will never know it before the ship is instantly destroyed and we travel to the next level of Humanoid existence!"**

The Reptiloids quickly scattered to get out of the way of the titanic explosion on the planet's surface that they knew by the immutable laws of physics was coming; even though they knew that if the alien went FTL; they were doomed and had no chance to escape the tremendous explosion when the ship's FTL propulsion systems reacted and interacted with the planet's gravitational and magnetic fields; immediately causing tremendous damage to the planetary crust; terrible planet quakes; and immense volcanic activity!

Even as Thud quickly descended into the palace's defense shelter deep underground to escape the expected coming eruptions; the Reptiloid's automatic translation earpiece indicated that it could not find any meaning for the words "Tanya" and "Rube"; causing Radak to wonder, *#Who or what is a 'Tanya' and what is a 'Rube'? If I survive the coming titanic blast, I* *must ask my advisors to find out what the strange alien words mean! I am intrigued that as he was probably about to die; the unknown Humanoid called Blow would use such unusual words that my usually reliable translation earpiece did not know what the unknown Humanoid terms meant and could not find what the unknown terms meant by instantaneously using its extensive data banks on Empire Prime and the Thunder Worlds! Apparently the words were not listed in that enormous documentation of Galactic words! SO WHERE DID THE HUMANOID GET THEM?!?!?#*

By all the normal laws of every branch of propulsion science, when it came to operating any known star drive; any ship capable of FTL could not suddenly go Trans-Light while resting on a planet's surface without the ship's drive unit producing the powerful magnetic field needed to go FTL causing tremendous gravitational and magnetic reactions that would literally destroy both the planet and the ship! It was impossible for almost any other ship in the Universe, but not impossible for one of Captain Gallant's so-called "Special Courier" Ships; which; as previously documented; secretly boasted alien technology that the Captain had obtained from grateful alien planets who he had helped over the long centuries of his service to the Empire! Through the centuries after he helped them; each alien race gave him an improvement for one of his systems in his propulsion unit; not knowing about the gifts of the other beings! (Meshing Imperial and alien technology slightly improved each system necessary for FTL travel and the net effect was all of the slight increases in efficiency together produced a ship that was far superior to anything the Empire or any of his alien friends would produce for many centuries! Because each improvement came from a different source; none of Cap and Cody's alien races, and the Empire's Imperial Navy; knew of the ship's far superior performance; which it had obtained very slowly over the decades and centuries! Because of the advanced shape and size of the ship's FTL drive field; (the secret of which was given to him by a small Snakoid race at the edge of the Great Dark grateful to him for saving the life of their ruler using Empire medical technology; when the Snakoid King was sick with the dreaded "Great Dark Fever"); as Blow's ship left the planet's surface, it did not fatally interfere with the planet's magnetic and gravitational fields; hence there was no fatal explosion!)

The faint humming noise suddenly stopped, with all the Reptiloids still alive, because the craft suddenly disappeared right before their astonished reptile eyes; with only a faint pop to indicate that the ship had vanished and planetary air had imploded into the sudden vacuum caused by the ship literally vanishing; without leaving a tunnel of suction that sucked objects on the surface of the planet far up into the atmosphere like one ship did on Empire Prime several years ago![4] But their possible physical dangers were not yet over! The next noise the much-relieved Reptiloids heard was much greater in volume as high overhead; just as Tanya figured; the entire planet's titanic energy shields exploded in gigantic sheets of atomic and electrical flame an instant after the small alien craft successfully penetrated the multi-ply kinetic and energy protection screens from the rear; the exact opposite side they were designed to defend! **Radak's defense engineers were either ignorant of; or forgot this vital fact!** Since the thick defense fields were not designed to stop any kinetic or energy weapon's slug or particle or energy beam traveling from the interior, all the screens reacted to the fast-moving small ship by pushing the magnetic defensive screens outward! Because of their one-way design; which was to resist material objects or electronic beams <u>coming in</u>; the electronic feedback from Admiral Blow's ship surging outward created a surge of raw energy that first flowed outward; then backward to cause the entire planet's protection fields to implode! The resulting titanic feedback surge of raw; untamed electrical power caused a severe explosion in every defensive installation on the planet; resulting in absolute chaos among every military base on the orb; when every electronic device in every one of their installations was fused to slag by the electrical feedback of a tremendous surge of raw electricity!!

The next nanosecond; dozens of satellite defensive batteries with FTL target imaging systems which ringed the planet; suddenly detected and tried to focus their weapons on the fast-moving escaping ship, but incredibly; and impossibly; the already trans-light speed of the craft was already moving too fast for even their AI controllers using FTL sensor technology! They could not track the phenomenal ship because compared to the speed of light; it was traveling faster than the speed of light as a ray of light travels faster than an Earthly snail! As such; it was no contest!!! The robot sensors could not successfully compute the coordinates of Blow's ship close enough so that they could shoot and destroy it; so all they could do was keep trying to calculate their target's path and the lasers and energy weapons kept moving without firing; which they would the instant a successful computation was achieved!

Next; from high orbit out of the way of the exploding defense fields; Reptiloid AI fighters with 20-gravity acceleration drives attempted to catch the escaping courier vessel; but again; it was so much faster than the planet's best; that it seemed like a sailboat on a lake during a calm was trying to catch a high-powered speedboat! Once again; the race was no contest! In just a few seconds the swiftly moving small ship disappeared from even the Thunder World's most powerful long range sensors which could detect and identify targets out to 1,000 light years; and could detect ships out to 10,000 light years!

As the Anchor Event continued across a tremendous stretch of the Cosmic All; the Winds of Destiny continued at gale force along the path of the infinitely swift small ship traveling at a speed higher than any other object had ever accomplished in the history of the Universe!! (With all the advanced alien technology at his disposal in the AI ship "Tanya"; since the day he got her at the Imperial shipyard; the Captain had never had any excuse to "open her up" and find out exactly how fast she could go; and so even the AI did not know, and could not compute; what her top speed was!) And now, because of the previously mentioned technology willingly given by grateful alien civilizations for Cap's service to them, far out in the Universe; when Admiral Blow had rescued the patrolman and needed raw **SPEED** to escape the Reptiloids from the Thunder Worlds; it was at his disposal!! The result of this speedy escape was that after the mission was over; Tanya was able to tell Captain Gallant just how fast she could actually go; (until it slightly increased when she was given the next upgrade by another grateful alien civilization!)

Plus, when the Destiny-altering mission was completed, and the Admiral was able to return to his house; he picked up his beloved wife and took her to the first cancer treatment appointment with Dr. Regal Strife! The couple was never disappointed by the decision to change doctors and change treatments! The gifted doctor specialized in treating all forms of cancer with microwaves that were tuned to totally destroy the patient's cancer cells and be absolutely harmless to normal Humanoid cells! After only a few short sessions with the doctor, Mary Pearl was totally free of her tumors and was ready to live a normal life and become a mother with at least eight children; (or more if Jonathan wished!)

CHAPTER 11

At the same instant; the scattered Time Points of the Cosmic All continued to drift; (or if you prefer, all of the Time Points on the Time Stream continued to drift along toward Eternity!) But, at the exact same instant in the Eternal Universe, at one particular extremely important Time Point, another related crucial Anchor Event was happening; impossibly connected to several other impossible and improbable events that were happening on one very important Life Path on the Main Galactic Time Line!! All of these Anchor Events were not "physically related" on the Time Stream/Time Cloud; but the effects of one Anchor Event happening in the "Future" impossibly affected the "preliminary events" and the "post event" happenings of several other Anchor Events; which in turn; affected the Anchor Events in the "Future"; in a way that the Imperial Seers could not have predicted in a million years of mental and computer computations! Because of the unprecedented "Time Manipulation" one set of events was actually duplicated!

The unique effects meant that something or someone was using ultra-advanced technology to literally go from one spot on the Main Galactic Time Line to another; in order to perform an act that would change the course of the Time Line and change the outcomes of other events that had already happened; as well as impossibly changing the outcome of events that on Imperial Seer visions of the Main Galactic Time Line had not yet occurred! But to attempt to prevent disaster; incredibly each time inert matter; or the sentient Humanoid; moved from one part of the Time Line to another; ultra-hot matter was somehow automatically deposited at the instant on the exact position on the Time Line that the inert matter or the Humanoid came from; in order to keep the energy and mass at both instants on the Time Line exactly the same! This had happened several times before on the Main Galactic Time Line; as a young Humanoid man named Watson[2] traveled across Time in order to change his Final Destiny; while a mature Humanoid man traveled across Time to save the life of his wife! Incredibly; at another instant on the Main Galactic Time Line, millions of Imperial dollars were suddenly added to the Humanoid's bank account! But at another instant on the Time Line; he was a very old retired man sending a large black object back into Time for a rendezvous with Destiny several hundred feet under an Egyptian riverbank at a time several thousand years before that instant! The old man was also sending information back to himself at the point on his Life Path when he was a middle-aged Admiral so that he would know exactly how to defeat and escape the Reptiloids with his patrolman who had been captured; instead of both of them being imprisoned or executed! He was also told to not take his wife to use the standard cancer treatment of surgery; radiation;

and chemotherapy; and instead use the advanced techniques of Dr. Regal Strife in order to heal his wife; without the terrible side-effects of the standard treatment of chemo and radiation! Then on another instant; he was a very, very young lad in elementary school and being bullied! At another instant he was middle aged and giving a younger naval cadet at the naval academy written instructions on how to live his Life Path!!! But just exactly what was going on?!?!?!? The wisest Imperial Seer who had ever lived could not have figured out just what the sentient Humanoid being was doing; throughout his life as an old man and as a middle-aged Admiral and as a young boy!!

And incredibly; as each Anchor Event on separate; widely spaced spots in "TIME" occurred; even though the happening was not physically "related" to the other Anchor Events; or happening very close "in Time"; **ALL THE CIRCUMSTANCES AND DETAILS OF EACH ANCHOR EVENT AND ORDINARY EVENT THAT CONCERNED THE SENTIENT BEING KNOWN AS "BLOW"; WERE INSTANTLY CHANGED; AT EACH AND EVERY POSITION ON THE TIME LINE! INCREDIBLY, THE BLOW IN THE "FUTURE" SENT INSTRUCTIONS TO HIMSELF IN THE "PAST" TO SAVE THE LIVES OF HIS PATROLMAN AND HIS WIFE; AND TO COMPLETELY CHANGE BOTH HIS "PRESENT" AND HIS "FUTURE" LIFE PATHS; WITH EACH CHANGE OCCURING AT EXACTLY THE SAME INSTANT ON THE MAIN GALACTIC TIME LINE!!!!** So what ultimately happened? What was the total effect of this cascade of eerie; literally impossible events?? If you are not an Imperial Seer and you can't observe what the total effect of the events now occurring has had on your section of the Main Galactic Time Line; ask an Imperial Magi in a thousand or so years when the Imperial Time Laws will allow the information to be released to Imperial Citizens when the Time Line "settles down" after all the unprecedented Time Manipulation used by Admiral Jonathan Baines Blow to rescue his wife and his life!!

But as this Anchor Event was reshaping Admiral Jonathan Baines Blow's Life Path; other Anchor Events scattered at several other points up and down the Main Galactic Time Line were also happening; and influencing points that were earlier and later than their positions on the Line! These Time Line-Affecting Events were happening at several other points of The Main Galactic Time Line that would also be important to the healing of Admiral Blow's wife of cancer and vastly improve and gladden both his and her Life Path! **Such as . . . . . at one ultra-important instant on the Main Galactic Time Line, an event that had already happened; because of a "Time Distortion"; was somehow reoccurring! But just how would this affect all the Future/ Past events of the Admiral's Life Path?!?**

CHAPTER 12

The Main Galactic Time Line was jolted back again to a very Important Anchor Event on the Main Galactic Time Line; at a position occurring before the previous happenings illuminated in this Imperial Document; in the main headquarters building of the Earthian fleet Admiral Jonathan Baines Blow was just finishing up the day's paperwork before he was scheduled to take his wife the next day to the base hospital for the first preliminary surgery to remove a large cancer tumor before it metathesized and spread to all parts of her body. But just as the Admiral was locking his desk, a brilliant pinpoint of light appeared in front of him just over his head and swiftly dropped to the desk's surface! Startled, Blow first jerked back; then reached forward toward and grasped the very familiar object on his desk that had suddenly appeared! The thing on his desk that had suddenly appeared was a single Manila paper envelope; with his distinctive letterhead on the side! Reaching forward the Admiral plucked the envelope out of the air and quickly opened it. Reaching inside he extracted a single sheet of paper which had very small writing on it--very familiar hand-written letters written in a particular shade of red that looked like it was produced by his favorite red pin in his desk!! It took him only several seconds to read and absorb the information that had somehow been written by himself; then his combat instincts took over and he stopped to deeply think about the information that he had been given--somehow impossibly written by himself at some point in the Future!! But his thoughts suddenly ceased because the instant after he finished reading the note from the Future, it unexpectedly blazed up and was instantly gone!! Blow ignored the fiery ashes that burned a hole through his desk; then dropped down to blacken a spot on the floor; and continued his important pondering! The note had to somehow; some way; have been written in the Future; because it contained very important information about cancer treatment that he had not heard of; before that instant!!! It also gave detailed instructions on how to rescue the patrolman who was captured by the Reptiloids while defending Earth! The note said that a frontal assault on the Thunder Worlds by the entire Earthian fleet would be easily defeated; but just one ship could make it through the Reptiloid defenses and successfully rescue his man by using the natural curiosity of the Reptiloids to allow just one small ship through their massive electronic defenses! It also gave instructions on how and where to get the ship that he needed! As he pondered how to use the information that had suddenly appeared on his desk; Blow thought, *#I have never heard of Dr. Regal Strife; but I will immediately postpone the cancer operation scheduled for today and contact Dr. Strife to see if he can operate on Mary Pearl's tumor ASAP!#* It took only an instant for him to gather up his documents and swiftly exit his office; even as the Winds of Destiny swirled around him and continued on at beyond light speed past Empire Prime; to the consternation of the Imperial Magi! And so it was that for the first time in the history of Creation, events in the "Past" that had already happened; were altered and completely changed by information sent to the "Past" by a sentient being in the "Future" who knew just what had happened in the "Past" and wanted to alter certain very sad happenings in the past; so that the "Future" extremely sad events that he had already gone through would be changed!! But just what effect would this have on literally all of Creation?!?

But as Sergeant Todd "Banjo" Biggens, the main protagonist on the weekly military series "Combat on the Planets" shown on satellite stations; says quite a bit to describe what was going to happen; **"if we fail in this mission; nutin' good will happen; only something extremely bad!"**

CHAPTER 13

And so it was that at another very Important Time Instant somewhere on the Main Galactic Time Line, the old navy veteran, Jonathan Baines Blow; always wore the same old faded military uniform and loved to daily travel by "old-fashioned walking" to go from his run-down shack in the East Texas woods in order to visit the famous Imperial Compu-Library in Madisonville to research his favorite subject; military history on the many planets in the Empire. For several years, every day the library was open; rain or shine; he came to the library; working very hard on all the research computers the library had; as if he were searching for something very, very important; **which he was!** Through the years the veteran librarian, Mrs. Barbara Larrison, the wife of retired Army General Jerry "Lucky" Larrison; slowly got to know the old man; who had a very dilapidated artificial right arm because of a botched raid he had lead against the Thunder Worlds many decades before. Gradually, over the months and years she learned that he was a widower whose wife had died of cancer many years before; and because of the radical surgeries, radiation treatments, and the chemotherapy used to attempt to save her life; before Mary Pearl had died; she had never been able to have children. The first few years Mr. Blow started coming into the library; whenever Mrs. Larrison was near the computer where he was working very industriously, she would hear him quietly mutter over and over again, *"I wish I had gone with Dr. Regal Strife's treatment using microwaves to kill the cancer cells and yet totally harmless to the normal cells; instead of deciding on the standard cancer treatment of radical destructive surgery; deadly radiation treatments; and very painful chemotherapy! Dr. Strife's technique was a treatment that I just found out about while researching in this library!! I wish I had just. . . . "* But gradually; over the long months and years; the old man stopped his muttering; apparently coming to grips with his beloved wife's death from cancer and accepting what had happened.

Then one fateful day the former Admiral Blow was relaxing by searching through old "Global Science" websites and ran across a huge article on the findings of Doctors McBroom and Blacklock; two archeologists who had worked at the same muddy bank of the Nile River for over sixty years; without finding anything of archeological value! They had painstakingly used small hand shovels and whisk brooms to examine literally every grain of sand and clod in a small area down to the bedrock and then fifty feet deeper; literally wasting their lives without finding anything of historical value! The article gave the exact location of the huge extremely thick bank of hard mud where the two men had toiled for many years to increase the information about early life in Egypt;

but alas; their toil was in vain; and for all their extremely hard work; they found literally **NOTHING!**

As the old man was reading about the useless toil of Blacklock and McBroom, the Winds of Destiny suddenly came to life around the old man as, for some reason; he saved all the information about the useless endeavor on the banks of the Nile River to his very small ''flash drive'' and left the library for the day!

Barbra found out from other visitors to the library that the man known as Jonathan Baines Blow had come from a very wealthy family but that as a teenager; instead of following in his father's footsteps into the family banking business, the young man had developed a severe case of ''flying fever''; just like so many young men, had joined the navy and had become a naval fighter pilot. After he had been in the military for many years, rising to the level of Admiral and tragically losing his wife to cancer; the family business had gone bankrupt and now the lonely widower had to live on was his relatively small navy pension. The librarian always warmly greeted him whenever she saw the faded man determinedly hobble into her research room where she was assigned to work at the Texas State Research Library near Houston, Texas; on the famous ''International Trading Highway 45''. He always acted like the gentleman that he was and was always very quiet while he researched; until the fateful day he blurred out, **"So that's who got my. . . . .** Oh, I'm sorry, Mrs. Larrison; after so many years of fruitless research in your fine library; I got excited when I finally was able to contact the proper Imperial data sources and get information about a historical battle against some rogue

Reptiloids that I was involved in--and lost; which is where I got this cyborg right arm!!"

Excitedly the old man started delving into the Empire's vast data banks concerning countless planetary; interplanetary; and galactic-wide battles; searching for more information about the alien race that captured and executed the young man under his command that was simply patrolling out beyond Pluto! Back then, Captain Gallant's old enemy, Thud; was the leader of the Thunder Worlds and he led most of their raiding parties.

The old man pondered to himself, #I need to calculate exactly what I could have done to prevent my patrolman from being killed by those Reptiloids! Fighting them on the way to the Thunder Worlds did not work; Earth's fleet did not get there in time; and my man was executed; in addition causing me to lose my right arm in the gigantic battle afterwards! But what could I have done differently to win the battle and save my man? At that time I did the best that I could do to defeat those huge Reptiloids so that I could rescue Johnny Trevor before they executed him! Could I somehow wipe the slate clean and try to do the job over again with this new information and using Captain Gallant's ultra-advanced ship?!? Now how can I use this information about Blacklock and McBroom's fruitless decades of toil? I wonder, could I send a ship deep into the muddy bank. . . . and then. . . . will this actually work?!? When I get some more pertinent information; by the rings of Saturn, I will find out!!! Now, how can I send that ship back in Time so that nobody else can find it except myself in that timeframe;

and yet it will still be serviceable for me to use against Thud? I think I know! I'll try to use the ultra-advanced time devices of my friend Dr. Chance Watson to send the ship that I need back in time to ancient Egypt! Then I will sent instructions to myself in my own handwriting so that I can find it under the Egyptian mud that Blacklock and McBroom are examining at about an inch of mud every ten years. Then I can use military equipment to dig up Captain Gallant's ship and use it; instead of the whole Earth fleet; in order to accomplish the successful rescue of Johnny Trevor! I believe I heard him say once during a private donor's conference that his latest devices can send something through Time and also act as a transposing device to send them anywhere on Earth!! Then I'll . . . .#

After many hours of meticulous research spread over many days; to make sure he had all the vital details correct; Blow carefully copied many hundreds of pictures and thousands of pages of material to his supposedly obsolete "flash drive" that he was issued while in the navy; which in actuality could hold every byte contained in every computer memory that could have been accessed by the library! On the fateful day when he was satisfied that he had all the pertinent information and had formulated a complex plan of what he could do to literally change history; if he had the right equipment; the old warrior hurried out of the library and got into a robot taxi to go to the proper communications building. Besides his friend Chance Watson, he wanted to also contact one of his old friends, an Imperial military man known as Captain Gallant; who happened to 'owe' him for a few favors he had been able to do for the Cap a few centuries ago when he was still an Admiral here on Earth and Cap was a roving spy for the Empire; who tried to find "Trouble"; literally anywhere in the entire Universe; before it became big enough to be of concern to the Imperial forces! One day a very long time ago, after a terrible space battle in which the Imperial forces had almost been defeated by the hordes of the "Moran", a sub-species of Reptiloids; "The Man" had crash-landed near Earth and was found in a totally wrecked advanced space craft on the moon by Admiral Blow's forces. The Admiral privately interviewed the Humanoid who identified himself as "Captain Gallant", an officer in a space navy from beyond the stars, and after hearing his explanation of why he had crashed on Earth's moon; and hearing his men's report about the spacecraft; following his "battle instincts"; had chosen to totally trust the Captain! Later in a private conference with the alien Humanoid Captain Gallant, Admiral Blow told him that his forces would give him the help that he needed to repair his heavily-damaged ship; or give him the resources to contact other units in what Gallant called the "Imperial Navy" of the Interstellar Condominium of Planets and Empires"; or "ICOPE". (The Admiral, and Earth, had never regretted his decision to trust an unknown Humanoid from beyond the solar system and literally give him almost anything he needed to be able to go back to where he came from!)

Following Blow's orders; the Earthian forces had given the previously unknown Imperial officer known as Captain Gallant all the help they could to "jury rig" his ultra-advanced ship so that he could return to the ICOPE. The Admiral also allowed Gallant to contact Imperial authorities; and his sidekick, Captain John Cody. (In return for the help, Cap had secretly allowed the Earthian forces to keep certain advanced Imperial electronic devices so that they could "reverse engineer" them!)

In his memoirs that were printed several decades after he finally retired; the Admiral reported that the instant that he had met the two men, they immediately became life-long friends. Thereafter, whenever the Captain or the other Imperial officer he introduced to the Admiral, Captain Cody, were "in the neighborhood"; (say within a few hundred thousand light years); and had ever needed materials, medical help, or ship repairs; the Admiral's forces had standing orders to always help them whenever they could; and conversely; the spies had helped the Admiral and his planet Earth whenever they could. Both Captains remembered the kindness that the Admiral had shown them; and they each privately vowed to help Blow at any time and in any way they could if it took a thousand years; because they **ALWAYS! ALWAYS! ALWAYS REPAID THEIR DEBTS—BOTH "GOOD", AND "BAD"--(ESPECIALLY THE "BAD")!!**

Visiting face to face electronically from galactic range with his former military comrade in a thoroughly screened holographic suite which was safe from sensor and telepathic intrusion, where each man was reproduced in a 4-D image;, the extremely old man who once had the nickname "Hurricane"; had a secret conference with his old friend he now knew as the famous Captain Bordoe Gallant; who with the help of "Interferon 777", still looked like a young man and was still working for the Empire! After conferring for many minutes, the old Earthian military man thanked the Imperial spy for giving him vital information and for promising him the temporary use of one of his "Gallant Courier Ships" that he needed in order to carry out his plan to "reclaim" his life! Blow then hurriedly left to contact another important figure in Earth's Time Stream, a man of world-renown scientific knowledge he still knew as a close friend; Doctor Chance Watson.

While he was in transit walking along the wide street to contact his friend; attempting to communicate across several hundred thousand light years using ultra-advanced Imperial technology; his pocket communicator indicated that several trillion Imperial Credits were suddenly transferred into his account from a secret and inaccessible "Unrestricted Account" backed by the Imperial Government who had made contact with the Earth a few decades before after the Captain had contacted Admiral Blow's forces! He inserted the proper password and was able to open and read an attached restricted and encoded memo with the deposit that stated several things. The money was to be used as the Admiral saw fit in the next few weeks; and the remainder of the funds did not need to be returned to the same mysterious "no limit" Unrestricted Account when his "mission" was finished; he could use the rest of the funds as he saw fit! (Captain Gallant still remembered how the Earthian Admiral had rescued him and had his injuries treated a very long time ago when he had crash-landed on the far side of Earth's moon, and now he was returning the favor! As was previously mentioned, the Captain **ALWAYS**

REPAID HIS DEBTS--BOTH "GOOD" AND "BAD"--ALWAYS PAYING THEM MORE THAN 'IN FULL'!!)** When he read and memorized the information, Blow permitted himself a grin; then he permanently deleted the encoded message. Then he used secret military computer "hacking programs" to make sure that the message was totally blotted out from all his computer's temporary files and all the covert "public domain" permanent record-keeping files; which the government covertly used to download private emails in order to help to keep track of planetary and interstellar "terrorists".

As he walked along to meet one of his old friends, a deep peace pervaded his Soul, and he permitted himself a short break to get a free senior cup of scalding hot black coffee at a local "Golden Arches" restaurant. After a short rest, the tired old man got up and hobbled down the street in search of his Dream, which over the decades had tarnished and almost faded from his memory. Almost, but enough of it remained to keep the old man working to resurrect his very important Ultimate Goals! As he walked, unknown to his regular Humanoid senses, the Winds of Destiny again started swirling around him; then gradually increasing their speed; causing the few "Proxies"[5] that were mental adepts on the small but extremely important planet Earth, to immediately raise their mental shields or risk physical injury or burn out of their ESP centers in their brains! **But just what could be happening on the small planet Earth that was of Galactic Importance?!?!? The weak planet was not yet a member; or even an associate member; of the ICOPE; i.e.; Interstellar Condominium of**

Planets and Empires; so what could its very weak ground and space forces do that was of galactic importance?!?

The Imperial Magi would never fathom the amazing answer until that section of the Main Galactic Time Line finally settled down--in a few thousand years or so after the very rare Mental Magic of a certain Imperial Seer was used to shield information about the secret rescue mission finally faded out; and their mental powers could once more visualize just what had happened to cause such a fuss of the Winds of Destiny on such a small and unimportant planet such as Earth!!!

But as the Imperial Seers had finally realized; during the long millennia they had been organized to research happenings on the Main Galactic Time Line and all its branches; victory in any sized military conflict does not always belong to the largest; strongest; or swiftest military force! Just one tiny incident or detail during a battle can make the difference between total defeat and total victory; either for a battle at the present time or amazingly, for a battle in the Past; which then would automatically change the ''Present''; OR WOULD IT?!?!?! JUST WHAT WOULD HAPPEN IF A SENTIENT BEING IN THE FUTURE PROJECTED SOMETHING BACK TO THE PAST IN ORDER TO LITERALLY CHANGE CERTAIN IMPORTANT PAST EVENTS! CHANGING THE EVENTS IN THE PAST WOULD THEN CHANGE CERTAIN EVENTS IN THE FUTURE THAT HAD ALREADY HAPPENED?!?!? NOT EVEN THE IMPERIAL

MAGI; USING THEIR MENTAL POWERS IN THEIR HEADQUARTERS THAT IS TWO HUNDRED IMPERIAL MILES BELOW THE SURFACE OF EMPIRE PRIME; COULD FATHOM THE ANSWER!!!

CHAPTER 14

As the former Admiral arrived at the front of a very large fenced house of the world-renown scientist, his old friend Doctor Chance Watson, Scientist Emeritus, Retired; the Winds of Destiny continued to blow at gale force; invisible and undetectable by the normal Humanoids on the small planet; but giving the Magi on Empire Prime fits!! At the large front gate that was locked Blow remembered the password from many years ago and punched in the numerical code on a keypad that was built into a raised concrete post; which identified him to the house's protection system; and the large gate immediately swung open. Walking up the long winding driveway amid very old trees, he finally reached the large wooden front door; and just beyond the door he observed a path leading into the forest through the lust undergrowth. As the old man approached the entrance, the door was opened by his associate's famous athlete daughter, Cleonardo Watson[4] Adams; who happened to be home with her husband visiting her dad between professional golf and tennis tournaments. Behind the beautiful young woman and through the wide doorway, he heard the faint sounds of a trumpet practicing a beautiful melody and having a very difficult time with most of the notes. The high notes were not quite on pitch and the low notes did not sound "quite right"; due to "warbling" up and down on each note; instead of being precise and steady on each tone until going on the next note. To the former Admiral, who over the centuries that he was in command had heard many trumpeters in military bands; the notes sounded like they were being made by an absolute beginner; not a mature man who had previously played in school bands!

The attractive young lady hugged him like the long-lost uncle she considered him to be and explained, "That's my beloved Daddy; still practicing all these years and still having his lifelong dream of wanting to play in a band somewhere!! He hopes someday to be good enough to start in one of those volunteer bands that play every Friday night at some cafes and hotels; like the ones that play in Madisonville! Off the record; he still does not sound very good when he attempts to produce very high staccato notes; but he keeps practicing and doing his best!"

With these words of explanation, Cleonardo Adams smiled and led him through the house to the famous "time laboratory" of the genius who pioneered "time research". Her father, Dr. Chance Watson started studying the fabric and the characteristics of "Time" after he himself was amazingly transported though time to a position on the "Time Stream", (or "Time Cloud"); to actually meet himself at a time in which he was a young boy in order to try to solve a terrible problem he had at that time in his life! (His problem was that the son of the mayor of the town was constantly bullying him![2] The technique that Dr. Watson had invented to cross "Time" had somehow been able to successfully solve the "Conservation of Mass" problem and also the time paradox problem of "meeting yourself"; which the scientist had actually done many years ago; apparently causing no damage to the Main Galactic Time Line; (**YET**)! Perhaps his Time device produced an electronic "Time Shield" like those Captain Gallant sometimes used in order to prevent "time paradoxes" that had allowed him to go back in time to help his younger self. Chance used one of his inventions to literally go back the time when he was a young boy and he actually "met himself"; with no apparent damage either to himself or the Main Galactic Time Line when he returned back to his Life Path position in the Future; which went against what Earth and Imperial nuclear physicists thought would happen!

Hearing the talking of his daughter and an unknown visitor as they approached; Dr. Watson put his trumpet down and smiled broadly as he saw who his visitor turned out to be. "Cleo, I want to thank you for interrupting your work with your author husband upstairs to admit my old friend! Admiral, it has been a long time since the last time we met! What brings you out here in the woods to visit an old scientist? You caught me practicing my trumpet because I'm still not very good; although I hope to be good enough someday to work in a band; just for the fun of it; and to entertain people! I played in my high school band when my lungs were younger; but after several decades since that time without any practicing; my former talent with the trumpet has not returned; no matter how much I practice and massage my lips; but I will never give up!!"

Cleonardo excused herself and returned back upstairs where she was helping Thomas Adams; her author husband; edit his latest novel; <u>The Time Box on Mars</u>!! While taking Blow to meet her Daddy, she had told the Admiral that her husband's last novel, <u>Time Key</u>; which had been published last year; had been a runaway bestseller for many weeks and they hoped his latest endeavor, <u>The Time Box on Mars</u>; would do equally as well!

"Chance, I have observed you work as a scientist for many years, and you have always been able to accomplish anything that you have ever wanted to do! I think that someday if you keep trying you will become good enough someday to fulfill your dream of being an accomplished trumpet player! From listening to you playing as I came in the front door; if I ever have somewhere for you to play and I need a trumpet player; I will hire you immediately! I hate to change the subject; but I need to talk to you about something very important! I need a little time because you would not believe what I am about to tell you without a long explanation!" said the old retired military veteran as they walked along.

"All right, old friend! Let's shoot the breeze for a while and let my lips cool off; then we can talk turkey and get serious! Like I stated a few minutes ago, one of my few hobbies is practicing so that I can be good enough to again play my trumpet in a band someday!" requested and explained the scientist.

"All right, it's a deal! If and when I need a band to play when I have guests at my small lakeside cabin, I will contact you!" said the Admiral. (For some reason, this statement caused the Winds of Destiny to surge around the large brass trumpet of Chance as he carried it along while he talked!)

After smiling and talking about the good times they had shared in the past for many minutes; the two former associates finally went behind locked and energy-screened doors for a very important discussion! After a short time of the two friends reliving old times and bringing each other up on the other's present circumstances; Blow explained to his old friend what had been going on and what would sound like totally impossible things that he needed to do in order to "make his life whole again"!! The world-class scientist listened to what only a few years ago he would have said were crazy ramblings; but now after completing his "Time Research" by studying the properties of the Main Galactic Time Line; he realized they were scientifically possible!! After he heard the whole plan of what the Admiral wanted to attempt; the gray-haired scientist asked to be excused to walk around on his wooded estate for a few minutes; where he could detach his thought processes from any other subject and deeply ponder the amazing actions that his friend was asking him to do! The old, retired admiral quickly agreed to let Chance ponder what he was asking and asked permission to look at his friend's private library while he was gone. The world-renowned scientist immediately gave his permission and then walked out a back door and onto a long curving path which would slowly wind through lush green foliage and tall trees and curved around to reconnect with the house sidewalk near the front door. Many years ago he had the long concrete path built to provide himself with a "Ponder Path"--a quiet pathway that he could use to get away from everyone and everything for as long as he needed in order to deeply think and ponder about whatever he needed. For an extended time one of the Alpha members of the Earthly Mesa Society; (the upper 1% Intelligence Quotient brains on the planet Earth); thought very deeply about scientific principles, and the possible consequences of using them to solve his friend's serious problems which had been caused in his past life; a failed military foray and his wife dying of cancer; which left him with absolutely no family and few friends. What his friend wanted to attempt were things that would have seemed far-fetched on the eerie new popular Tri-Vid science-fiction program "The Stranger Still Zone"! They even seemed to be extremely dangerous to the Main Galactic Time Line by moving certain objects back to the Past to change certain events in his past life in order to change the Future! So why his friend would even think about doing something so dangerous that could possibly disrupt and maybe even destroy and disrupt the entire Time Line?!? Chance realized that he would have to deeply ponder just exactly what would happen if he gave his friend the equipment to accomplish what he wanted to attempt to do--change the "past" by sending a note and devices from the "future" to himself!!

But as documented before in many Imperial documents; Dr. Chance Watson had not had an easy life; and he had gone through rough periods in his life and was present today because someone had given him help when he needed it! So after carefully weighing all the facts; the Time Scientist decided that he would do all he could to help his friend! Then he started deliberating just what he could give his friend that he could use to solve his very, very complex problem! It seemed as if his friend Johnathan would need to travel to at least three wildly-scattered points in his Life Path and somehow "reset" each Anchor Moment that had disrupted and changed his life; caused the death of his beloved wife; left him without a family; and had caused a military foray to fail that would have rescued one of his pilots from the Reptiloids on the Thunder Worlds! Chance continued slowly walking among his beloved trees for an extended amount of time before he came to several conclusions and realizations that were only possible because his unique life experiences and his one-of-a-kind self-education on the ultra-complex "Time Physics of the Universe" on the Main Galactic Time Line! For a few moments more; the tall graying scientist gathered his thoughts and retraced his steps to his study; where his friend awaited his presence.

Dr. Watson and his retired friend sat down before a warm fireplace to discuss extremely important matters that; if it did not disrupt or destroy the Main Galactic Time Line; would covertly change the past; present; and future Course of History for literally the entire Cosmic All! It was a weighty and awesome challenge that the scientist and the retired military man faced!! Could they actually accomplish the changing of several events in the past in order to radically change Admiral Blow's past Life Path from being painful and fruitless; to being joyous and productive? Could they actually do what Blow wanted to attempt? But the question was: SHOULD THEY TRY IT; SINCE IT POSSIBILY COULD DO MORE HARM THAN GOOD? INSTEAD OF HELPING

HIS FRIEND'S LIFE PATH; IT COULD POSSIBLY CAUSE THE ADMIRAL'S DEATH!! IF THE DARING FORAY WAS ONLY PARTIALLY SUCCESSFUL; WAS IT WORTH THE ULTIMATE COST-BOTH MONETARILY AND THE POSSIBLE LOSS OR IMPRISONMENT OF HIS LONG-TIME FRIEND BY THE REPTILOIDS? All these questions had to be honestly and completely answered in his mind before Chance could say yes or no to the requests of his friend!

Dr. Chance started the conversation by being completely honest with his old friend. "Even after all my deep ponderings, I don't know how your using my inventions for the purposes that you have explained to me will exactly affect or change the Space-Time Continuum or the Main Galactic Time Line!! It will be very interesting to try because the order in which you will accomplish your objectives in the Past will mean that if you are successful; absolutely no one; including yourself; will ever know what you have done and the Time Continuum will not be harmed! If you are unsuccessful, you literally will cease to exist and again; the Time Continuum will not be harmed; only radically changed when it comes to one Jonathan Baines Blow; because all of your kinfolks; every shred of evidence of your existence; and all of your accomplishments; will no longer exist! They will all vanish!! There will be no record of you being born or any record of your accomplishments as an Admiral! Automatically some other naval officer will be literally inserted on the Main Galactic Time Line and take your job as Admiral of the Fleet; and every naval person that formerly knew you will not remember you!! I will even forget that I was your friend or that I have helped you! All of your written and information that you have written in any of your computers will vanish and if I have made any notes about what you will attempt to do, they will also vanish! In addition; neither of us will remember this meeting!! But everything will instantly go back to a normal Time Line and be exactly the same as it was before you attempted these Time Thrusts, if you are ultimately successful in your quest; and everything you attempted to change is successful!! But the effects of this 'time foray' will be a weighty matter! You must give me some more time; I must make and print out more precise calculations on my electronic equipment before I attempt to do as you ask and construct the microcircuits that the subatomic electronic mechanisms require in order that you can accomplish what you require!"

Leaving his friend to chat with his daughter Cleonardo and her husband in his comfortable den by the warm fireplace; Dr. Watson went down to his very secure laboratory that was shielded against hackers, telepaths, transposers, kinetic and energy weapons, and physical invasions; to help his friend by performing certain calculations on his computer about the transference of matter and energy in such transpositions along the Main Galactic Time Line. After many minutes of very complex computer calculations on a scientific spreadsheet; he came to a final conclusion and printed out the rows and columns of Calculus symbols and extremely large numbers that he had carefully thought out and had constructed on an advanced physics spreadsheet. (Imperial Editor's note: Probably no Humanoid on Earth could interpret and comprehend those computations; and only a few Seers on Empire Prime!) Chance walked across the laboratory to the advanced "Ink Transpose Printer"; (which used very tiny electronic transposers to obtain ink from designated ink sources in the room and place them on the paper in the proper required patterns for numbers; letters; and symbols!) Stooping down; he retrieved the very complex multi-colored print-outs from the exit paper bin; slowly walked back to his desk; and spent time going over the computations that no probably Humanoid or AI computer analyst in the world could have understood and deciphered! He quickly scanned all the complex calculus computations; then he took a short rest to drink some coffee and relax. Then he returned to his desk in order to go over them once more slowly; so as to completely absorb the results and to check for any mistakes in his calculations or in his logic. Any mistake at any part of these calculations could literally be deadly--to his friend Jonathan or the entire Universe!

Then finally; when Dr. Chance was sure all his calculations were correct; he pondered the ultimate meaning of the fateful very large numbers, unique symbols, and complex diagrams on the sheets of paper in his hands! He deeply thought about the important questions: *#Were these flimsy scientific principles worth the life of his valued friend, retired Admiral Jonathan Blow; or worth not to know him? Would these actions by his friend actually change a failed navy career to one of success?!? Could it give the Admiral back the joyful life with his wife; and the wonderful life that he had with her before she died of cancer* *when the operation performed to remove and cure her cancer was unsuccessful?#* The gifted scientist **DID NOT KNOW AND REALLY DID NOT WANT TO TAKE THE CHANCE AND POSSIBLY LOSE THE FRIENDSHIP OF THE ADMIRAL FOREVER!** But to change the life of his friend for the better; he would probably have to lose the friendship of his very old and dear friend! He had known and valued the friendship of the Admiral for many, many years; and he hoped that what JB was about to attempt to do would not simply erase the life of the man; and all evidence that he had ever lived; from the face of the Earth; and from his own memory!

Finally, after much deep thought; the talented scientist went back to the den to face his friend with the results of his extremely difficult and very intricate calculations; calculations that nobody else on Earth; or anywhere in the Empire could examine and realize the fact that the hundreds of mathematical symbols in Dr. Watson's formulas contained a small error-**PROBABLY A FATAL ERROR!!** (One small mathematical sign at the center of Chance Watson's unique Time Formulas was incorrect! That part of the very complex "Time Equation" should have contained a multiplication sign before the next group of formulas; instead of an addition sign! Which meant that the reaction to Admiral Blow's "Time Jumping" would be much greater than Dr. Watson had calculated--MUCH; MUCH; **MUCH GREATER; AND VERY, VERY DESTRUCTIVE!!!)**

After thoughtfully weighing the ultimate consequences of his actions; Chance had finally decided to offer his friend what he was asking for; and allow the old military man to make the final decision to use what he had ascertained; (not knowing about the one small error in his calculations!) Chance entered the den; thanked his daughter and her husband; quietly closed the door when they left; then he said "Jonathan, my final computer calculations constructed by my Time Computation Algorithm Program; and my back-up hand-drawn diagrams both agree with my earlier hastily drawn-up figures! They both indicate that what you want to attempt, if totally successful; will apparently only affect the life paths of the beings that you have made contact with and will not physically or mentally harm anyone! If you are successful in your quest, both of us and my daughter Cleonardo will probably forget this meeting and it will be as if it never happened! If you are not successful on such a dangerous expedition through Time to single-handedly invade the Thunder Worlds and save the life of your patrolman; and save the life of your wife; you will be dead or imprisoned on the Thunder Worlds; and we will probably still remember you!! But it could happen that if you fail in your journey, you; and all evidence that you ever lived; will vanish from the Cosmic All, because you will have never been born! But it could be that what you are attempting to do will just work to accomplish what you want to do and it will not terribly affect you! You will forget what you did to change your Life Path and no one else will know that you did anything!! So many variables in the Time Equation are extremely hard to understand and fathom as to what will ultimately happen! So even though it is an extremely dangerous mission and you want to try to succeed by literally changing several different events on the Main Galactic Time Line; **I have to tell you that THE ODDS ARE**

THAT YOU WILL FAIL; and you will die in the rescue attempt; since your patrolman is guarded by thousands of Reptiloids on the capital planet of the Thunder Worlds and there is no way you can defeat them all! Plus; it could transpire that the effect could be that every facet of your Life Path would just be blotted from the face of Time as if you had never been born! But it is your Life Path and your ultimate decision to make!! If I were in your shoes, and had the opportunity to accomplish what you probably could be able to do; I CONFESS TO YOU THAT I WOULD ALSO TRY IT!! I had to make a similar decision many years ago when I decided to try a reckless journey through Time^2 to change history and correct my Personal Time Line, and incredibly; I won; apparently with no damage to the Main Galactic Time Line! In that particular instance traveling the Time Stream in order to salvage my wrecked life; I won; and incredibly; I remember what I did; but that does not mean that you will! The odds are heavily stacked against you; probably one in a thousand against success; but you and I both know that given the wonderful things that you could accomplish if you are successful; you have to try!!!"

"Because you have helped me so many times in the past when I needed materials in which to accomplish my scientific goals; as a favor to you, I will gladly and willingly do as you ask; because it is what you want to do; and if you are unsuccessful; it will harm you and only you; even though it means that probably I will never see you again and will totally forget you; since you would not have been born; or we would not have ever met! I will get the required objects and devices that are in my back storage shed and meet you in front of the house! **Good bye, my friend; perhaps forever; since I am about to relocate out west to the Federal Research Center under Cheyenne Mountain**[15]**!!** The Science Institute wants me to take all my documentation and equipment down into that U.S. government facility for security reasons in order to keep the 'time technology' from falling into the wrong hands! They will allow Cleonardo and her husband to visit me several times a year while I am down deep in the mountain working on my time projects; and I can do research and work on literally anything that I wish to!

I wish you luck! If you succeed, our Earth will be better for it! If you fail, we will never know that you failed; but we also will probably never know if you are successful; since Reality on the Main Galactic Time Line will have been changed and we will not remember what the "Old Reality" was!" Replied the galaxy-wide renowned scientist to his friend of many years; as he shook his hand.

And so it was that in order to change his Life Path for the better; by saving the life of his beloved wife; and to obtain his revenge against the Reptiloids who killed his patrolman by changing the past in order to save him; Blow was given several very small unique devices; and one very large enclosure; the principles of which had been patented both on Earth and far away on Empire Prime several decades ago by his friend who just shook his hand, Dr. Chance Watson! Using the Doctor's expertise and the very precise information that he had downloaded at the Imperial library after many years of work; together the two friends of many decades adjusted the extremely advanced sub-atomic electronic devices to perform certain heretofore scientifically impossible feats of locomotion on material objects! Their work was tedious and exacting; but they kept working! When their task was finally finished, the two good friends again shook hands; one with a shaky cyborg arm and the other with a normal Humanoid arm; as if it were for the last time this side of the Curtain of Death; which they both knew that it probably would be!!! Then the extremely old military veteran known in the past as Admiral Jonathan ''Hurricane'' Blow, took the amazing devices that he needed to change his Destiny and walked outside to meet his Karma head on in the usual ''Blow Style'', which was **"Hang the danger; full speed ahead; no matter what happens; until Victory or until Defeat; or Death!"** But in this case, there were several other possible outcomes: as Dr. Chance said, the **MAN** known as Jonathan Baines Blow could disappear forever from the face of Time; because he would have never been born! He could be killed trying to rescue his patrolman; or he could be captured and his right arm again severed by the Reptiloids and imprisoned for life and/or executed!! The odds were very, very slim that he would be totally successful; but the Admiral surged on anyway!

As the two friends parted company for what would probably be the last time this side of Eternity; the Winds of Destiny surged around them, invisible and undetectable by them; because as ordinary Humans of the Earthly branch of Humanoids; although of above average intelligence; with only the ''5 standard Humanoid senses''; these sentient beings did not have the sensory perception to sense and visualize the presence of the famed Winds of Destiny! So Admiral Jonathan Baines Blow walked out of Chance Watson's house to attempt to rescue his patrolman; change his own Personal Destiny; and resurrect the Life Path of his deceased beloved wife; not knowing just exactly what would happen!! But no matter what Fate had in store for the brave Imperial Admiral; when the Main Galactic Time Line settled down after Blow had inserted several "time devices" at different points on the Line and they had activated in order to attempt to change certain Anchor Events; he would not know if he had succeeded or failed; or simply ceased to exist; because after the Main Galactic Time Line had settled down after all of the effects of his "time tinkering" had gone into effect; he would remember only one Life Path and he and any other sentient being in the Cosmic All would not know that it had been changed!!! Plus; all of his friends and his enemies also would not know exactly what happened; because:

1). He had never been born
2). He had failed but he had survived
3). He had been totally successful!
4). He had been executed by the Reptiloids!
5). He had been imprisoned by the Reptiloids until he died.

And so; philosophically "the die was cast"; "the torpedoes were about to be launched into the water"; and the Final Life Path of one former Admiral Jonathan Baines Blow was about to either be extinguished or be radically changed . . . for the good . . . . or probably for the **BAD**--and the odds were that it would turn out to be terrible! (One-in-a-hundred thousand odds against Blow's total or even partial success would be tough odds to overcome!)

But there was a saying that Admiral Blow liked to state again and again throughout his career: **"In war; most of the time; bad odds will not make an air or ground or naval combat mission a defeat; because with their skill and daring and the right equipment; good soldiers and good sailors and good flyers CAN SUCCESSFULLY DEFY THE ODDS SO THAT ANY SO-CALLED IMPOSSIBLE MISSION CAN BE A SUCCESS!!"**

But after a lifetime of successfully cheating the odds to stay alive in deadly combat situations; could the Admiral tempt Fate and successfully cheat the odds one more time?!? Not even the Winds of Destiny knew the answer to this question because most of the visualizations of the Main Galactic Time Line for the galaxy in which the Empire resided were still not in operation; with virtually every Life Path and Time Line either blank or totally black; for the first time since Creation!!

But just what was the Humanoid known as Jonathan Baines Blow going to do in order to "buck the odds" and renew his Life Path"?!? Well. . . . far back in Earthian history; as the famous Old West gambler known as "Maverick" was prone to say: **"When it all comes down to the very important 'Final Hand'; either on your very important 'Life Path' or at a gambling game of chance in a Dodge City saloon; when you realize that you are being dealt the 'Last Hand' and whether you win or lose is 'up** for grabs'; TO HAVE ANY CHANCE OF SUCCESS; YOU LITERALLY HAVE ONLY ONE OPTION!!! When it is your turn to play, you have to shove all your 'chips' to the center of the table and play out the hand to the very last card to know for certain just what will happen! You have to do it; even if you have been dealt a 'bust hand'! WHILE YOU ARE LIVING YOUR LIFE; IF YOU HAVE ANY BACKBONE AT ALL; YOU CAN'T GIVE UP AND GIVE IN WHEN YOU FACE DIFFICULTIES AND HARDSHIPS!! GIVING IN IS NOT THE WAY TO LIVE OUT YOUR LIFE SUCCESSFULLY WHEN YOU ARE BUCKING THE ODDS! YOU HAVE TO LOOK YOUR OPPONENTS IN THE EYE AND PUT ALL YOUR CARDS AND RESOURCES DOWN ON THE TABLE OF LIFE TO HAVE ANY CHANCE OF WINNING--EITHER AT CARDS OR IN LIFE!"

So one Admiral Jonathan Baines Blow was about to play out what could be his "Last Hand" or carefully play a "hand" that would completely change his Life Path on the Main Galactic Time Line--FOREVER! But no matter how his actions affected his Life Path; when all of his calculated actions were finished; BLOW WOULD NEVER REMEMBER ALL THE THINGS HE DID ALL ACROSS THE MAIN GALACTIC TIME LINE THAT RESULTED IN DRASTIC CHANGES IN HIS LIFE PATH AND NONE OF HIS FRIENDS OR ENEMIES WOULD REMEMBER THEM ALSO!!! IF THE RESCUE MISSION WAS A FAILURE; THE

TOTALITY OF ADMIRAL BLOW'S LIFE PATH AND EVERY MEMORY OF THE HUMANOID WOULD BE TOTALLY ERASED FROM THE COGNITIVE BRAIN OF EVERY SENTIENT BEING IN THE COSMIC ALL--FOREVER!! IF HE WERE SUCCESSFUL; NO SENTIENT BEING WOULD EVERY KNOW THAT THE TIME LINE HAD BEEN CHANGED; WITH HIS WIFE'S CANCER BEING CURED AND THE PATROLMAN BEING RESCUED!

AND SO, IMPERIAL CITIZEN!! AT YOUR POINT ON THE MAIN GALACTIC TIME LINE; HAVE YOU READ YOUR OFFICAL IMPERIAL NAVY HISTORY BOOKS AND DO YOU KNOW WHAT ACTUALLY HAPPENED TO THE ADMIRAL AT THIS ULTRA-IMPORTANT TIME IN EARTHIAN HISTORY; WHEN JONATHAN BLOW TRIED TO REPAIR HIS LIFE PATH?!?! EVEN IF YOU THINK YOU DO KNOW; OR YOU DON'T KNOW; READ ON; AND BECAUSE BLOW ALWAYS FOLLOWED THE "MAVERICK RULE"[30]; WHICH ORIGINATED DURING THE SPAN OF THE EARTHIAN "OLD WEST"! BECAUSE OF BLOW'S "TINKERING WITH TIME"; MAJOR CHANGES WOULD OCCUR ON THE MAIN GALACTIC TIME LINE; CAUSING ALL THE INFORMATION IN THE MEMORY OF EVERY SENTIENT BEING;

EVERY ONE OF THE RELEVANT HISTORY BOOKS; COMPUTER HISTORICAL FILES; AND ALL PERTINENT WRITTEN MATERIAL TO BE CHANGED; AND NOT A SINGLE SENTIENT BEING IN THE COSMIC ALL WAS/IS/WILL BE; AWARE OF THIS AMAZING FACT-EVEN YOU; IMPERIAL CITIZEN!!!

ERGO; ALL YOU CAN DO IS READ ON TO FIND OUT THE IMPORTANT HISTORICAL INFORMATION YOU ARE MISSING-IMPORTANT INFORMATION THAT ESTABLISHES THE FACT THAT; USING EARTHIAN "BASEBALL TERMS" TO DESCRIBE WHAT HAPPENED; ADMIRAL JONATHAN BAINES BLOW EITHER STRUCK OUT; FLIED OUT; GROUNDED OUT; OR HIT A HOME RUN; IN HIS EXTREMELY IMPORTANT 'GAME OF LIFE' THAT AFFECTED VIRTUALLY ALL THE GALAXIES IN THE COSMIC ALL!

So what was it?!?!? Was the Admiral successful or did the result of his failure to change the past simply erase his entire history from your memory?!?!?! READ ON, IMPERIAL CITIZEN!!!

CHAPTER 15

On the permanent official yearly government tax accounts, it is recorded that on a certain day on the Main Galactic Time Line; the Supreme Commander of Earth's Space Fleets, Admiral Jonathan Blow bought a very expensive and very advanced "Galactic Tour" sports craft and paid cash with a direct draft from his own private account. He then had it transported to his mansion in the woods for storage and placed it in a large black container to protect it from the weather. (The amazing fact was that the Admiral did not need such a civilian craft to travel around; he had literally hundreds of military craft with which to use to travel anywhere he wished!) The transfer of funds was only done on electronic computer memories and no actual "money" exchanged hands. (Seer's **"OFF THE OFFICIAL RECORD"** note: "Actually our exhaustive investigations over many years indicate that it was a cover to allow him to obtain from an unknown source the temporary use of what our exhaustive research indicates seemed to be one of the fastest ships in the Universe! It has been calculated that the ship was faster than the fastest class of Imperial courier ships as those ships are faster than an Earthian snail!")

The official investigation document then states that apparently Admiral Blow next went to the only place on Earth that he owned; a large house situated on 200 acres of pine trees that he had purchased next to the Sam Houston International Forest, and had the brand-new ship that he just bought delivered to that spot. He told everyone at headquarters that he hoped to eventually be able to retire to that scenic spot when his military days were over.

But it is apparent that other important details were somehow omitted from the official investigation! Almost at the same time; two flatbed "Fed-Extra" delivery trucks delivered two strange black containers only a few inches longer and wider than the sports craft obtained from Captain Gallant; that was already stored in a similar-looking container in the barn. At the direction of Blow; the unknown cargo boxes were carefully unloaded on an open field several hundred yards from the main house. The driver and his helpers also unloaded a very large and powerful electric pallet jack for Blow to use to maneuver and store the very heavy cargo that had been just delivered. The pallet jack was scheduled to be retrieved in a few days after Blow had finished his projects and had contacted the Fed-Extra office down in Houston, Texas. But because of certain changes in the Main Galactic Time Line, the existence of what had been delivered would also be erased and forgotten from the face of the Universe!

When the delivery truck had gone; Blow sat next to one of the large boxes in the shade and carefully thought out his very complex plan! While a cool breeze blew past his location; Blow plugged his flash drive into the side of his small portable computer and carefully studied the information that he had researched about Blacklock and McBroom's fruitless archeological digging on the banks of the Nile River in Egypt; writing down the exact geological location of the large river bank and how it had changed over the long centuries; so that he could use the data to carefully repair his sorrowful Life Path!

When he had written down all the information that he needed in his notebook; the old man carefully wrote on a piece of paper detailed instructions to himself; using data that he had obtained by his exhaustive research over many long years in the Imperial Compu-Library in Madisonville. When Blow had finished writing the important note at his desk using his favorite red pen to help himself in the Past recognize who had written the note; using his very shaky bionic arm he had carefully written out instructions to himself in very, very small printing; using his unique style of printing certain letters! On that single piece of paper the exact location on the Nile River Bank to dig was specified; as well as how deep under the mud the ship probably would be. The old military man had also put down the military procedures that the Reptiloids would use against the small black ship that he would get under the Egyptian mud; and what to do to counter them and rescue his patrolman--how to go in by himself to the most heavily defended planet in the Cosmic All and successfully rescue his patrolman! He had put all the intricate information; known data about the hot and cold layers on the Reptiloid's home planet; a diagram of Thud's palace; and other instructions on how to pull off the daring raid on just the single sheet of paper that; if successfully carried out; would allow him to rescue his patrolman! He also had stated that the small ship had a very large surface blow-back when it started FTL on the surface of a planet; but it would not harm the planet!

When he had finished with that set of instructions to attempt to successfully rescue his patrolman; on the same sheet Blow started on the second set of instructions that he hoped would save the life of his wife; first detailing that the regular cancer treatment that Mary Pearl would receive would ultimately cause her death! Writing in his style of writing, he then told himself to instead opt for the cancer treatment performed by Dr. Regal Strife instead of the standard destructive chemo and radiation treatments! He described what would happen if his wife's cancer was treated by Dr. Regal Strife; whose procedure used microwaves tuned to the exact frequency in order to kill the cancer cells and leave the normal cells unharmed; and with absolutely no side effects; such as nausea and all of her beautiful blond hair falling out! He described how Dr. Strife's treatment would cure Mary Pearl of her cancer forever; and again told himself in the note to cancel her regular treatment and opt of that of Dr. Regal Strife! That Fateful Day when he had written down all the instructions to himself; Blow then placed the note inside the mailing envelope with the "hypergolic chemicals" that would ultimately ignite the sheet of instructions soon after the air reached inside the envelop; i.e.; after being mixed in the envelope during shipment; the moment that the envelope was torn open and air touched the paper; a chemical reaction would immediately start that would flare up and destroy the paper a few seconds after it was opened! (But he knew that with his superior reading speed and cognition; it would be long enough for him to read all the information on the page before the chemical reaction destroyed the paper and probably burned a hole in any desk or floor which happened to be below the reaction!)

Carefully attaching the envelope to a small device which he had obtained from Dr. Watson, Blow had slowly twisted the location dials below a LED screen on the front of the device to get certain readings on the readouts so that the note would suddenly appear in front of himself in his military office at the specific time in the past that he had received it--when he was working in his office and was about to take his wife to the hospital for unsuccessful cancer surgery that would probably cause her death! He had carefully put the package down on the ground in the sunlight; and had run toward his house to escape the implosion that he knew was coming. After a few seconds there was a soft plop, as a small amount of extremely hot molten matter suddenly appeared in place of the time-traveling envelope! To automatically balance the energy and the matter whose levels are always the same throughout all of the Space and Time Continuum; the Time Entropy had automatically replaced the envelope's matter in the present with a balancing amount of matter from the position on the Time Stream-Time Cloud which the envelope had suddenly appeared; which prevented the Main Galactic Time Line from being completely disrupted and destroyed! Taking a deep breath; the veteran military man again went back into his house to continue his very complex plan-a plan that after it was complete; he would never know if it was successful or a failure!

Next the Admiral again had gone outside and attached a small electronic device on the front of one of the large black boxes that had been delivered; (both of which had come from his friend Captain Gallant); while unhooking what looked like a remote control for a television from the device. Then he used a stick to mark the outline of the stasis container in the soft dirt around the box. He retreated back to a position next to the house; then, a touch of a small control on the remote control device caused the large black stasis box in the dust in front of him to mysteriously disappear! At the same instant a mound of extremely hot magma appeared in the yard to balance the matter/energy levels in the two points on the Main Galactic Time Line that had exchanged matter!

Then the Admiral slowly took the other large black box apart, revealing what looked like an advanced black aerospace plane secured on a stout metal pallet! The radical craft had *"Tanya"* printed in blowing script on both sides of its tail section. Next, using the electric pallet jack Blow maneuvered the black spacecraft on its pallet until it was completely inside the outline that he had marked in the dirt; then he detached the ship from the sled; hoping that it would be in exactly the same location that the black container had occupied. If it weren't; he would quickly know; since two solid objects cannot occupy the same space without a terrible reaction!! Blow then went back inside large dwelling and waited for just over an hour for an indication that he had successfully positioned the box. A bright flash, instead of a large explosion; told him that he had been successful in positioning the ship so that when the stasis field container reentered the present time; it completely enclosed the ship! At the same instant the hot magma in the yard disappeared; moving back to its former position somewhere on the Time Line! Blow then firmly secured the sides of the stasis box to the sides of the metal pallet using metal clips. To finish his extremely complex plan, Blow then attached several small devices that he obtained from Dr. Watson on several positions around the side of the stasis container. Then he again twisted small dials on the front of each device to obtain certain numbers on the LED panels on the front; so that the box would be transposed to a specific geological position on the Main Galactic Time Line; several thousand years in the "past"; as well as being situated in a certain spot along the Nile River so that the spring floods would completely cover it until it would be found thousands of years later outside the box; but only minutes to the AI Tanya waiting for him inside the box; because of the time stasis field totally enclosing the small black ship!! As the military man worked, he fervently hoped that somehow, some way his complex plan would work! The physical part of the plan done; the man then quickly went back inside his home in order to rest and cool off from the heat of the day and to again escape the expected Time Implosion; which should be much larger than that produced by the envelope!

At the instant that Blow shut the outside door and picked up a cold drink; the stasis container containing the ship disappeared with another loud POP! Simultaneously, across the entire Cosmic All it sounded as if the Heart String of the Universe had been plucked; and a strange event occurred a quadrillionth of a second after the mysterious container disappeared; on its way to a riverbank in Egypt several thousand years before Jonathan Blow's present position on the Main Galactic Time Line!

Suddenly, the Entire Main Intergalactic Time Line and literally all of its branches throughout the entire Cosmic All and throughout all of recorded and unrecorded History were literally shaking and in a turmoil because of the Admiral's unprecedented time manipulations of changing 'Past' events by sending information from the 'Future' to the 'Past'; which then would alter the 'Future' events!! The Main Line was in such turmoil that one important event was replicated! This was because the one small error in Dr. Watson's calculations meant that the time disruptions would be much greater than he thought; nine times greater; instead of just adding nine to the gyrations! The "time gymnastics" of one Jonathan Baines Blow moving objects up and down the Main Galactic Time Line; in addition to moving large objects vast physical and time distances with the devices of Dr. Chance Watson; had permanently disrupted every portion of the regular Time Continuum and nothing could be done by any mortal; sentient being to completely heal it! As the Time Tremors gradually increased in their intensity, all across the "Second Heaven" total chaos ensued; causing major physical damage on every planet and moon in the entire Cosmic All; and even including those in the "Great Dark" at the edge of the Created Universe! But the destruction did not affect the "Third Heaven"!! But then, as the Time Tremors were reaching their absolute maximum force and all Creation was about to be completely destroyed; they reached the edge of the Second Heaven, i.e.; the section of Creation containing the suns, planets, and moons; and started entering the "Great Dark"!

Instantly another fantastic event occurred that had not happened since before the present Creation!! From the edge of the Great Dark there suddenly appeared a large glowing cloud, several thousand miles across; then swiftly coalesced into an extremely large member of the "Citizen One Race"; an extremely physically, and mentally powerful sentient being whose name was Adama[11]! The instant the eerie transformation was complete, the result was what looked like an ordinary sandy-haired very tall Humanoid male floating in Interstellar space; **WITHOUT ANY AIR SUPPLY OR PROTECTION FROM THE VACUUM AND THE RADIATION OF SPACE!** The strange being looked around; immediately sensed what was going on; then he **ACTED!** The eerie being quickly cupped his hands to his mouth and seemingly moved his lips as if he were shouting something; without being able to produce sound in the vacuum of space! **But what was the powerful being doing or what could he do in order to quell the turmoil, chaos, and total destruction occurring all across the Cosmic All?!?** The entire Universe was literally being destroyed because of the unprecedented and physically impossible object manipulation all across the Universal Time Line!!! Instructions and physical objects were being sent from the "Future" in order to change the "Past"; which in turn: completely changed events in the "Future"!!!

In response to the Citizen One being's powerful "mental shout" of what several thousand years later Imperial scientists would call "Panabeing Waves"; INSTANTLY; all across the entire Second Heaven; in each of their own minds and each in their own language; each and every sentient being on each and every planet; planetoid; moon; and spaceship; heard in their own mental or verbal language, *"PEACE, BE STILL! BE AS YOU WERE; I ORDER YOU TO REPAIR ANY DAMAGE; AND AFTERWARDS; FORGET THIS HAPPENING!"*

The unique so-called "Panabeing Waves"[24] produced and projected by the almost infinitely powerful mind of the "First Citizen" being, instantly stopped the destructive gyrations of the material objects!! INSTANTLY; because of the unique healing properties his unique shout; which was produced by his unique extremely advanced brain structure; all the tremors on the Main Galactic Time Line ceased; all physical damage throughout the Second Heaven was somehow repaired; and every sentient being; animal; and insect did not remember the events of the past few moments when their surroundings were in turmoil and were being totally destroyed!! Then suddenly all the sentient beings in the Universe subconsciously heard the Citizen One being's mental Command and everything was miraculously healed!

So the damage to the Cosmic All was repaired; but did this mean that Admiral Blow's complex plan was also halted or destroyed; or did it mean that he would have to construct the note again and send all the large objects through Time again in order to reconstruct his destroyed

Life Path? The passage of "Time" would eventually reveal this to the entire Cosmic All!!

But elsewhere on the Main Galactic Time Line; as the tremors ceased and all material objects were returned to their former state; other important events were happening--events that would reshape the Past; the Present Positions on the Main Galactic Time Line; and the Future!!!

CHAPTER 16

Back in the ordinary Space-Time Continuum; at a specific point in Time; immediately after the black stasis container containing the black spaceship disappeared, the large estate of former Admiral of the Fleet Jonathan Blow suddenly shrank to only a few acres of dry ground overgrown with weeds! The expensive mansion that had existed in a previous "Time Point" on the Time Stream-Time Cloud was suddenly shrunk and looked like a run-down tar paper shack! Inside the ancient hovel, the now old former military man was still enjoying his cold drink; but Time and the strain of his working extremely hard the last few days finally caught up with the suddenly-transformed former Admiral! He started having chest pains and regretfully had to use his old-fashioned cell phone to call 911 for medical help! Twenty-nine minutes later an emergency vehicle roared up in front of the weather-beaten shack, after getting lost several times while in route; until finally their base used Blow's cell phone to get a fix on his position so that he could obtain emergency medical help in order to save his life! Upon finally arriving; two EMTs rushed inside the shack, tearing the front door made of tar paper off its rusty hinges, and quickly carried the old man to the nearest civilian hospital; ignoring the strange bare spot among the weeds in the side yard. They had been gone a little over 30 minutes when that bare area where the strange black container that had vanished from off of the face of the Earth and started moving down what some experts call the "River of Time"; others the "Cloud of Time"; suddenly had an equal amount of extremely hot "raw" matter suddenly appear to replace the vanished large black object! Again, the exact reason for the strange emergence was that the Time Stream/Time Cloud had to adjust; and do so immediately and automatically; using the natural forces of Entropy; or there would be an energy imbalance during one "instant" in "Time"; causing a Universe-wrenching explosion of titanic proportions! But, thankfully; the exact amount of solid matter contained in the equipment that was transferred through Time was exactly balanced out with an equal amount of extremely hot molten material. (Seer's further note of explanation: the same exact amount of matter had to be automatically taken from the exact moment in Time that the matter was going, and sent along the Time Stream-Time Cloud to arrive at the exact position that the stasis container moved from; or this movement in Time by the container would have violated the Conservation of Energy Law and a tremendous subatomic explosion would have ensued, completely destroying that phase of the Main Galactic Time Stream!)

After a few days in the hospital; the old man with the very worn and shabby cyborg right arm was identified by his old faded military identification in his empty old-fashioned money wallet as the formerly famous retired Admiral "Jonathan Baines Blow". The wallet was found to be empty of any physical currency or credit cards; and did not contain the standard "universal money debit card" that by international law every citizen of every nation was required to carry. Apparently the old man had lost or misplaced his card; which every citizen in each country on Earth was required to carry at all times for identification. While in the military hospital; the military veteran was examined and found to be physically disabled enough to be transferred and admitted to the famous Earthian Aerospace Force Veteran's Hospital, where he remained living as a total invalid having virtually no visitors for several years, until one day, as previously documented; he very mysteriously vanished while quietly eating by himself in the dining room; and all written or photographic evidence that he had ever lived was totally erased off the face of the Earth--**TEMPORARILY!!!**

All memory of his former existence was also somehow selectively removed from every hospital personnel's memory and amazingly all personal information about the man was also physically erased from every hospital and government retirement computer record! All of his school records and pictures instantly vanished, leaving no blank spaces in any of the annuals and school medical records! It was if the man had never been born! It was as if he had never existed during that span on the Time Line/ Time Cloud! **THE ACTUAL TRUTH ABOUT THE SITUATION WAS SIMPLE—-AFTER THAT PARTICULAR, BRIEF MOMENT HE HAD NEVER BEEN BORN IN THAT "TIME FRAME",**

I.E., THAT ONE SMALL POSITION ON THE MAIN GALACTIC TIME LINE/TIME CLOUD!!!

So what had ultimately happened to one "Jonathan Baines Blow"? Just what had happened if his "Time Travel" was successful in changing what happened to both the man that the Reptiloids kidnapped; and also what happened to his wife because this time; if his complex plan succeeded; he would choose the right surgery to combat her cancer? Did this mean that he was nonexistent in all possible Time Lines/Time Spots; or he could possibly only exist in only a few Time Regions? Perhaps only the Winds of Destiny could possibly know the answer to this Time Paradox, **(AND THEY ARE NOT TALKING; YET! MAYBE IN ANOTHER THOUSAND YEARS OR SO; AFTER THAT SECTION OF THE MAIN GALACTIC TIME LINE FINALLY SETTLES DOWN AND THE IMPERIAL SEERS CAN GET INFORMATION ABOUT THE INCREDIBLE UNIQUE TIME EVENT THAT HAD JUST HAPPENED!!)**

These very intricate idiosyncrasies in the Time Line/Time Cloud are described in certain Ultra-Top Secret scientific audio and mental articles available to Imperial Seers on Empire Prime with the required seniority and Intelligence Clearance. Amazingly such advanced scientific information has also been described on several sci-fi episodes on television; (such as the episode "Dr. Watson's Time Paradox"; last year being voted the most popular episode on "The Stranger Still Zone" television series; and the top-secret volume, Dr. Chance Watson's "Time Travel is Not Logical"[17])! This was published by the monopolistic Imperial publishing company on Empire Prime only for Imperial Seers to read or visualize; since they are the only ones who can fathom and completely understand such far-out knowledge; such as the extremely complicated "Life Line" through "Time" of one "Past"; one "Present", and one "Future" Jonathan Baines Blow; that can only be explained by an Imperial Seer of at least a thousand years seniority; having a post-doctorate degree! But if one waits just about a thousand years from now; after the manuscript is declassified; even after hearing the complex explanation of how any sentient being can successfully travel up and down the Main Galactic Time Line given by the veteran Magi Sanjo Mocmoc; (who uses words that only exist in the future); most non-scientific persons will not know any more about "Time Travel" after hearing the explanation than before! Plus; they will not be able to "Time Travel" because they do not have the proper "mental" and physical equipment and the legal authority to do so!!

But the information about Admiral Jonathan Baines Blow's amazing "Time Travel" to repair his Life Path is; and will be; available in the "Future" on Empire Prime; if you have the proper credentials and security clearance and will vow before the Imperial Magi Librarian that you will never tell anyone what you have learned; on penalty of **DEATH!** At the same time you should also want research about the other amazing exploits of the extremely famous Earthian Admiral Jonathan Baines Blow; and what actually happened to him when he literally skipped up and down and around the Main Galactic Time Line; deliberately changing events in his Past; in order to change events in his Future! On the Capital Planet; behind guarded doors; after certain nondisclosure forms have been filled out; the information can be viewed on the Imperial Library media or mentally scanned or using audio equipment; listened to with "old-fashioned" ears! (Because the Admiral apparently is still active on at least one constantly shifting positon on the Time Cloud/Time Stream; the information available to interested parties is constantly growing!)

So just what happened to Admiral Jonathan Baines Blow? Was he successful; partially successful; or did he totally fail in his endeavor to change his past from loneliness; sorrow; and pain; to joy and gladness with a large family?!? Just what was the result since the Admiral did not remember just what he attempted to accomplish in the "past"; using unique equipment that he obtained from his friend Dr. Chance Watson? Plus, at that position on the Time Continuum; none of his friends could remember anything about him that suddenly changed--from "pain to gain"!! In his mind and the minds of every sentient being that has ever heard of him; **NOTHING IN HIS LIFE PATH HAD EVER BEEN CHANGED FROM WHAT THEY NOW KNEW ABOUT THE FAMOUS ADMIRAL!!**

So Imperial Citizen; at this instant that you occupy on the Main Galactic Time Line; do you remember what has suddenly changed about the Admiral?!? No?!?!? Because if you don't remember any pertinent information; **IT IS NOT IMPORTANT**; because no one that was/is/or will be; connected to the Ultra-Life Path of one Admiral Jonathan Baines Blow; does either! So don't worry about not being able to understand the idiosyncrasies of "Time Travel"; just relax; take a deep breath; and turn the page!!

Then; at one particular very important "Anchor Moment" on the Main Galactic Time Line; a "Moment of Destiny" which had been caused by the unusual and unprecedented use of "time manipulations" from Future positions on the Time Line in order to change Past events which would then change sorrowful events to joyful occasions in the Future; the Life Line of one Admiral Jonathan Baines Blow took a sudden fantastic turn for the better; with most; if not all of his past woes erased!!!

And so. . . . . . .

EPILOGUE

While there was chaos; confusion; and disorder on the three or four related positions on the Time Line that had affected the Admiral's Life Destiny and literally the entire Main Galactic Time Line; elsewhere in the Cosmic All on one particular instant on the Time Stream/Time Cloud; his Life Destiny on his Life Path had suddenly radically changed--from chaos and sadness because he lacked a family; to peace and happiness with a very large family and literally hundreds of naval personnel and friends continually around him; 28/8; (to use the Empire's hours in a day and days in the week on Empire Prime)!!! Amazingly; nobody on the entire planet of Earth; (or in the entire Cosmic All!); remembered the Admiral's very sad past life; **(BECAUSE IT NO LONGER EXISTED; AND ON THE "SLATE OF THE ETERNAL UNIVERSE" ON THE UNIVERSAL TIME LINE; IT HAD BEEN LITERALLY ERASED AS IF HIS MISFORTUNES HAD NEVER EXISTED!!)**; and nobody on the planet; or the entire Universe; was cognizant of the sudden change when his Life Path was completely changed in less than a quadrillionth of a second! The two Anchor Events of successfully rescuing his patrolman; and his wife being cured of cancer; suddenly appeared on his Life Path; replacing the military debacle and the cancer surgery that had failed!!

Then . . . . . .it was as if an Angel had plucked the heartstrings of the Cosmic All; and no sentient being; (except one "Citizen One" being living in the Great Dark); in the Universe was aware of the change as suddenly; things started happening on one particular section of the Main Galactic Time Line; and nobody was aware of the vast differences and changes from one quadrillionth of a second to the next! On the minor planet Earth; the house at one particular site had suddenly been transformed; from an abandoned tarpaper hut in the middle of a small field of dry weeds; to a luxurious ranch house in the middle of a very large estate; that was suddenly filled with the Admiral's FAMILY; FRIENDS; HAPPINESS; MUSIC; AND JOY!

Then as the Main Galactic Time Line continued to settle down; in the next quadrillionth of a second; it came to pass; as the former painful events were literally erased from the Main Galactic Time Line and every Time Branch in the Cosmic All. . . . .

SOMEWHERE IN "TIME"

It was the usual extremely exciting last-Friday-night-of-the-month celebration at retired Admiral Jonathan and Mary Pearl Gallant Blow's elegant mansion overlooking crystal-clear Lake Conroe at the edge of the beautiful Sam Houston International Forest in eastern Texas! For some reason the clear Texas air seemed to somehow literally tingle with excitement as the musicians for the evening played their hearts out to the millions upon millions of twinkling stars above; and the extremely excited large crowd spread out over the Admiral's large and beautiful wooded estate! The electricity in the air could have been caused by the lively music; it could have been caused by the effects of the line of thunderstorms several hundred miles away around Fort Worth and coming down toward the lake; it could have been caused by the Winds of Destiny surging at record speed around all the party goers; or it could be a combination of all three possible reasons! Whatever the cause; the place was literally **ROCKIN' WITH EXCITEMENT!**

As usual, for the Admiral's locally famous parties, usually called "Blow Outs"; "Blow-Ins"; or "Blow Ups"; almost all the regular Friday night "gang" of his friends were there; except for the ones on active duty around the planet; patrolling elsewhere in the solar system; and those serving their planet almost literally beyond the stars; with a star or two between them and their Home Planet; up to; and beyond the boundaries of the Interstellar Condominium of Planets and Empires; (ICOPE)!

Operating by the normal "Texas Tradition" schedule for party musicians honored to play at the Admiral's shindigs; a combination of the party's regular "A-Team", "B-Team", and "C-Team" of jammin' musicians was keeping the joint jumpin'; hopping; and dancing; with everyone having a fan-tab-u-lous time!! Around the large expanse; the rest of the guests were a large crowd of just "eaters and dancers" that consisted of "volunteer guests" made up of any of their many friends and present, past, (and future!) military personnel who had ever served under the Admiral! Literally all of them were always welcome! Tonight, even the present Grand Admiral of the Fleets; Johnny Trevor covertly dressed in civilian clothing so he could enjoy the evening in peace; was present with his beautiful wife, Susan.

Among the large crowd; each person of whom had to have photographic identification and a special electronic pass to enter the closely guarded and electronically protected house grounds of the very famous retired military man; was a person who came from many hundreds of thousands of light years away! He was a man that only his sister; the former Admiral; the present Admiral; and their families; knew was there! The important visitor was Captain Bordoe Gallant; dressing incognito in civilian clothes; instead of his fancy Imperial uniform; to avoid creating another incident like what happened a few decades ago when all the experienced Earthian military persons could not identify his "Standard Galactic" insignias and numbers and would not let him enter! But at the present time, "The Man from ICOPE" had decided to take a break from the strain of his top secret missions on the edge of the Empire to have a good time and relax for a few days in the home of his close friend; who he had nicknamed "JB" a few decades ago after he had first successfully completed an important covert mission against the Hunan with the Admiral's full cooperation! It was one of many times through the centuries that Jonathan had helped him and his partner, Captain Cody; before and after Earth officially came into the ICOPE. Most, if not all of the incidents where the Admiral had helped him were not historically recorded on any military computer or archaic paperwork; and would never become a part of the official military or civilian historical video, paper, or mental records of either Earth or the Empire! But that is the way Captains Cody and Gallant always worked through the centuries—together, carefully, patiently, and above all; **COVERTLY**; so as not to attract attention; (which is always extremely bad in the 'spy business')!

Several things combined to always make Admiral Blow's very famous Friday night parties into great celebrations! Each party was always given on the very large estate of the now semi-retired military man; which meant that there was always plenty of elbow room for the large crowds that were always composed of his many friends, ex-military personnel, and very famous personalities who had been invited. The Admiral when originally designing the layout of his 20,000 square-foot house made sure that around the spacious covered dance floor outside the back door; there were large spaces to allow all his guests to relax on the many sofas, padded chairs, and old-fashioned swings that were provided; while also allowing plenty of room for the guests to "maneuver around Texas style", talk, dance, and eat--**Texas food!** The very large vertically sliding doors on each side of the dancing area could be opened up to allow anyone who wished to go outside on an extremely large, covered patio to eat or dance to the music which was sent outside on large cordless electronic speakers hanging from the rafters.

As always, the Admiral's Lady served lots of great traditional Texas food; mountains of brisket, ribs, Bar-B-Q, baked ham, pork loins, baked beans, tortillas, pecan and apple pies, iced tea, coffee, and such; compliments of the owner of McKenzie's Bar B-Q in the nearby town of Huntsville, Texas; United States of America, Earth. (Rocky Blaine, the present owner of that particular store, was a retired veteran who had also served under the Admiral for many years.)

For those who wanted to dance; there was the new and traditional Western dance music; always provided free by a local band made up of military veterans; was sometimes fast and furious for the line dances; and sometimes slow and mournful for the newly in-fashion tear-in-your-beer "Texas Waltzes".

As the evening wore on, many observers at the edge of the dance floor remarked that the Admiral's beautiful wife was still a very good dancer; in spite of her present medical condition of being "very pregnant". During these get-togethers; especially for the last eight months; when the music slowed down; Mary Pearl Blow loved to relax and very slowly dance cheek to cheek for at least half an hour with her husband; letting each Life Partner talk softly and privately into the other's ear; reminiscing about their amazing past-life together; making future plans; and talking about anything they wanted to. She would dance until someone "cut in"; then she would slowly walk to the edge of the dance floor; sit down in one of the comfortable chairs, and quietly talk with her many close friends about the coming blessed "event". When everyone in her close group of friends had "talked out"; then Mary Pearl would go searching for her beloved husband in the usual places that he and his close friends congregated and confabbed during these "Blow-Ups"!

This evening the couple were able to follow their usual tradition of very slowly dancing together for half an hour at the side of the large dance floor without interruption; catching up on their needed conferencing and sharing of information. Then breaking tradition; they split up to take turns dancing with their three older children and their many friends and neighbors. Following the rules of the party, everyone would have a partner to dance with and everybody would have a good time and a good exercise workout.

At the end of having fun carefully dancing with all his children who wanted to have him teach them the dance steps; Jonathan also followed his usual modus operandi that whenever he got tired after his wife and his children had "danced his socks off"; he always looked around the large dance floor and the surrounding rest areas to see if Cap; one of his retired military friends; or some other veteran spacer; was on the premises so that they could quietly and privately "talk shop" by themselves; especially if his Omni-phone had quietly beeped a certain signal. Sometimes; after he received the small covert beep that indicated that Cap or Cody was around; it was a challenge to find and recognize either of the Imperial spies because as usual, for protection they were wearing their Imperial defense belts; which meant that both "The Man" and "Coe" could use their belt's ultra-advanced electronic ECM circuits and solid holographic circuits to look like anyone, (or literally anything); that they chose! It was always interesting for Blow to use his keen trained powers of observation to determine if just one or both of the covert Imperial spies were present! It took all of his intellect and mental resources to be able to spot the clever disguises used by the wily Imperial spies! Sometimes each spy only changed his hair and beard color; sometimes they also changed their height and weight, and the tone of their voice. But each spy did not always change his basic mannerisms which through the long years the former Admiral had come to know well! To the retired admiral's sharp eyes, Captain Cody and Captain Gallant; the famous Spy of Spies; always moseyed around the large entertainment area the same way; no matter what their size or shape! Almost always they first cased the food area; then cruised around "on the prowl" with a large plate of goodies carefully balanced in one hand; along with a delicious drink in the other. Potent Sada Juice[9]; (in moderation), was their favorite beverage; but they rarely could get the exotic and expensive drink except on Empire Prime and one of the Imperial pleasure planets. At the Admiral's famous Blow-Outs, the Sada Juice dispenser was always controlled by the same bartender who was in charge of the alcoholic beverages; retired Master Sergeant Johnny Storm. For each of his large "whing-dings" the retired Admiral had **THE Juice** transported in especially for the two Captains and made sure it was on the menus whenever they graced his parties with their presence. If either of them did not show up, **The Juice** was stored in a triple-locked refrigerator down in the main house's basement, until the next blow-out. Stored in the refrigerator The Juice; because of its peculiar molecular makeup; would keep its unique flavor and last a minimum of 100 years after the Sada Berries had been picked and processed!

The Admiral also had another method of spotting the two sneaky Imperial Spies! Each of the two Imperial agents, although casually walking around incognito; always covertly looked around at his immediate surroundings the way an experienced warrior did, constantly looking around; not wanting to be the victim of a "sneak attack". All three of the warriors enjoyed their little game of "hide and seek" whenever the spies could attend the Admiral's parties!

But it was only a few times a year on Friday nights that the very busy Captain Gallant could make it; Captain Cody a few times more than his Imperial spy partner. If Cap was within communications range any time during the week before each party; he always sent the Admiral a FTL com message saying whether or not he could attend the next bash; so that Blow could be on the lookout for him. When the Spy of Spies could attend, as previously mentioned; penetrating his disguises became a game that both the military veterans enjoyed. The Captain and the Admiral would unobtrusively search for each other; but the rare times the Admiral could not find his disguised friend; after the standard interval to search, the Admiral and The Man would use their pocket coms to rendezvous at any quiet place outside the raucous dance floor to reminisce about the "Good Old Days"; to "talk shop"; to discuss what was going to happen next in galactic politics; and debate about the local, state, national, and ICOPE politics.

A few of the times that the two; or sometimes three military friends were able to rendezvous; Admiral Trevor; the present leader of Earth's Aerospace Force; would attempt to find them hidden in one of the nooks and crannies of the mansion's large dining room and connecting covered patios; in order to obtain certain "private information". If and when he found the Admiral Emeritus and the one or two spies that were conferring; the young admiral would openly approach their chosen rendezvous spot and carefully pull back the portable sound-proof curtain and 'sound mixer' that they always installed around their "confabs" in order to shield their conversations from prying ears and electronic eavesdropping. But even though Admiral Trevor was the most powerful military commander on the planet, out of respect for his friends; he would ask the war veterans inside for permission to join in the private conversation; which was always immediately given. Then usually, after being polite for a few minutes and listening to their banter about past combat missions; most of which he did not know anything about or understand just what they were saying when they talked "shop" using their covert military "jargon" or even talking in the very guttural Reptiloids language of Thunderese; the young Admiral acted! When he could politely interrupt the string of exciting reminisces between the combat veterans talking in the guttural Reptiloid language; with the excuse to increase his military knowledge; the active military man would start asking the two experienced Imperial officers questions about their top-secret military experiences in the last few hundred years. Since Admiral Johnny Trevor probably had the highest ranking security rating on the planet; if they chose to, the old veteran soldiers could always answer most of these questions, except those regarding the Emperor; as per the strict Imperial Laws concerning the Ruler of a million-million worlds. Realizing why the young man was asking them sensitive military questions; the two; and sometimes three; experienced soldiers never minded sharing with the young Admiral the hard-won knowledge that they had gained from their vast and varied combat and diplomatic experience; most of which was lived beyond the stars that were visible from Earth!

And so it was thus decreed by their Karma? Fate? Or Kismet; that one fateful night when the young admiral found the two particular military veterans together in a quiet corner room of the extremely large dance floor and, after following the usual preliminary oral traditions; he again finally "took the bull by the horns" and asked them "point blank" for answers to the riddle of "Blow's Miracle" that had been bothering him for almost two decades!

"Captain Gallant...Admiral.......Sirs; I sure would appreciate it if you could please enlighten me on a few things that I have to know! Admiral Blow; please think back many years ago to the virtually impossible event on that fateful day that you somehow performed that literally saved my life so many years ago! I do not remember how you rescued me from that terrible Reptiloid prison since I was unconscious most of the time from their beatings; which unsuccessfully tried to make me tell about Earth's defenses; although they did examine my ship!! Before the Reptiloids broke into my ship I had managed to hit the 'capture switch' which destroyed all my computer and paper records; so the Lizards did not get much useful Intel! I also remember waking up for only an instant in total darkness when you were apparently easily carrying me with just your very strong right arm through the totally dark corridors of the Reptiloid's labyrinth like a rag doll; then I lost consciousness from the pain!! To this day, I never can figure out how you could see when it was totally dark in Radak's labyrinth and find your way back to the so-called black 'Mystery Ship' that showed capabilities beyond what we have even today!! None of the available Earthian or Imperial military records that are available to me can tell how you penetrated the impenetrable Reptiloid planetary defense screens and escaped after you rescued me! The screens were such that even an Imperial Battle Ball warship attempting to go through them would have exploded and been totally destroyed! So how could your small mystery ship that you used for the rescue mission accomplish that literally impossible feat?"

When there was no immediate reply; Johnny Trevor paused to take a deep breath and continued, "After the so-called 'Blow's Impossible Mission' was over; I was still asleep or unconscious when the official hospital entry records document and identify that you were the person that dropped me off at the base hospital into the care of the Emergency Room personnel! The official log entries also indicate that you quickly left without any explanation to the military police; which for some reason; against regulations; let you go without you having to give any explanation of where my terrible injuries occurred and who assaulted me!! It's as if they already knew what was going on and did not need for you to tell them what had happened!! I woke up several days later after several surgeries that finished up what the doctors at the hospital said were merely procedures to finish up reconstructive surgeries on my severe injuries that had somehow been done; by <u>somebody</u> or <u>something</u>; to stabilize my medical condition before you got me to the hospital; **WHILE COMING ALL THE WAY FROM THE THUNDER WORLDS TO EARTH!** Their preliminary examinations before their exploratory surgeries indicated that extremely advanced micro medical techniques that had been done immediately after my rescue to my severe injuries had to have been done by some pretty amazing computer-controlled medical facilities, or I would not have survived; even as a vegetable; mercifully given a quick death; or fed intravenously and existing forever in a permanent coma! Because of this documentation I guess these so-called 'advanced medical techniques' were somehow done by someone or something on your mystery ship that somehow; some way; completely vanished off the face of the Earth after what all the insiders secretly call 'Blow's Miracle' was complete!!"

"Other than the information that I have just repeated; the base security police would; or could only tell me that something or someone wearing an Ultra-Top-Secret security badge and a security radio helmet; and also wearing a large and bulky 'Haz-Mat' suit; whose 'build' looked somewhat like yours; had rescued me; brought me in; and immediately rushed me to the base hospital! Searching military records several years later I found out later that several of them had previously served under you for many years; so they should have known who you were even if you were wearing a helmet and totally covered up by the 'Haz-Mat' suit! But for some reason when I asked them who had rescued me, they first hesitated; then they politely refused to identify my rescuer by citing 'Area 51 Rules'; as if they were ordered not to tell me who it was who saved my life! When I interviewed them later separately; they each told me not to worry about it and they all used the exact same term; saying **'don't worry because everything was in the green'**! They each used exactly the same military jargon; as if they were briefed on what to say! By the time several weeks later that I was able to leave the base hospital using a solar battery-powered chair with my wife Susan; as I left my room I was told by the hospital commanding surgeon Doctor Martha Wagstaff[10] that because of 'national; international, interplanetary, and interstellar security'; the incident involving my rescue had been declared ultra-top-secret and any information about it could never be legally published on Earth; or even orally given by any medical person to anyone--even to ME; an admiral with the highest security clearance on the planet; and the recipient of said secret military operation!"

"After all these years; even now with my supposedly ultra-top-of-the-line security clearance as the Supreme Commander of the Earthian Aerospace Fleet; I have only been able to garner a few more hard facts! I have never been able to find out just where you got that unique and seemingly impossible FTL ship that you used to rescue me! At that time, Earth, and supposedly even the so-called 'Empire' that Captains Gallant and Cody still work for; which had contacted us several decades before; did not have the technology to produce such an advanced ship that could do what the official Reptiloid and Imperial records state that it accomplished without blowing up! From the few photos that I have been able to obtain; taken by the base's security cameras from several miles away; and magnified until an indistinct; fuzzy image is obtained; it looks like Captain Gallant's regular ship; but its operational and physical characteristics were, and are; absolutely different from any Earthian or any standard Imperial courier ship physical specifications known! But even though the blurry photograph looks like an exact copy of the outside shape of Captains Gallant and Cody's unique 'Courier Class' ships; Imperial Naval Experts have since told me; for some reason 'off the record'; that the mystery ship's exhibited capabilities were far superior to theirs; so it couldn't have been Gallant's or Cody's ship! They also stated 'off the record' that its performance will be untouchable by their ships for at least a century or more; until there is further research and the theoretical physics equations that determine how fast a ship can go are further refined; or entirely new FTL propulsion equations are constructed that will allow for faster speeds! That mystery ship that you piloted to rescue me sure was not the expensive "Galactic Tour" sports craft that you bought with some of the extremely large sum of money that suddenly appeared in your bank account and then vanished as soon as you amazingly sold the ship back to the dealer for a slightly larger sum that you paid and re-deposited the money! **What a deal!** Sam Bow; the owner of the gigantic "Ships Trading Lot" where you purchased the tourist craft; never would tell me why he purchased the used ship back for more than you first paid for it; except he did mention that it was an extreme honor to do so; since he owed you so much! I checked his records and he also had previously served under your command for many years and on several air bases in faraway places; but that was the only possible connection he had with you!"

"The transaction records indicate that you somehow made a very large profit on a roughly-used, lightly-constructed civilian ship that supposedly had just traveled several hundred thousand light years in a very short time! Imperial and Earthian records indicate that somehow; some way; the tiny ship had impossibly burst through the literally impenetrable defense shield of the Home World of the Thunder World Reptiloids; then it had successfully evaded the impenetrable robot defenses of Thud's planet; and to top it all off; the mystery ship had outrun the fastest Imperial and Reptiloid AI and being-controlled naval destroyers in the Universe! Yet; in his back office when I checked back with him a few days later; Sam Bow's records show that the civilian ship that you returned to him was in 'mint' condition; as if it had never left Earth or flown very far! To top it off; it did not have 'Tanya' printed on the left and right rear parts of the fuselage; and it was not painted black; as was reported by dozens of reputable witnesses of the event! It was not scratched up, the paint was still shiny, its very limited protective weapons created by Earthian science had not been fired; and some of the protective shipping covers on some of the interstellar and planetary flight controls had not been removed; indicating that the ship could not have possibly been flown for very long or flown out of the Earth's atmosphere! Through the years Earthly intelligence; and probably Imperial spy forces; both have not been able to find out where the advanced ship came from; or just what happened to it after you dropped me off at the hospital of the Aerospace Command and mysteriously left! For some reason; the Top Brass or any administrators have not officially pressed you about the subject; although I suspect this indicates that they already know all the answers; or they have been told that the mission was of such importance that any mention of any facet of the incident is illegal under the Imperial/Earth Treaty and ICOPE law!"

Admiral Trevor stopped talking to take a deep breath; then continued, "The official records report that after you had dropped me off at the hospital emergency room; you had been given the green light by the base's control tower to take off for an atmospheric trip and were a mile or two above the base when suddenly the ship impossibly vanished from the base's sensors; apparently going FTL while in the Earth's gravity well without the ship exploding or the entire continent going up in a titanic explosion! Only a relatively few hours later, with no explanation; the official base records show that you were back in circulation at the base with no ship; and attending to your regular command duties at your desk on the base as if nothing extraordinary had happened; and with no official record of you entering the base through any gate or from the base air strip! There is no record that either the civilian craft or the other amazing ship received permission to exit Earth's atmosphere and there is no record that the unknown craft was stored anywhere on Earth; **it just disappeared!** There is no official record that you received permission to exit or again enter Earth's atmosphere from the proper planetary flight control tower at Yeager! With all the sentries and sensors at the base; there is no possible way you could have returned without someone or some sensor observing or recording your entry to the base; unless you did something like an episode on the "Stranger Still Zone"; where a government man was given a transposer device by aliens after he did them a favor and he used the device to secretly spy for the government and evade detection by the enemy agents of Comrade X!"

Johnny was getting red in the face; so he again stopped to calm down by taking a slow breath; then continued, "After all these years; at the present time; I'm at a literal roadblock in my personal investigation of just what literally impossible events occurred to allow you to rescue me! It still **'sticks in my craw'** that I can't find out exactly what happened and I feel like I must find out exactly how you performed the literally impossible feats of ship-handling; penetrating the electronic barrier around the

Thunder Worlds; and medical treatments that when they were all combined on the ultra-secret mission; **LITERALLY SAVED MY LIFE!!** If you will fill me in on what happened; I won't ever tell anyone; I just need to know exactly what happened that saved my life!! For some reason; none of the pertinent Imperial records are available to me! I still can't fathom just how you came alone into Radak's palace and; amid hundreds of Reptiloid guards; and single-handedly rescued me; apparently without firing a shot!!! Somehow; some way; apparently you literally talked your way out of Radak's throne room; surrounded by hundreds of Reptiloid guards; without one talon, claw, or sword being drawn to stop you!!! Then you retraced your steps; carrying me by yourself with no help; through the labyrinth to the outside! Then before all of Radak's guards you apparently put me aboard the black mystery ship and somehow penetrated the planets impenetrable energy screen to bring me home in a medical cabinet that partially healed my extensive injuries and saved my life!!!!!! **I can't imagine how you managed to accomplish all those feats of daring without any help from anyone; but I am sure glad that you did!!"**

"No matter how much I have argued with you in the past at these Friday night parties; neither of you would ever tell me any of the facts of how you pulled off the ultra-secret impossible rescue that will be forever covertly known in the Earthian Aerospace Fleet as the Top Secret legendary fleet mission called 'Blow's Miracle'! In addition, the whole thing has been declared 'Ultra-Top Secret!' and a lid put on the whole thing by both Imperial and Earth militaries; so further research is literally impossible! But since I was the one that was rescued, I sure would like to know how you accomplished that impossible string of physical and electronic feats of daring! Again; if you tell me; I will never tell anyone what happened!"

While hundreds of people laughed and danced outside soundproof walls of the small room; the Supreme Admiral of Earth Defense "vented" and spouted out to the only two beings in the Cosmic All who really knew exactly what happened before, during, and after; that legendary mission that had happened so long ago; which had saved his life!!

Silently looking around at both the Captain and the Admiral; he continued, "After fruitlessly digging for the facts for decades; I find the whole impossible, improbable, and eerie story of my rescue contains so many impossible happenings; super-human feats of physical strength; and illogical Humanoid behavior of military personnel; that it is impossible for me to find out just who did it; exactly what did it; or exactly how I was rescued!!"

Taking another deep breath to try to calm down; Admiral Trevor continued, "To tell the truth, Sirs; it would sure help me to sleep better at night, knowing how you one or two veteran military men impossibly pulled it off; without constantly using every scientific resource on Earth and every brain cell that I possess trying to figure it out! Any illumination that you both give me about just how it was done will forever be sealed up in my memory until I pass on to the next level of existence; without telling anyone; including my wife, Susan; and my five and one-half children!!"

When the young Admiral's words ceased; there was a heavy silence in the immediate enclosed area for a few minutes as the two older men settled back in their chairs; relaxed; and enjoyed their refreshing cold natural fruit drinks without speaking. Their attitude caused Johnny to start to get a sinking feeling in his stomach that this meeting would end like all the others--with no new information about his impossible rescue!!! This time if they would not tell him anything else; the thought crossed his mind that maybe he ought to resign from the EAF!

The silence was interrupted from time to time as the very loud happy sounds of the dance floor reached their ears even through the efficient extra sound-proofing installed between the canvas walls to allow the retired Admiral and his friends a quiet place to talk. But tonight; for some reason; the large crowd was being extra joyful; thus the noise was louder than usual!!

Then, finally; the slightly graying Admiral Emeritus Jonathan Baines Blow spoke and broke the deafening silence inside the soundproofed area. **"Johnny, Johnny! You should know that some things are better left in the past; especially things that pertain to the hot-blooded Reptiloids of the Thunder Worlds!** Some of those incredible events that happened many years ago that allowed you to be rescued; if the secret facts were uncovered and brought to light at the present time; would do more harm than good! What's the use of stirring up old war stories again and getting some of our people and the Reptiloids on the Thunder Worlds mad at Earth and the ICOPE again? When you are young and hot-blooded; like I was during that long ago mission; you always want **REVENGE** when something like this happens; instead of accepting the happy ending of the rescue mission; letting things cool off; and living your life to the fullest! But as you grow older and wiser; you tend to cool down; start to think; and realize the "big picture"! Right now, things are still 'touch and go' on the Thunder Worlds; peace-wise; although; thankfully; Thud was finally deposed from the throne of the Thunder Worlds a few years ago by his brothers! Maybe it's the peculiar lightning storms that continually strike the surfaces of the Thunder Worlds; along with the super-hot and super-cold currents of air that also continuously crisscross the planet's surface that keep the population stirred up! I don't know! But his younger Reptiloid brothers who are now together ruling the Thunder Worlds might not like us rehashing and circulating old stories that would literally rub salt in their wounds by bring up the historic fact that a supposedly defenseless Earthman alone on a very small ship with no armor or weapons; invaded their heavily-defended Home World; and successfully breached all their titanic impenetrable electronic defenses and somehow evaded the cryogenic temperatures and ultra-hot layers in the atmosphere without instruments; while descending to the dangerous surface of the Thunder Planet! Then alone on foot; after he had somehow destroyed his ship so that the Reptiloids could not capture it; the unknown invader successfully navigated the dark labyrinth around Thud's palace; successfully snatched a prisoner from the palace; and toted the prisoner back through the labyrinth like a small sack of Earthian potatoes!! But to top off the story, the unknown invader somehow; some way; very quickly reconstructed his destroyed ship; then took the prisoner back through their planetary screens by successfully smashing the very small; supposedly obsolete ship back through their powerful planetary energy forces that could stop an Imperial Tytano Battle Ball!" Blow stopped his explanation for a few moments to take a breath. At that instant; Admiral Trevor's many requests for information were finally granted as Jonathan started explaining what had troubled the young man from many years!

"But, OK! OK! OK! I guess 'spilling the beans' at this particular time will be for a good cause! To help Earth's Top Head Honcho Naval Commander; to help you sleep at night; and to stop you from continuously using up valuable military computer resources sending useless FTL messages seeking information from top-secret Imperial data banks; Cap and I will give you enough information to let you rest easy for a few centuries! As always, anything you hear tonight in this room has to stay here!" The retired Admiral quietly stated and asked after first looking over in Cap's direction and getting a quiet nod of assent from him to tell Johnny what he wanted to know.

"But if it would help the young man to sleep better at night, Cap; let's see if we can relieve the young man's anxiety! What do you say, Bordoe? Do we tell him all that secret information so that he can sleep better at night?!? Yes or no? I'll go with what you say about the situation!"

Blow and the young Admiral both looked to the Imperial spy for a final verbal answer; but Captain Gallant only again quietly nodded his assent to the important question of whether or not to let the young military man know how he was impossibly saved from Death so many years ago; while he sipped the very; very small amount of potent Sada Juice that he had just poured into his glass of old-fashioned lemonade to lessen the potency of the popular intergalactic juice.

In response to the silent and almost imperceptible dip of his jaw that indicated that it was OK to "spill the beans"; so to speak; after Cap took another slow sip of the potent alien-produced beverage; across the from him the retired Admiral Blow continued; **"JUST REMEMBER!! WHAT IS SPOKEN IN THIS ROOM; STAYS IN THIS ROOM!!! UNDERSTOOD?"**

When Johnny Trevor nodded to indicate that he agreed with the secrecy; Jonathan Blow continued, "As your commanding officer at that time, I was responsible for your safety and I took it very, very personal when you were attacked by unknown forces and taken to the Thunder Worlds! So when the Reptiloid that Cap and Cody had nicknamed 'Thud' had you kidnapped way out in the edge of our solar system when you were only doing your job to protect Earth; I called in a few 'favors'; found out what happened; and who did it; and gave it a whirl myself since I did not want to endanger the lives of anyone else under my command! I was extremely lucky; because the conditions that I happened to face on that mission were very unique! I doubt if I could do such a thing again because on that mission many; many things somehow happened together in just the right way for me to be successful! Just be glad that I was successful and let sleeping dogs lie! Also as to the question of where the ship. . . . . ."

He was interrupted by the very confident military voice belonging to Captain Gallant; which employed all the Command Tonals the Imperial spy had learned over the centuries! **"Nah, MAN! For one of the few times in your life; you are dead wrong!** (Oops! I'm sorry!! That was a poor choice of words!) On that solo trip, with your nerve, just plain guts, and your **SKILL**; using your 'never-say-die attitude and Titanium backbone', **YOU** made your own luck, **JB! You; YOU** did it entirely on your own; I did not help you after I temporarily loaned you the money from my Imperial Emergency Fund to obtain the decoy ship to throw off any investigators and loaned you that other 'equipment'; including my 'Tanya'; who had been painted black; the toughest; the fastest, and most advanced AI Courier-Class ship in the Empire! I always give silent thanks to the grateful alien races that I have helped through the centuries for giving me their ultra-advanced tech to secretly combine with the Empire's best to make such a unique ship; and my trusty old defense belt which gave you the power to knock down the steel door of the Reptiloid's palace; find the only safe way through Thud's deadly maze to get to his palace; and then after suckering Thud to let Johnny go; get out again; using super strength, infrared vision, and other ESP powers provided by the belt! (Tanya told you during the mission briefing about the covert alien devices on our ships that greatly improved their performance!) The equipment on your belt could give you the means to have such powers; but you had to have the guts, the 'moxie', the intestinal fortitude, the backbone, the will, and the 'sand' to use the belt and the ship to carry out your dangerous plan; (which now I can tell 'ex post facto'); Tanya's separate military tactics computer on the ship indicated to her before the mission started that it had an almost zero, nada, zilch; chance of success; and the mission would be a total failure and the ship destroyed!!! **But she did not tell you this and she went with you anyway!! Amazing!! Simply amazing!** That bag of computer chips knew that she would probably be destroyed while trying to rescue your man; **BUT SHE WENT ALONG WITH YOU ANYWAY!!! TANYA WAS WILLING TO SACRIFICE ALL HER EQUIPMENT AND GIVE UP HER EXISTENCE FOR YOU TO HAVE A SHOT AT A MUCH HAPPIER LIFE!! I'd say you owe her some new computer diodes or something, the next time you two meet; like maybe give her the first dance at the next Emperor's Ball in a few months!** If she had been destroyed then I would have needed an entirely new ordinary ship built in the shipyards on Empire Prime and I would have had to break in another AI ship again; with a different personality and no secret alien devices to produce unmatched speed!! The whole Imperial Fleet could not have done the job because they could not have successfully penetrated the electronic defenses of the Capital Planet of the Thunder Worlds and dodged the layers of super-cold and super-hot atmospheric layers of the planet and get to Johnny before Thud executed him by feeding him to his 'pets'! You attempted the only desperate plan that had an even 1% chance of success! Only one man using Tanya's advanced navigation aids and my defense belt could possibly get down to the planet's surface without automatically being destroyed by the planet's advanced defenses! But with just one small unarmed ship attempting the rescue; the Reptiloids would be curious about why one Humanoid being would try to penetrate their defenses; so they would not destroy you without first talking to you! Then you could use Thud's dull mental facilities against him again by using my defense belt to attempt to execute the plan to get Johnny and escape! You bravely attempted the plan; the only one that had a snowball's chance in a blast furnace of succeeding; knowing that you would probably be killed!! I still can't fathom how you successfully talked your way out of the throne room; somehow getting Thud to let you go with his captive; with none of the hundreds of Reptiloid warriors lifting a single talon to stop you!! But you impossibly succeeded; against the impossible odds! When you started the mission and left Earth, you were absolutely and positively on your own! Tanya gave you a quick instruction in how to run things on the ship and how to operate my Imperial Defensive Belt systems, and **AFTER THAT VERY SHORT BRIEFING, YOU DID IT ALONE WITH NO HELP FROM THE AI SHIP! MY BRAVE TANYA TOLD ME IMMEDIATELY AFTER THE MISSION THAT SHE DID NOT HELP YOU IN ANY WAY; OR CONTROL ANY OF YOUR FLIGHT MANEUVERS DURING YOUR ENTRY TO THE PLANET'S SURFACE OR WHEN YOU WERE SUCCESSFULLY LEAVING THE PLANET! IT WAS YOUR PILOTING SKILL AT THE CONTROLS; NOT HERS; THAT RAN THE GAUNTLET THROUGH THE TOUGHEST SPACE DEFENSES THIS SIDE OF EMPIRE PRIME'S ELECTRONIC RAMPARTS! YOU**

ATTEMPTED LITERALLY AN IMPOSSIBLE RESCUE MISSION AND SOMEHOW; SOME WAY; YOU SUCCEEDED!"

Lowering his voice, the veteran spy continued, "Afterwards, that cryogenic-headed, solid holographic sassy AI had the gall to tell me that even I could not have pulled the mission off better than you did!!! That two-bit hunk of computer chips had the nerve to tell me that I could have equaled the outcome of your mission; but I could not have done better! What gall; what chutzpah; what audacity; what boldness; what nerve!! **WHAT AN AI!!** She told me that your pilot skills and combat timing of your attacks on the interior of the defense shield and the ground installations graded out to almost 100%! What nerve; what a worthless pile of sub-atomic circuit chips! **I am do amazed that I have to say it again; what chutzpa; what a ship; and what a MAN--YOU ADMIRAL; YOU!!!** Jonathan, you have to realize that any action that gets such a complimentary statement from that bag of lackadaisical several hundred year-old computer circuits; man; **is quite a compliment!"**

Cap took a small sip of Sada Juice; then continued, "In several hundred years of working with that bucket of bolts and sub-atomic chips that I christened "Tanya" the first day the AI was brought online, she has never given such a compliment to anybody, including me! **SO BELIEVE IT, MR. ADMIRAL EMERITUS!! THE REASON SOME CALL YOUR ULTRA-SECRET HISTORIC MISSION 'BLOW'S MIRACLE', IS BECAUSE IT WAS; AND MANY YEARS LATER; IT STILL GRADES OUT TO BE SUCH!! THERE WAS NO WAY YOU COULD HAVE**

SUCCEEDED AGAINST SUCH OVERWHELMING ODDS-- BUT YOU DID! YOU WERE COMPLETELY ON YOUR OWN; WITH NO, NADA, ZIP, ZILCH; ZERO; HELP FROM ME, TANYA, OR ANYONE ELSE! YOU DID IT COMPLETELY SOLO! YOU BEAT THE ODDS THAT SAID YOU COULD NOT SUCCEED; BUT YOU DID!!!"

"Although I could have done so, I did not secretly follow you in one of my other personal advanced courier ships protected by advanced Imperial Phantom Screens so that I could get you out if you ran into trouble because, officially; I was supposedly on another important mission for the Emperor! You can look at the official records of the Imperial Pleasure Planet of Alpha Quadrant! I was supposedly vacationing at the time on that paradise planet in order to watch certain other planetary agents; who it was thought, were "double agents'! It was my job to find out if they were 'clean' or 'dirty' Imperial Empire agents! When you started for home with Johnny; Tanya sent me a coded FTL signal to my spare defense belt and I quickly tied up a few 'loose ends' and checked out of the luxury hotel; all rested up and tanned from being under the UV rays of a real sun for a few days trying to find the traitorous agents; and headed at emergency speed in your direction! At the proper time, you rendezvoused with the courier ship from the Imperial Navy reserve fleet that I was temporarily using and I retrieved my Tanya and my defense belt that I loaned you! Then I transposed you back to the sport ship that you had temporarily purchased as a cover for the real ship; which we had stashed close to Bow's Ship Store where you supposedly bought it; (in an open field, undetectable by anything on Earth, by putting one of my little gismos that caused it to always reside exactly one second in the future on the Local Time Line! You quickly took it a few feet back to where you originally got it; compliments of your old military buddy; and then I covertly transposed you back to your office from beyond the moon's orbit! (But for some strange reason, I found out later that the supposedly poor, new and used ship dealer actually gave you more for it used when you brought it back, than you paid for it new! **Say! Wait just a MINUTE!!** Come to think of it; my several hundred years-old brain just remembered something important to solving this puzzle! One time fifty or sixty years ago, I believe that I remember seeing an ultra-secret Earthian intelligence report that said that as a new recruit many Earth years ago you had risked your life on a rescue mission in the short-lived Republic of Lower Brogan in Africa to save another recent recruit named Samuel Jackson Bow! **YEA!! THAT'S IT!!!** Now after a few decades; I finally get it! Perhaps the now-very-rich ship dealer in new and old vessels was paying you back for rescuing him at the expense of a few months in a military hospital to let your multiple bone breaks and wounds heal up! You ought to donate the extra money that he gave you to the Retired Imperial Spy Retirement Home or something!"

"But, seriously, despite all the spouting that I am doing; it was your combat savvy; quick thinking; and nerve that won the day and allowed you to rescue Johnny; escape Thud; and successfully ram your ship through the powerful electronic barrier around the Thunder World capital planet! The only thing I have done to help you is to call in a few favors in order to 'put the quietus on the mission! That legendary undercover mission everyone calls 'Blow's Miracle'; is buried so far under a bureaucratic blanket and the Official Signet Ring of the Emperor that even the Imperial Seers can't visualize it! (The Emperor owed me for a dangerous favor I performed for him a few centuries before and I collected!) After the mission was over, I even called in a favor from the top head honcho Imperial Seer Kantorie Smi-Th-Jo-Nes; one of the few Magi with ancestors on both sides of the Royal Line! That particular Seer has extremely rare mental powers that almost none of the other Magi possess; or even probably know about! I saved his life a few hundred years ago from a Hunan assassin when he was only a first rank Seer! At that time he told me after the unsuccessful assassination attempt that if I ever need a favor to look him up on Empire Prime! On principle, you know that I always pay my debts to other sentient beings and I also collect my dues from them also; so after you pulled off your "Miracle"; I conveniently remembered what he promised and I looked him up on the Capital Planet! When I asked him to mentally veil your brave rescue mission for security reasons; he agreed; and with no questions asked; he did some 'mumbo-jumbo' with his far-out mental powers that will keep other less-powerful Magi from visualizing exactly what happened for a few thousand years! After that span of time; who cares?" Cap injected.

Captain Gallant took a deep breath and added, "But even so, I bet you still have enough moxie and you could do something like it again, even these many years later!"

When the Admiral ignored the compliment; The Man quietly added, "And remember, Admiral Trevor; what JB and I have just told you, what you have heard in this room, stays in this room; not to be discussed with anyone, **FOREVER**, by an Imperial Order of the Emperor; sealed by his Majesty's Official Signet Ring in the Empire; somehow sealed with mental mumbo-jumbo by a top Seer; and protected here on Earth by the Earthian Secrets Act! We told you all this Ultra-Top-Secret Stuff for your own personal benefit; not because you are now the head military honcho here on Earth! We only told you so you can sleep!"

The extremely serious off-the-record talk about extremely important top secret happenings in the distant past was suddenly and unexpectedly interrupted! All the participants of the arguments stopped their jawing and looked around toward the exit when they heard the low grating sound of the security curtain being slowly pulled back across the rough rocky floor! (The scraping sound made by the door rubbing the floor started several years ago when a new curtain was installed and was deliberately not fixed, and the grating sound was tolerated, so that the military men conferring and talking about ultra-secret "Old Times" could tell when anyone was attempting to enter!)

Immediately after the grating sound, in the background the threesome heard the sound of a tenor trumpet being played; and played very expertly! The basic Staccato note patterns of the tune were very complicated and the song was apparently being played by a master trumpeter; with several bass guitars skillfully playing softly in the background to back him up! But even above the vibrant notes of the rousing song; the three men heard and immediately recognized a low and sultry voice speaking from inside the room above the din! From long experience with dealing with **"THE LADY"**; the beloved wife of the retired Admiral known in Earthly military circles as **"THE MAN"** to have on your side covering you back in a battle"; the three men in the room instantly knew that the voice belonged to the beautiful Mary Pearl Gallant Blow; secretly Captain Gallant's sister; (and kept a secret to keep Cap's enemies from taking out revenge on him through his sister!) It was a very low Alto range voice that did not employ hypnotic command "tonals"; but, somehow, some way; it effectively exhibited the "do it or else" quality rivaling that of the toughest Imperial Marines Drill Sergeant; or even that of her husband; the retired Admiral Emeritus Blow!

THE LADY firmly stated, "I don't care what ultra-sky-high top secret military information you military men are always talking about stays or leaves this room! I don't care if when he was active in The Service of the Emperor; my brave and trusty husband could or couldn't single-handedly and/or bare-handedly outfight, out fly, or out swim; every Reptiloid, Insectoid, mutant Humanoid, Snakoid, or Colloid Cloud in the Universe; or save the little waif Annie Spacey on that science fiction television program, "Orphans in Space"; from Terrible Ted the famous alien meanie always featured on cliff-hanger episodes of the popular new daily tri-vid program called the 'Children's Stranger Still Zone'!"

The very pregnant lady with beautiful long blond hair was panting slightly; so she had to take a breath before she continued,

"All those important matters don't matter, now! Right now; this very instant; my very own famous "Hurricane Man" of recent Earth military history has something **REALLY** important to do; instead of attending to some small, trivial matter; like saving the Universe from the migrating reptiles called "Hunans" or the rambunctious Reptiloids raiding from the Thunder Worlds!" The soft, but commanding woman's voice said from just inside the covered doorway.

Mary Pearl again stopped to pant and catch her breath; then continued, "All I know is that before this shindig, **MY WONDERFUL MAN**; my beloved husband for so many wonderful years and the father of our seven and one-half children; gave me a thrill when earlier in the evening; before we came to this wonderful confab; while alone in our bedroom; he promised me the last dance of the evening, and the band of your former aide, retired Major Admiral Marty Ballesteros; along with his son, our God-son; Colonel Marty Ballesteros, Jr.! (He is on extended leave after being awarded the off-the-record Planetary Congressional Medal of Honor for bravery during a little-old Top Secret Mission that for security reasons can only be described as occurring somewhere in or out of the Solar System!) Marty Sr. and Marty Jr. are subbing quite well on the electric bass and backing up the master trumpeter; who is one of our old friends! Brave father and brave son, after taking their last break for the evening; are about to rev up to play absolutely the last band number of the party! It was just announced that our very famous; traditional and favorite song called; naturally; 'Absolutely-Got-to-be-the-Last-Song!' is to be masterfully done in a few minutes; with a very difficult trumpet solo by our old friend Dr. Chance Watson; who is now playing those wonderfully-sounding; and very difficult to produce; staccato notes with his trumpet! He is one of our old friends from the distant past that we 'chanced'; (sorry, a bad pun!); to meet a few months ago and on the spur-of-the-moment; when he told us that he still played the trumpet; we invited him to be the regular solo trumpeter and start playing his hot tunes at our get-togethers; starting the next Friday night; which is tonight!! So my husband gave him a copy of the 'Official Blow-Outs; Blow-Ins and Blow-Ups Music Book'; for him to start learning; and the rest is history!!! Dr. Chance Watson has been literally a sensation ever since he started playing at the start of the evening show! I know you heard that difficult and extremely fast staccato music that he just played that sounded great; with just a week or two for him to practice the difficult music! If he can play that number; he can play anything!! But now, this evening; if you ask him; after his trumpet solo which is now playing; he might be so kind as to help the locally-famous 'Marty and Marty' band play the 'Absolutely-the-Last-Dance-Number'! So now, time's a-wasting; so come on, My Darling Husband; Brother Cap; and Admiral Johnny! **LET'S GO; TIME'S AWASTING!** Our eldest daughter Mary also requested that her Godfather; secretly **my brother**; whom other people in the Empire also call **"THE MAN"**; give her the pleasure of this last dance; since he promised it to her last month and uncharacteristically did not deliver; somehow disappearing on a supposedly important mission before Marty and Marty played the last piece! Also; another wife is impatient to slow dance with her husband"; nodding to Admiral Trevor; "and since the first two dancing slots for the guys that I mentioned are already taken; you ought to guess who she is and who she wants to dance with!!"

Mary Pearl Gallant Blow's words had the desired effect as the back meeting room quickly emptied just as the beautiful trumpet solo ended! Arm-in-arm the Admiral Emeritus with his hairy and suntanned right arm gently around her shoulders; carefully led his beloved wife out to dance with her one more time; (probably the last time for a few months until after the baby was born)! Bowing to seniority, Admiral Johnny Trevor let Cap exit next.

It took a few minutes; but Cap; Blow; and Johnny Trevor finally rendezvoused with their dance partners; just as Dr. Chance Watson and Marty, senior; and Marty, junior; started playing the traditional last number for the Blow Get-Togethers. As Mary Pearl and her husband started very, very slowly dancing on dance floor with Jonathan's hairy and very strong right arm supporting her; the beautiful mother-to-be suddenly had a thought about something that had been bothering her for about fifteen years; but she had never remembered it when she was around her beloved husband--**until now!!**

As the couple were slowly waltzing around the dancefloor she gently pressed her mouth up to her much-loved husband's ear and whispered, "Honey, I need to know about something that happened a long time ago! That fateful day I was scheduled for the standard "cut and burn" cancer treatments; what caused you to suddenly and unexpectedly cancel my cancer treatment from the standard surgery, radiation, and chemo regiment; and immediately arrange for me to be treated several days later; (after you got back from a super-secret mission that I still officially don't know about; but probably heard about a few minutes ago); with an entirely different procedure?!? You opted for Dr. Regal Strife's revolutionary technique employing a new treatment using microwaves that are tuned to the correct frequency so as to simply kill the cancer cells and leave the normal cells unharmed! I have always wondered what made you change the type of treatment; but every time I remember, you are not around! But I am not complaining because the treatments were a total success; with no side effects; and I did not lose any of my beautiful long blond hair; like I would have with the radiation and chemo treatments!!! Plus, I would not have been able to have our lovely gang of beloved kids! For my own personal information I would just like to know how you apparently very suddenly found out about that successful treatment technique and decided to use it; probably saving my life!!! You never have told me what changed your mind about my treatments! On that fateful day while I was waiting for you to pick me up; I had prepared myself for the terrible side effects and losing all my long; beautiful blond hair!! I was all set to 'go under the knife'; then you telephoned me at home about the new plan that I would have; after you came back from an unspecified mission; which; (as I said before); strictly following the military code for secrecy; I still don't know anything about even today!!"

Her husband waited a few seconds until he was facing away from the band; then he slowly bent down and whispered in her ear,

"I haven't told you about this all these years because I didn't think you would believe the remarkable and utterly impossible event that suddenly happened to me to make me change your cancer treatment!! The Fateful Day of the scheduled surgery; just as I was about to go out of my office door to pick you up for your standard 'cut and burn' cancer treatments that probably would have caused all your beautiful blond hair to fall out and would have eventually killed you; **something incredible happened**! I was seated at my desk when literally out of thin air; I received a mailing envelope on my desk with a note inside having remarkable information on it that completely changed what I wanted to do in order to completely heal your cancer; instead of treating it for years with painful and destructive radiation and chemotherapy! Apparently it was somehow; someway; in a way that even today I still don't know; sent by me in the Future to myself in the present; in order to tell me the correct cancer treatment that would save your life!! It also had detailed instructions on how to rescue Johnny Trevor from the Reptiloids on the Thunder Worlds and how to get a literally amazing ship to accomplish the daring raid! The note suddenly appeared in the air in front of my desk with the information just before I was all set to pick you up to take you in for surgery and before I would have taken the entire Earthian fleet to rescue Johnny! Thank Heaven; I completely trusted the information on the note; I followed the note's directions; and all the instructions were totally correct; since I apparently wrote a note in the Future that told myself what not to do in the past that did not work; and advised me to use the tactics that were extremely successful!! It was written using one of my unique red pens that I have specially made; and using my own style of handwriting that Mrs. Murphy taught me in the third grade at Oaklawn Elementary School; so I guess I somehow accomplished the impossible and sent the vital information to myself; even though I don't recall doing it; and I have never been able to find out how I did it!!! I would have kept the eerie sheet of paper that apparently came from my supply of paper; but as soon as I had read and memorized the entire paper; the whole sheet suddenly burst into flames and was totally destroyed as it burned a hole in my desk and dropped to the floor! Through the years I have never had the hole fixed; because it helps me to remember just what went on during that fateful span of time; and be thankful for the two miracles that happened--your successful cancer treatment and Johnny's successful impossible rescue!!!"

The Admiral paused a moment as they gently moved around the dance floor; then Mary Pearl spoke up; "**Wow! What an amazing thought!! Such a scenario seems impossible; but you are a witness that it actually happened; and the hole in your desk is a constant reminder that it did happen!!!** Through the years I have wondered what caused it and why you didn't get it repaired! But I am not complaining, my beloved; I believe you! I believe you because Dr. Regal Strife's method of treatment was a total success; all my cancer was killed without any of the usual side effects of disabling pain; nausea; loss of appetite; and losing my long blond hair; and I was able to have our beloved children! Ergo; it means that the information you somehow received from the future was totally correct; so it had to be from you!! You somehow learned about the new treatment in the future and somehow; some way; you sent the note back to yourself so that you could save Johnny and me!!! This sounds like an eerie episode on 'The Stranger Still Zone'!!! But enough of talking about the past; life is too short to dilly-dally and worry about such trivial things!!! **Let's calm down and enjoy the exciting events that are happening and about to happen in the present; and forget the terrible things that did not happen; thanks to your bravery in the past; and in the future! Give me a tender hug, BABY!** You know, I just can't wait to have to do those 2 AM feedings again for our baby-to-come! As each of the rest of our much-loved crew was born, I was able to drag myself out of bed; while you were either sleeping or out of town on a classified mission; seven times before the present birthing-to-be; so doing early morning feedings for number 8 should be a snap; since I have done it so many times that I can do it while I am sleeping! But say!!! If you really <u>want to</u>; since you are now retired, you could volunteer to get up a few times to do it by yourself; but only if you <u>want to do it</u>!!"

Jonathan totally ignored his wife's suggestion and the couple continued talking about other trivial matters while gently clinging to each other. (Both Mary Pearl and Jonathan knew that he would get up by himself to feed the baby with a bottle; or to help her and at least hold her hand while she fed the baby!) So as the Admiral and his beloved wife again silently danced, the calm Texas air again became electric and magical, as the introductory trumpet notes of the famous "Absolutely the Last Dance Number"; written together by Doctor Chance Watson and Marty Ballesteros, Sr.; carried into the warm air! Perhaps the magic was created by the talents of a pair of military veterans who were skillful guitar musicians; a father and son duet softly playing in the background; which blended harmoniously with a world-class scientist skillfully blowing a tenor trumpet very quickly up and down the high scale staccato notes very precisely; exactly like he did while long ago in the high school band; which produced a breathtaking masterpiece ending to the almost impossibly fantastic evening! Later as the dancers slowly moved around the dance floor to the hauntingly beautiful sounds of the now-muted trumpet and the soft guitars; playing the gang's favorite the "Absolutely-the-Last-Dance-Number"; overhead the Eternal Stars twinkled magically in the clear Texas night; even as the first wisps of the storm clouds coming down from the north started moving overhead! Dr. Harold Taft the skillful meteorologist at the Channel 5 WBAP television station said the first rain would hit the Metroplex around 1 or 2 A.M.; so everyone hopefully would have enough time to get home before the so-called "squall line" would come through.

The Winds of Destiny around the retired military man were once again stilled over the entire Earth as the Karma of one Admiral Emeritus Jonathan "Hurricane" Baines Blow, for the moment; was complete and fulfilled! His Galactic Destiny was, for the moment; "achieved"; "in the groove"; and "on track"! At that instant on the Main Galactic Time Line, former Admiral Jonathan Baines Blow, the family man; was very contented and in the one position in the Universe where he most wanted to be! He had his beloved family and friends around him, and he was having a good time, dancing arm-in-arm and cheek-to-cheek with his beloved wife Mary Pearl; who he loved with every fiber and atom of his being and Soul!!

He did not remember any of the heart wrenching events of his former past history when he was totally alone; because it was totally erased from the Main Galactic Time Line and therefore all those painful events did not happen; because the successful events automatically replaced the totally disastrous ones; ergo, the rescue mission was a total success; and his beloved Mary Pearl's stage 4 cancer was totally obliterated! Nor did he remember visiting his friend, the present trumpeter; in order to get the time devices that literally remade his tragic Life Path in the Past; to one of fulfillment, joy, and peace; because in the new "reality" he did not visit his friend to get what was needed!!! He did not remember his ill-fated mission in which he lost his right arm and was unsuccessful in rescuing his patrolman; because it no longer existed on the Main Galactic Time Line! Only events of the successful mission remained on the Time Line; which when they happened, totally erased any effects of the unsuccessful mission! He did not remember losing his right arm when the Thunder Worlds fleet ambushed the Earthian fleet that was coming to attempt to rescue the man who; in the Future on the "revised Main Galactic Time Line"; would ultimately replace Jonathan as Admiral of the fleet!! It was as if his unsuccessful actions and the failed rescue mission had never occurred--because when the preliminary actions about the cancer treatment and the rescue attempt on the Thunder Worlds had changed; the slate had literally been wiped clean and **THEY**

HAD NEVER OCCURRED!! He only remembered the other virtually impossible; the dangerous; and the successful; solo mission to save Johnny Trevor that literally somehow changed his former Life Path from emptiness; loneliness; and "wreck and ruin"; to the present Life Path filled with fulfillment; a large, wonderful family; and joy and happiness!!!

Even **Dr. Chance Watson** also did not remember helping his friend remake his **Life Path** by giving him small electronic time devices that allowed an important note and several large solid objects to be sent along the Main Galactic Time Line that literally changed galactic history; because those actions were also literally "wiped clean" from the Time Line and had **not happened!** Mrs. Barbara Larrison also did not remember Jonathan toiling for many years in her library to ultimately find the information that he needed to change his Life Path!! His Life Path had been changed to one of peace and joy; hence he did not need to use her library to get information; hence, those events also had been literally **wiped clean** from the Main Galactic Time Line! Also; everyone who had ever had any contact with the Admiral Emeritus did not remember any of the tragic details of the failed rescue mission and the aspects of his former life that were changed by his "tinkering with Time" by using Dr. Chance's devices to go back through Time and literally change the preliminary events that caused the debacles in his life; hence, they no longer existed!!

The beautiful mother-to-be dancing with the Admiral Emeritus also did not remember how her previous Life Path had suddenly changed from sadness and death caused by metastasizing cancer and the extremely painful and unsuccessful surgery and radiation and chemo treatments; to complete fulfillment; because her old **Life Path** with disastrous cancerous treatments also no longer existed!! She only remembered that on the fateful day of her scheduled first regular cancer surgery the procedure was canceled at literally the last possible instant by her beloved husband; who did not tell her beforehand!! Then after her Jonathan had come back from a mission; the type of cancer surgery was changed; from one that would cause many different painful side effects; such as nausea, diarrhea, loss of appetite, skin rashes, vomiting, and the loss of her beautiful blond hair forever; to a new non-invasive medical procedure that; after several treatments; quickly killed the cancer tumor; and all the other cancer cells that had metastasized throughout her body; with literally no side effects!!!

As the couple clung to each other with loving arms and slowly danced; again and again the same fantastic joyful memories kept going through Mary Pearl's mind! She remembered that with the 180-degree change in her Life Path; she had fought cancer before the birth of their first child a little over fifteen years ago and had won; being completely healed of the dread disease; when her doctor at the base hospital used the advanced cancer surgical techniques pioneered by Dr. Regal Strife! The skilled surgeon had used microwaves; (tuned to the proper frequency which he had determined beforehand by observing live cancer cells through a miraculous microscope which Dr. Regal Strife himself had invented); to kill all the malignant cancer cells of the tumor inside her body and leave all the healthy cells in the surrounding tissue unharmed!! Such treatment had no terrible side effects; such as deadly degradation of the immune system; severe infections; a lack of appetite; or the loss of all body hair! The miraculous technique completely destroyed her cancer using a few treatments without any physical side effects; or any damage to any of her other body organs or glands!! This fantastic operation made it possible for the beautiful young woman to have their present "seven and one-half" children; the "half" being the one she was expecting and due in about a month! (After Dr. Strife's successful treatment, she also started drinking alkaline water, to prevent further cancer growth! Medical history records that Dr. Octon Peaceburg, a German medical researcher; won the "Zolander Prize for Medicine" in 1931 for discovering that if a person's body pH becomes alkaline, cancer will not grow or, if present in your body; it will harmlessly die off!!

A few yards away; their eldest daughter Mary was finally getting a priceless thrill she would record in her diary and literally remember the rest of her life by having the last dance of the evening with her childhood hero, close friend, uncle, and legal Godfather; the literally ageless Captain Gallant; (compliments of the Empire's Interferon 777!) Across the large dance floor, as the Winds of Destiny swirled around the couple; Admiral Johnny Trevor was dancing cheek-to-cheek with his lovely wife Susan; who was expecting twins in a few months. In the corner of the dance floor; Mary Pearl and Jonathan's three younger teen-aged children, Jonathan, Jr.; Bordoe, (named after Captain Gallant) ;

and Marty, (named after his good friend); were also having a good time dancing to the latest slow Texas waltz music with some of their school friends they had invited to the carefully chaperoned party. While up above on the very large mansion's second floor; their two other very young children Susan and Amber with their nanny, Mrs. Barbara Larrison; were very busy playing educational computer games after they finished their pre-middle school homework online; while Mary Pearl and Jonathan's eighth male child-to-be; whom they planned to name "Johnny Trevor Blow"; according to their pediatrician; Dr. Gene Bl-Air[32]; was doing very well and was due very soon hopefully in about a month; or perhaps less; depending on the stork!! (All in all, it was setting up to be quite a busy summer for the Blow family; and one that every member was looking forward to!)

But the very important career of one Admiral Johnny "Blow-Up" Trevor; despite his "rocky start" as a patrolman almost two decades ago when he was kidnapped by the Reptiloids; was just beginning!

If you are curious; get permission from your Senior Mage; and have an extremely strong Seer Vision Talent, to you; several of Admiral Trevor's Main Future Lines of Destiny on the Main Galactic Time Line will be extremely strong, instead of being "fuzzy" like they are to lower rank Seers! Also, if you are an Imperial Seer of at least five hundred years or more experience, and are interested; you could take the time and the mental energy to visualize the Primary Time Stream that indicates that Admiral Trevor's Karma, or Ultimate Historic Destiny; at this position at this position on the

Main Galactic Time Line; was fated to be even more spectacular than that of his former mentor, Admiral Jonathan Baines Blow! The Imperial Magi visualize that, sometime in the distant future, the young admiral would command the combined Imperial and Earthian fleets against a rogue fleet from the Thunder Worlds! He would also personally go against the Reptiloid Thud in mortal combat and ultimately completely change the hazardous ultra-hot and cold layers above the Thunder Worlds by. . . . . (But that is another story to be documented in the Future; **AFTER THE FACT; AND NOT BEFORE; AS PER INPERIAL LAW!** (Any documentation about the future "Thunder Battle" all across the Thunder Worlds could seriously affect its outcome!) Seers of the proper security rating may mentally scan and visualize Imperial Seer's Earth Volume #2,342,120-B, and on Empire Prime, access Imperial Volumes XX through DCLVII for further data! Admiral Trevor's past, present, and future; records are quite lengthy; so plan on spending at least three months to view and ponder the important data before you can grasp the Total Picture of his Destiny and make any significant decision using the information!)

After many centuries of serving the Empire, wanting to stay busy; Captain Bordoe Gallant will retire[28] with his wife Dru to take over the administration of one of the Empire's agricultural planets.

As always, all the Imperial Time Laws are totally in affect for ordinary Humanoids; Reptiloids; Insectoids; and Snakoids; which means; if you are able to visualize the future Life Paths for Admiral Trevor; you may not tell him, or anyone else; either now or in the future; by any means of messaging; i.e.; mental; electronic;

or manual; what you have visualized! Any person breaking these important laws; anywhere in the Imperial sphere-of-influence or outside its jurisdiction; whenever and wherever the breaking of such law is discovered; perpetrators are subject to arrest any time; day or night; 28/8; then swift judgement by Imperial Courts who are in session 28/8; who will then immediately send all guilty perpetrators to the nearest prison planet for the rest of their lives; with no chance for release by a pardon or a parole!

And so; Imperial Citizen! Just what does the data that you have been given in the preceding Imperial document mean to you?!?! If you are interested; read on; and carefully ponder these additional facts!

POSTLUDE

So, Imperial Citizen! Have you answered for yourself the question given above: "Just what is a **Time Winner**"? Is it some being, such as a Reptiloid, a Snakoid, a Humanoid, an Insectoid, or even a Colloid Cloud; (the major 4, perhaps 5 species of sentient beings in the Cosmic All classified by Imperial scientists); that impossibly goes through time to accomplish deeds of daring? **Yes, it can be!** Bravery is not lacking as a trait in any of the 5 above mentioned species of sentient beings!

Is it any one of those sentient beings existing somewhere in the Cosmic All who "wisely uses their time" that is allotted to them during their relatively brief lifespan to accomplish something; the effects of which will last until the last sun in the Cosmic All fades and all radioactive materials transmute to lead? **Yes, that can be one of the characteristics!**

Is it one of those "gallant beings"; **(not the Captain!)**; who treats every other sentient and animal being like they would want to be treated? (AKA the "Golden Rule"!) **Yes, absolutely!**

Is it any one of those beings whose daring exploits that accomplish virtually impossible feats that stir the fabled and extremely controversial Winds of Destiny[6] to action? **Yes, indeed!**

Is it one of those beings who does not ever take Defeat lightly and will keep on "Hanging Tough!" and keep on "keeping on" until Victory is finally snatched from the Jaws of Defeat? **Yes; that can be one of the characteristics!**

It is one of those beings who does not quit even when literally facing Death or even when more that half-Dead and literally walking through the Valley of the Shadow of Death[7] in order to accomplish their mission? **Yes; that can be one of the characteristics!**

Is it all of the above characteristics? The answer to that question given at the first of this document was: **Yes and more!** The "Yes" answers have been explained above, while the mysterious **"MORE"** answers will have to wait for the next installment relating the Life Path of another courageous "Time Winner"! In the meantime; **THINK DEEPLY AND PONDER ABOUT WHAT YOU HAVE READ; AND ALWAYS DO AS THE MASTER SAID AFTER HE TAUGHT THE GOLDEN RULE:**

"GO THOU AND DO LIKEWISE!"

IMPERIAL SEER EXPLANATION ADDENDUM

(The following quote is from a privately published document by an unidentified Seer to provide further information for Imperial researchers about the preceding very strange document: "Forgive me if I seem to 'ramble' in the following narration! It is very difficult to state the perplexing, confusing, and totally impossible information in the document below without 'back tracking' and 'blathering'! After much tedious, (and personally dangerous), research; I can state the following about this very perplexing and totally unexplainable 'Anchor Event' in the very minor Earthian Time Stream; which has had so much influence on the Main Galactic Time Line that it literally changed the major line's direction; as related in the previous Imperial document:

1. Certain critical parts on the specific ship that apparently the alien Humanoid named "Jonathan Baines Blow"; supposedly from the minor planet "Earth"; the third planet from a very

small sun; used to go interstellar distances was found to be manufactured somewhere in the Empire under Imperial license circa 412,000 A.F.E., (After Founding of the Empire). I use the term "supposedly"; because the being's ship exhibited powers and abilities far beyond those capable by other ships produced by the Earthlings; (and even beyond those of the advanced Imperial "Courier Class ships that are piloted by Captains Gallant and Cody!)

2. But certain devices on the strange ship, (such as the apparently highly-advanced ultra-fast FTL drive which openly displayed the presently utterly impossible ability to outrun non-inertial and extremely fast robot AI fighters and the presently impossible ability for a Humanoid-manned ship to dodge 100% accurate computer-based energy beam weapons; exhibiting the presently impossible ability to penetrate a powerful planetary defense shield powered by zero point energy; and (perhaps invisibility screens); could not, and cannot have been produced at that time by any planet in the Empire; any planet in the Empire's sphere of influence, or on Earth!

3. NONE OF THE ABOVE MENTIONED AREAS COULD PRODUCE SUCH A SHIP EVEN TODAY BECAUSE MOST OF ITS EXHIBITED INCREDIBLE CAPABILITIES ARE SCIENTIFICALLY AND/OR PHYSICALLY IMPOSSIBLE IN THIS PRESENT TIME-FRAME; EVEN WITH TODAY'S ADVANCED TECHNOLOGY! SIMILAR CAPABILITES TO THOSE EXHIBITED BY THE UNKNOWN SHIP ARE NOT EVEN IN THE PLANNING STAGES BY IMPERIAL SHIP

YARD NAVAL ARCHITECTS! IT IS BELIEVED BY IMPERIAL NAVAL ARCHITECTS THAT A SHIP WITH SIMILAR SPEED CAPABILITIES COULD BE BUILT BY THE EMPIRE IN, SAY; 100 YEARS AFTER MUCH DEDICATED SCIENTIFIC RESEARCH ALONG THE MANY AVENUES OF KNOWLEDGE NEEDED TO INCREASE THE CAPABILITES TO MATCH THOSE EXHIBITED BY THE MYSTERY SHIP; which include the ability to go through a planets defense screens that were powered by Zero Point Energy sources; with very little or no damage since afterwards it outran speedy manned ships; the ability to evade FTL energy weapons with a kill rate of 100%, and the ability to outrun AI robot ships with over 100 G drives!

4. IT IS HOPED THAT OUR TECHNOLOGY WILL PERHAPS CATCH UP TO SOME OF THE EXHIBITED CAPABILITIES OF THE MYSTERY SHIP IN A FEW DECADES! IMPERIAL ADMIRALS ARE EXTREMELY INTERESTED IN POSSESSING A SHIP WHICH CAN SOMEHOW PENETRATE A PLANET'S ENORMOUS AND POWERFUL ENERGY SHIELDS WITHOUT BEING DESTROYED BY THE MUCH STRONGER ZERO-POINT ENERGY SHIELD PROTECTION POSSIBLE ON A PLANET!

5. When fuzzy photos of the ultra-advanced unknown courier ship that was used in the Anchor Event are examined; the unknown ship had an outer design shape very similar; if not an exact copy of the outside design characteristics to those flown even today by Imperial Captains Gallant and Cody! It was then

somehow; some way; successfully sent undamaged through the very small and unimportant Earthian Time Stream to Earthian time circa 8,000 B.C. while protected in an advanced Imperial-class total stasis field; which the alien Humanoid known as "Jonathan Baines Blow" had somehow impossibly gotten hold of! The ship could not have been an Imperial courier design like those flown by Captains Gallant and Cody because their ships have never exhibited such capabilities and when examined very closely during each yearly inspection and equipment update on Empire Prime's shipyard; have not ever been found to have any nonstandard equipment that would enable them to perform beyond standard specifications of the ultra-advanced "Royal Courier" Class of small ships.

6. Possession of such an advanced and dangerous scientific instruments able to "shift through time" using the "Watson Effect"; is limited to licensed Imperial scientific investigators and certain of the Empire's expertly-trained covert military forces that know its dangers and must operate within accepted Time-Shifting Guidelines; so as not to cause significant permanent damage to all parts of the Main Galactic Time Line! All of such equipment has been accounted for; was heavily guarded during the interval the super ship was observed; and therefore Imperial-produced devices were not used to perform such feats of time-shifting to the past in order to be buried in mud by the banks of Earth's Nile River!

7. But, impossibly; as stated above; the same ship was somehow found buried next to a politically and militarily unimportant

archeological dig only a day before the diplomatic mission left Earth! Our secret Imperial Seer History records that the ultimate commanding pilot of the ship, the previously mentioned local military man named "Jonathan Baines Blow"; with some sort of legal documentation supposedly somehow obtained from "Emperor Jones XIII"; (who happened to be the reigning Emperor on the throne of the ICOPE at the time!); somehow persuaded the head archeologist to give up the archeological find of the millennium; if not the millennium! Archeologists McBroom and Blacklock then proceeded to start digging at another nondescript river bank; which they apparently chose at random; where they are today still fruitlessly digging in the mud along the same large river on the Earth called the "Nile River"; looking for fossils and priceless Egyptian relics; (but as of this moment; not finding a single piece of debris to help their historical research!)

8. It is unknown; even at this later date; just how Admiral Blow of Earth got a "legal document signed by Emperor Jones XIII"! How a Humanoid not a citizen of the Empire and living millions of light years from Empire Prime could somehow get a legal paper giving them title to what is now a missing legendary super ship; is unknown! (Because of Imperial Law; we have not been able to ask Emperor Jones XIII anything about the strange happening! Also, for some unknown reason, the visualization channels of the Main Galactic Time line that pertain to the unknown ship or any phase of its legendary mission are totally blank, blackened; or blurred so much that

any useful information cannot be obtained about the legendary mission or the amazing ship!)

9. Again, to recap the totally impossible, yet, improbably true facts about the case: the only problem with our Intel that the ship was somehow manufactured somewhere in the Empire is the fact that no known ship that has ever been produced anywhere in the Empire; or the "Empire Marches"; or the Imperial Sphere of Influence; that has the ability to do certain things the unknown courier ship exhibited!

The unknown ship twice exhibited the almost unheard of capability to take off and go FTL in the gravity well of a planet without self-destructing or causing a chain reaction explosion that would penetrate the planet's thin crust and cause interior magma to cover its entire surface!!!

The fantastic ship also somehow had the capability to successfully penetrate the very strong planetary inner defense screens of the main Thunder World and escape! It was so fast that the FTL robot defenses orbiting the main Thunder World could not track it with their instantaneous tracking devices; much less successfully attack it! By showing these capabilities, this inscrutable ship was also evidently much faster than the fastest Imperial ship, apparently even those of the aforementioned ultra-fast ships of Captains Gallant and Cody! When its average speed was calculated using the time it left the Reptiloid "Thud's" planet; until the time it reappeared back on Earth with the injured pilot; it was found to be at least one hundred per cent faster than the fastest Imperial courier ship! It was even faster than any ship the Empire's computer designers are conservatively projected to produce during the next one hundred years!

The problem with producing faster ships presently seems almost insurmountable! Although the 'Propulsion Wave Theory Drive'; the foundational basis for all the civilian and military FTL drive units produced in the ICOPE; presently provides the fastest FTL speed of any of the literally dozens of different types of FTL drives available; Imperial Naval Architects are stymied in their efforts to produce more speed! They are hindered by the solid fact that all of the capacities available in every facet of the Propulsion Wave Theories have been thoroughly explored and utilized; with no room for any improvements in speed! This means that entirely new propulsion theories; using entirely new scientific principles will have to be worked out in the Theoretical Laboratories of the Imperial College; whose central building is on Empire Prime. Then propulsion systems using the new discoveries will have to be tested for years before they can be safely used in the Empire's naval ships and civilian craft! This titanic effort must be accomplished in order to improve the fastest Imperial ship speed to equal that of the unknown "stranger"!

10. Work is still being done **VERY** covertly by the Imperial Seers to find out just what exactly went on during this complex and baffling Time Event to see if any Imperial Weapons Laws or Imperial Time Laws were broken; such as any Imperial agent or official giving advanced weapons to primitive cultures; or

illegally taking objects from the 'future' to the 'past' and thus illegally altering the Cosmic Time Stream!! Updates to this Above Top Secret informative document are being drafted and the changes will be posted on all official Seer Mental Websites and Public Information Transfer Sites as additional information is being researched.

11. But there are obstacles to this effort! Somehow; as previously mentioned; this important Time Stream/Time Cloud Event is extremely 'vague' when any Imperial Seer attempts to visualize it! Something strange and unprecedented has caused any possible vision of any part of the actions of mystery ship; being used to perform an unknown mission; to be 'muddled and literally unusable for investigation by any Seer; no matter what their rank or mental capability! I know of no Seer other than the extremely powerful Imperial Seer Kantorie Smi-Th-Jo-Nes who could have somehow produced such an unusual and unprecedented effect with their powers! (Seer Smi-Th-Jo-Nes is so powerful that it would not be wise for me to ask him anything about the strange episode or the reason that all visions about it are extremely vague or blank!) If that weren't enough, the whole 'Blow's Miracle' has been designated 'Ultra-Top Secret — Not To Be Investigated' by an Imperial Order of the Emperor; and sealed by his Official Signet Ring, so that any research on this subject now or in the future will be extremely limited and it could prove to be literally very dangerous to any prying researcher's health; because of its extremely high security rating!! (Prying researchers have to take into consideration the

possibility of one of several things that could happen, including being arrested by Imperial Soldiers at any time of the day or night; pre-tried without the accused being there by a Compu-Judge on Empire Prime; and said perpetrator executed on the spot by a Royal Marines firing squad for 'Treason' against an Imperial Emperor's Order!)

12. (Any interested covert researchers need to check this ciphered document again in a few weeks for data updates on this mysterious "Historical Time Event!" to be absolutely safe from Imperial legal prosecution or any possible 'off the record bad luck or illness'; any interested party needs to use covert; multiple relay points, false passwords, multiple firewalls; with some real and some dummy; and any other defense their talented programmers can come with in order to hide their original and/or present location! Also using multi-layer encrypted communication programs using "squirts of information" to hide their identity is also a very good idea! Otherwise the person requesting the information will instantly be identified; instantly prosecuted by Imperial authorities; tried on the spot using a so-called fair and balanced Comp-Judge; who will then send Planetary Police officers arrest you and send you to the prison planet for eternal imprisonment or instant execution; with no legal way of appealing your sentence!)

Again, I want to apologize for the above essay! I had to let you know just what had happened and what could happen if the identity of any interested party is found out by the Imperial Government authorities! So I did my best to document the fantastic chain of events that happened! Check with me again in a few hundred years; if I am still publishing and/or alive!!!"

Respectfully,

The Unknown Seer,
OF NECESSITY; to protect my Life Path!

JUST WHAT ARE THE WINDS OF DESTINY?

In the long history of the Cosmic All; among the conscious sentient beings; very little has ever been universally known or published about the legendary and controversial "Winds of Destiny"! All of the sentient telepathic races that instinctively have the extra mental "senses" to detect anything about the invisible so-called "Destiny Makers", by rigid and unbreakable custom; will not say anything about the strange phenomena to any of the "non-sensory races" of the galaxies! The extremely long-lived group of mages known as "Imperial Seers" will say absolutely nothing to the non-telepathic of the galaxy about the unknown energy strands! They seem to believe that the "brick wall" brains of the Universe; (i.e., the non-telepathic members of the Humanoid; Insectoid; Reptiloid, and Snakoid races); would not understand about the eerie wisps of energy that constantly seek out important happenings in the whole of Creation! (Just why an invisible and eternal energy source would be interested about anything about weak-minded sentient beings in the every-changing finite Material Universe is also not disclosed; if they know!)   In the Universe there are many races of beings that have senses beyond the ordinary veil of light and sound senses. Only the most mentally gifted of the ESP races, which have organized a group known as "Seers", "Mages", or "Shamans" by their less powerful peers; can detect the ebb and flow of the strange curtain of energy that apparently exists below the lowest level of the atomic structure and is in every atom of the Cosmic All! It is said that the invisible, (undetectable by ordinary sensory organs, and scientifically controversial), streams of energy; (nicknamed the "Winds of Destiny" by some "Science-Fiction" writer in the Empire hundreds of thousands of years ago); blow constantly and eternally through the Cosmic All! The effect of the powerful sub-atomic energy on every living being in the Universe is largely unknown; but the Seers logically believe that the legendary powerful streams of sub-atomic energy must exist for some important reason or they would not have been created and they would not exist! The Society of Seers records every important event to analyze their effect on the Main Galactic Time Line, and tries to detect any outpouring of the Winds before, during, and after the important "Anchor Event"; which literally changes the direction of the Time Stream!!!

Even after many millennia of researching the enigma **of THE WINDS OF DESTINY**; no physical being, i.e., no Reptiloid, no Insectoid, no Humanoid, and no Snakoid member of the Magi will offer any explanation for their existence! It is said that even after many millennia of careful study; no species of beings in the Royal

Seers has any solid and substantial knowledge of; or can even imagine the source or solar system where such eerie energy beings originated! Even the eerie "Colloid Cloud" beings from the "Great Dark" also relate that they have absolutely no unique information about the unique infinitely tiny energy beings! No physical, semi-existent, or energy beings in the Cosmic All; no one except the legendary, eternal and invisible Winds of Destiny sweeping through all the solar systems of the Universe know the reason for their existence; where they originally came from; or what effect they have on the entire Cosmic All by their observation of important events that can happen virtually anywhere in the entire Cosmic All!

The only possible source comes from the earliest lore of the oldest interior planetary galaxies in the Empire! Rudimentary knowledge about what is called by dozens of names; such as the "People from Nowhere" and the "Event Beacons" has been orally passed down from each older generation to the younger generation of shamans, witches, warlocks, and other beings of power on dozens of scattered planets in the dense interior regions! Vague oral stories and verbal sagas handed down from generation to generation hint that these legendary cosmic ionic streamers were apparently somehow produced and/or originated on/by the Core Suns in the interior galaxies; during the first few moments of Creation. For the first few millennia they were unfathomable to all, and their presence could only be vaguely sensed by scattered groups of mentally gifted sentient beings. After the founding of the ICOPE an extremely small number of expertly trained Full Prime ESP Operators was organized to serve the Empire by using their mental powers to study what came to be called the "Winds of Destiny"!

In the Cosmic All there are many races of beings that have senses beyond the ordinary veil of light and sound senses. Only the more gifted of the "Extra Sensory Perception" races, known as "Seers" by their less mentally powerful peers, can detect the strange curtain of energy that exists below the lowest level of the atomic structure! (By Imperial Law, every being which lives in the Sphere of Influence of the Interstellar Condominium of Planets and Empires with the slightest latent ability to sense the "Winds" must be trained and become a member; or an "associate member"; of the official group of "Imperial Society of Seers" or unofficially just called "Mages" or "Magi"). The invisible, undetectable by ordinary sensory organs and scientifically controversial; streams of energy are thought by many scientists to blow constantly and eternally through the Cosmic All, unseen and unfelt by most sentient beings! (One source says that the eerie energy creatures were nicknamed the "Winds of Destiny" millennia ago by the ESP-gifted race of Reptiloids called the "Rone") The Imperial Seers theorize that the wisps of energy only seem to appear just before, during, and for a short time after, extremely important, destiny-changing events in the Cosmic All; seemingly whirling and swirling around the immediate vicinity of the happening; at speeds many; many times the speed of light; being able to travel from anywhere in the Empire's Sphere of Influence to Empire Prime in mere seconds!!! When the Cosmically-important Event is over; the Seers say the mysterious Winds vanish as quickly as they appeared;

apparently back into the deep recesses of the atomic structure of the Cosmic All! The effect of the powerful sub-atomic energy on every living being in the Universe is still largely unknown, but the Imperial Seers; who have been studying the phenomena for many thousands of millennia; believe the legendary powerful streams of sub-atomic energy must exist for some important reason or they would not subsist! It is not known if they secretly use their power to directly intervene in the affairs of the solid sentient beings of the Cosmic All[8]!

For hundreds of thousands of years, the Society of Seers has tried to record every important event to analyze their effect on the Main Time Stream by sensing when and where the Winds of Destiny rise up and trying to find out just exactly what was happening at the particular location where they were blowing. But important events occur that they cannot visualize or possibly know about beforehand; because the speed of the Winds of Destiny does not increase until just before or just as the Cosmically Important Event is happening! When the so-called "Anchor Event" has progressed so that its importance on the Local Planetary or Solar System or Galactic or Interstellar Time Line/Time Cloud has lessened; the mysterious Winds of Destiny vanish as quickly as they emerged to blow; before the Imperial Sages can visualize just what is going on or even what went on!

It is hoped that in the future at some point; sub-atomic electronic devices using laser circuits to tune in on the exact extremely low-level frequencies on the radiation spectrum in order to detect The Winds of Destiny can be developed by the Corps of

Imperial Mental Scientists! Such fantastic futuristic equipment will allow the Magi to quickly zero in on just where each extremely important event is happening so that the Seers can use their mental powers to visualize just what is going on and why the Event is important! But even if possible; that development is somewhere in the far; far future!

PONDERINGS BY A FRUSTRATED SCIENTIST

66 Ah, the concept of 'TIME' will probably always remain an extremely controversial subject, no matter how much cutting-edge research is done by many thousands of talented Imperial scientists in many ultra-advanced laboratories! It can be proven scientifically and demonstrated with the results of certain very involved experiments authored by me, and confirmed by dozens of eminent Earthian and Imperial physicists; that the entire 'span' of the Cosmic All; which can be described as extremely small intervals of 'Time'; can also physically be described using the metaphor of a 'torrent of separate time points' flowing like a stream of water forever; with all events on the 'stream' happening at the same time! That 'parallel' water metaphor used to describe 'Time' is an exact duplicate of what the exacting scientific experiments prove is actually happening!

However, it can also be proven scientifically, and demonstrated with the results of certain other entirely different intricate experiments carefully performed by me, and confirmed by other reliable scientists, that the commodity known as 'Time' can also be physically illustrated using a metaphor of an infinite number of points of "Time" that have been shot and/or flung all through the Cosmic All as if the Creator was using a shotgun; again; with all events and/or happenings in each "Time Point" occurring at the same time! Both physical parallels and logical analogies can be proven with equal logical reasoning and with equally solid scientific experiments by the same reliable and gifted scientists; that seems to indicate that somehow; some way; both analogies, a "Time Stream" and a "Time Cloud"; are physically; and scientifically correct; even though this logically seems **PHYSICALLY IMPOSSIBLE!**

Regardless of which scientific proof you believe; since both analogies are apparently both impossibly true; this meant that an unimportant and obscure event in TIME could suddenly become very important; like a large rock dumped in an ordinary stream of water causes the water to be radically diverted! But, conversely, the most important Historical Anchor Event that is known by millions of historians all across the entire Universe could suddenly disappear and become like an obscure pebble cast up on an uncharted island; unwanted and forever forgotten by all inhabitants of the Cosmic All; and removed from all recorded mediums; as if it had never happened!!

Simply put; any event in accepted 'History' can suddenly vanish as if it had never existed; because if one small event on one point on the Time Stream is somehow changed;

it can affect and change or delete any important Anchor Event Time Point or any other Time Point in the Universe!!

If all of the above explanations seem 'far-fetched'; impossible; and like something out of a present-day popular television science-fiction show called 'The Stranger Zone'; **YOU ARE RIGHT!** The preceding explanations of the many possible facets of 'TIME' may seem like a fantasy story; but it is as close to the absolute **TRUTH** as the language used to convey the meanings may express!"

The above paragraphs are excerpts compiled from the published and unpublished papers of Earthian Science Chair Emeritus Doctor Chance Watson[2]; noted Time Investigator and Inventor for many decades on his home planet Earth; and reprinted by the Emperor's own Personal Publishers for His Highness's own information with the gracious permission of the said esteemed Doctor Chance Watson! At the present time; Dr. Chance Watson is the one and only Earthian authority and actually; one of the few authorities on the important subject of "Time Travel" in the entire Cosmic All! He may be reached for discussion about "time travel" at either his Earthian office or his office on Empire Prime.

THE TIME TALENTS OF DR. CHANCE WATSON!

66 The following is an excerpt from the extremely low circulation; (but extremely relevant and important); mental newsletter physically projected out to all the Imperial Mages of the necessary rank throughout the Empire and also, because of its importance; eternally stored on the imperishable pages of the extremely secret "Annals of the Magi"; which is stored in the Headquarters of the Imperial Seers; located at a secret location at least two hundred miles somewhere under the surface of Empire Prime!

"This reprinted article is the first document accepted and published by the imperial Seers that has been authored by a scientist from the planet "Earth"; a relatively new member of the ICOPE, i.e., the Interstellar Condominium of Planets and Empire. It is an extremely interesting article on the extremely controversial subject of "Time"; which it states "Time"; using an analogy; can be described as either a "Time Stream", or a "Time Cloud"; since either analogy can be correct! It presents a new and interesting "slant" on the very important subject of "traveling through time" and documents a new line of research by Dr. Chance Watson, the very gifted Earthian scientist who discovered an obscure scientific principle that he successfully used to actually go through "Time" himself! In several conferences that he has attended both on his home planet Earth and on Empire Prime; Dr. Watson has explained in great detail; in scientific and terms that a "non-scientist" can understand, just how going back and forth in "Time"; using the correct "technique"; can actually be done successfully and without almost any danger to the 'Time Traveler' or to the "Time Stream"!

In each of the conferences that Dr. Chance has addressed, literally all the representatives in each conference were very impressed with his new; (and controversial); findings about 'Time'; and 'Time Travel'! But at each conference, the participants could not argue with one fact--Dr. Chance did travel back in time and he returned[2] to his original point on the Time Line with no apparent side effects to either him or; as far as we can tell; the Main Galactic Time Line!!" – Imperial Seer Rona Wad-Dee.

JUST WHAT IS AN "ANCHOR EVENT" OR "ANCHOR MOMENT"?

he following Imperial document has been translated from the Galactic Standard language to the reader's native language.

When Imperial citizens read their printed material or listen to their electronic media; several very important terms can be sometimes observed or heard. Just what does the term "Anchor Event" or the term "Anchor Moment" mean? Whenever an ultra-important event happens on the Main Galactic Time Line; in Imperial Seer documents this very important happening can be called an "Anchor Event"; "Anchor Moment"; or "Moment of Destiny"; which is literally a significant happening; i.e.; an ultra-important event; that literally changes; "swings around"; and/or alters the direction of the Main Galactic Time Line!! Such an extremely rare happening also changes the Life Path of each of the literally trillions upon trillions of sentient beings who live all across the Interstellar Condominium of Planets and Empires; i.e.; (ICOPE)!!!

Such an important event that happens in the "Future" can be "injected" back into the "Past" by using ultra-advanced electronic equipment or very rare and powerful mental abilities; which will; in turn; change the original event on the "Future" Time Line!

But can such an event happen to just one sentient being? The Historical Imperial Magi records illustrate that many times in the history of the Interstellar Condominium of Planets and Empires, just one sentient being[19] caused the Main Galactic Time Line to be radically changed!

And so Imperial Citizen, quit just "standing around"--GO OUT INTO YOUR AREA OF SOCIETY AND TRY TO ACOMPLISH SOMETHING SO THAT WILL BE AN "ANCHOR EVENT"; WHICH WILL CHANGE AND IMPROVE YOUR LIFE PATH AND THE LIFE PATHS OF MILLIONS OF OTHERS!

FOOTNOTES

1 "Space radar", a very long range sensor that uses Trans-light speed waves to obtain accurate tracking information of near and far away objects that are light years away!)

2 Documented in <u>Three Time Winners - "Story 3"</u>

3 **Ajax Chrome** is a very physically and mentally advanced Humanoid to be documented in a future novel.

4 Documented in <u>Cleonardo the Trecian Witch.</u>

5 "**Proxies**" were Imperial Citizens who were sent to Earth To secretly live and be on the lookout for anything that Would affect or be dangerous to the Empire.

6 Documented in <u>Matt Dixon the Time Cop.</u>

7 Documented in <u>The Trecian Witch and the Imperial Admiral.</u>

8 (Although such an occurrence is documented in the Imperial documents <u>One Time Winner!</u> and <u>The Trecian Witch and the Imperial Admiral!)</u>

9 (Sada Juice is described in <u>The Cy-Soldier</u>)

10 The exploits of the very talented and caring Dr. Martha Wagstaff are documented in <u>The Cy-Soldier!</u>

11 Adama's exploits and those of other similar beings are documented in <u>Jeopardy in the Empire! - "CITIZEN ONE"</u>

12 The exploits of Marshal Samson Blair are documented in the Imperial document <u>Samson Blair the Time Marshal!</u>

13 "AI" stands for "Artificial Intelligence"; which can be used in Imperial robots and computer CPUs to increase their performance and speed!

14 (Such events are documented in the Imperial document <u>A Blow in Time!</u>); and other similar historic documents!

15 Documented in <u>Pursuits Through Time!!-"Fancient Earth!"</u>

16 "AKA" stands for "Also Known As".

17 Documented in several secret Imperial Seer documents.

18 The official definition of an "Anchor Event"; also known as an "Anchor Moment"; is presented in this book's section entitled "Just what is an Anchor Event"?

19 Imperial Citizens interested in individuals that ICOPE history records caused "Anchor Events" may research the following sentient beings: Cleonardo Zantrick Watson; Samson Blair; Admiral Jonathan Baines Blow; Matthew Dixon; and literally dozens of others; all of whom by their actions changed the course of Empire and Trans-Galactic Histories <u>FOR THE BETTER!</u>

20 Documented in several Imperial Document including <u>Samson Blair The Time Marshal!</u>

21 A similar chain of events is recorded in the Imperial document <u>The Cy-Soldier!</u>

22 "FTL" stands for "Faster Than Light".

23 "IN THE CLUTCH" is a sports term meant to describe an athlete that comes through when the going gets tough and the game is on the line; and wins against impossible odds!

24 "Panabeing Waves" are the unique mental waves produced by "Citizen One" Humanoid beings that can pierce the Space-Time Continuum and control matter and energy.

25 28/8 stands for the 28-hour day and the 8-days each week on the Empire Prime calendar.

26 The discovery of "neo-electricity" is documented in the Imperial document <u>Gallant and the Apaches!</u>

27 "Getting the road on the show" is a joke with the answer: that is when an asphalt-laying paving machine runs over the Muppets!!

28 Documented in the Imperial document <u>The Old Man and the Dragon</u>.

29 "AFE" stands for "After Founding of the Empire".

30 The "Maverick Rule" supposedly originated with a gambler who operated during the span in Earthian history called the "Old West". It states: "When you are actually gambling, and you know that you are playing the last hand of the game; SHOVE ALL OF YOUR CHIPS TO THE CENTER OF THE TABLE AND LET YOUR BET RIDE; AND NEVER; EVER; GIVE UP UNTIL THE GAME IS ACTUALLY OVER! Similarly, in the Game of Life; when you know that you are near the end of your lifespan; DO NOT GIVE UP OR GIVE IN!!! DO EXACTLY WHAT YOU WOULD IN A GAME OF CHANCE! SHOVE ALL OF YOUR "CHIPS" TO THE CENTER OF YOUR LIFE AREA AND DO NOT GIVE UP UNTIL THE FINAL SCENE IS PLAYED OUT!!"

Imperial Magi's addition: "If either facet of the Maverick Rule is hard for you as an Imperial Citizen to understand; just wait until you are actually gambling or you sense you are nearing the end of your lifespan! At that instant on the Main Galactic Time Line; YOU <u>WILL UNDERSTAND</u> WHAT IS MEANT BY EACH PART OF THE Maverick Rule!! If you do not; please contact your local Imperial Magi that is stationed in your town, for illumination!

31 According to the Imperial Magi, "Time" can be described as a "cloud of infinite Time Points" or a "straight line of infinite Time Points".

32 Dr. Gene BI-Air's medical practice is described in the Imperial Document <u>Samson Blair the Time Marshal!</u>

Books, Novellas, and Stories by John R. Carden available for purchase, now or in the future, either in local book stores or online:

1. The Seasons of Space – 1976 - Out of Print
2. Three Time Winners! - 2006
3. Space, Time, and the Empire! - 2008
4. Samson Blair the Time Marshal - 2010, 2019
5. Jeopardy in the Empire! - 2011
6. Two Time Winners (And a Seer)! - 2015
7. One Time Winner! - 2016, 2018
8. The Cy-Soldier - 2020
9. Cleonardo the Trecian Witch - 2021
10. Two Warrior Time Winners! - 2021
11. The Trecian Witch and the Imperial Admiral! - 2021
12. Pursuits Through Time! - 2022
13. A Blow in Time! - 2021
14. The Sunman! - In preparation
15. The Man from Infinity!! - In preparation
16. The Adventures of Captain Gallant! - In preparation
17. The Empa! - In preparation
18. Rex and Regina! - In preparation
19. The SWAP Team! (Special Weapons and Powers!)
20. The Filly from Sand Dari! - In preparation
21. The Forest Foundling - In preparation
22. The Blue Road to Infinity - In preparation
23. The Invincible Fleet - Not published yet
24. The Four - In preparation

25. The Com Bats of Sand Dari – In preparation

26. The Ca-Tes of Sand Dari - In preparation

27. The Reptiloid and the Child - In preparation

28. Joseph and Cleopatra - In preparation

29. The Visitor - In preparation

30. Fairday! - In preparation

31. Old Blood - In preparation

32. Tales of Earth! – In preparation

33. Tales of the ICOPE! – In preparation

34. Tales of the Empire! – In preparation

35. The Adventures of Sunman! - In preparation

Many other books, novellas, and short stories are being worked on!

So long for now, and as they say in the 50th:

"Be there! Aloha!!

So what is "Time"? Will it ever be possible for any sentient being to "travel" from one point in "Time" to another? If such a journey could be undertaken, could any individual travel back in "Time" in order to save the life of someone who had drowned; or go back in order to sell stock that had greatly decreased in value one fateful day; before it went down? Or, conversely be able to buy stock the day before it skyrocketed in value?

If such trips could be accomplished, what would be the effect of events that had already happened being suddenly changed to greatly alter what had actually happened; changing important events that had happened to billions and trillions of sentient beings?

And what would be the effect of individuals who had died, suddenly being saved from death by a person coming to save them from the "Future"? Would the effects of such trips through time be "good" or "bad"?

And if any of these unique events happened; what would they cause when one point on the Main Galactic Time Line suddenly had more or less energy and mass that other points on the Time Line?!? (Nothing good!)

So, Imperial Citizen; read the following Imperial Document; carefully ponder its meaning; and after carefully reading this record, be prepared to contact any Imperial Seer on Empire Prime using the facilities of your local Imperial Library and tell them about your ponderings that occurred in your mental facilities after you read this document!

So just what is a "Blow"?

Suppose you are a military person and your career has not been very successful. You have a missing arm and several scars all over your body as evidence that you have not been a very successful warrior for your country. **BUT!** With "20-20 hindsight" you have used to ponder over the past years what you did wrong in each defeat; if you could somehow contact yourself before each defeat that happened in the past; and give yourself advice on what to do to change your defeat into a victory; WOULD YOU?!? BUT HOW COULD YOU DO SUCH AN IMPOSSIBLE FEAT OF COMMUNICATION DOWN THE CORRIDORS OF TIME?!? What would the effect of such tampering with the Main Galactic Time Line do to the rest of the Cosmic All? Would the literal "Fabric of Time" be somehow disrupted?!? But would such a daring ploy be worth it? Could it actually be done?

To one discouraged former naval admiral; the risk would be worth the try; and if the stratagem were successful; that would indeed be a **"Blow in Time"**!!